Praise for
Emily Belden's first novel,
Hot Mess

"A fun romp through the world of food, love, and luxury."
—PopSugar, The Best New Books You Should Read This Spring

"[F]ull of fire and fury…. Belden's excellent tell-it-like-it-is
read is perfect for foodies and entrepreneurs alike."
—*Library Journal* (starred review)

"Combining the wit and insight of Stephanie Danler's *Sweetbitter* (2016)
with the drama of Jessica Tom's *Food Whore* (2015), Belden's first novel is a
glimpse into the fast-paced fine-dining industry…. Full of heart, heat, and
passion, this restaurant rom-com in novel form is an exhilarating debut."
—*Booklist*

"[A]n engrossing, slow-burn read that yields a very satisfying
emotional payoff…. Rich with perfect details, balanced between
the various different relationships and presented in a well-
crafted narrative, this novel is meant to be savored."
—*RT Book Reviews* (Top Pick)

"Emily Belden serves the decadence and drama à la mode in
Hot Mess. The full-bodied novel takes the resilient Allie Simon
on a journey of sex, love, secrets, and the high-end culinary
world. You'll savor every word of this provocative story."
—Abby Stern, author of *According to a Source*

"[E]very bit as juicy as the dishes it describes."
—*SPLASH*

"[A] fun read filled with romance, drama and plenty of food."
—*Chicago Parent*

Husband
Material

Also by Emily Belden

Hot Mess: A Novel

Eightysixed: A Memoir about Unforgettable Men, Mistakes, and Meals

Husband Material

a Novel

EMILY BELDEN

GRAYDON
HOUSE

**GRAYDON
HOUSE**

Recycling programs
for this product may
not exist in your area.

ISBN-13: 978-1-525-80598-1

Husband Material

GraydonHouseBooks.com
BookClubbish.com

Printed in U.S.A.

Dedicated to my husband, Matt. I appreciate you.

Husband Material

Chapter 1

Well, that's a first.

And I'm not talking about the fact that I brought a date to a wedding I'm pretty sure didn't warrant me a plus-one. I'm talking about grabbing a wedding card that just so happened to say "Congrats, Mr. & Mr." on my way to celebrate the nuptials of the most iconic heterosexual couple since George and Amal. This—and a king-sized KitKat bar from the checkout lane—is what I get for rushing through the greeting card aisle in Target while my Uber driver waited in the loading zone with his flashers on.

It's Monica and Danny's big day. She's my coworker, whose gorgeous face is constantly lining the glossy pages of *Luxe LA* magazine. Not only because she's one of the leading ladies at *Forbes*'s new favorite company, The Influencer Firm, but because this socialite-turned-CEO is now married to Daniel Jones—head coach of the LA Galaxy, Los Angeles's professional soccer team. If you're thinking he must look like a derivative of an American David Beckham, you're basically there. Let's just hope their sense of humor is as good as their looks when they see the card I accidentally picked out.

Before I place it on the gift table, I stuff the envelope with a crisp hundred-dollar bill fresh from the ATM. Side note: I think wedding registries are bullshit. Everybody wants an ice cream maker until you have one and never use it, which is why I spring for cold, hard cash instead. I grab a black Sharpie marker from the guest book table, pop the cap off, and attempt to squeeze in a nondescript *s* after the second "Mr.," hoping my makeshift, hand-drawn serif font letter doesn't stick out like a sore thumb. I blow on the fresh ink, then hold the pseudo Pinterest-fail an arm's length away. *That'll do,* I think to myself.

I lift a glass of red wine from a caterer's tray as if we choreographed the move and check the time on my Apple Watch, which arguably isn't the most fashionable accessory when dressing for a chic summer wedding. But aside from the fact that it doesn't quite match my strapless pale yellow cocktail dress, it serves a much greater purpose for me. It keeps my data front and center, right where I want it, not on my phone buried somewhere deep in my purse. Bonus: the band, smack-dab on the middle of my wrist, also covers a tattoo I've been meaning to have lasered off.

Other than telling me the time, 7:30 p.m., it also serves up my most recent Tinder notifications. I've gotten four new matches since this morning, which isn't bad for a) a Saturday, since most people do their Tindering while zoning out at work or bored in bed at night; and b) a pushing-thirty New York native whose most recent relationship was the love-hate one with a stubborn last ten pounds. That's me, by the way. Charlotte Rosen.

Though present and accounted for now, the battle of Tide pen vs. toothpaste stain went on for longer than I intended back at my apartment, causing me to arrive about half an hour late to the cocktail hour. Which means I for sure missed Monica and Dan's ceremony in its entirety. I, of all people, know that's

rude. I'm someone who is hypersensitive to people's arrival tendencies (well, to all measurable tendencies, to be honest; more
on that later). But I'm sort of glad I missed the *I Do*s, as there
is still something about witnessing the exchange of vows that
makes me a little squeamish. I got married five years ago and,
well, I'm not married anymore—let's put it that way.

The good news is that with time, I can feel it's definitely
getting easier to come to things like this. To believe that the
couple really will stay together through it all. To believe that
there is such a thing as "the one"—even if it may actually be
"the other" that I'm looking for this next go-round.

Late as I may be to the wedding party, there are some perks
to my delayed arrival. Namely, the line at the bar has died
down enough for me to trade up this mediocre red wine for
a decent gin and tonic. Another perk? Several fresh platters
of bacon-wrapped dates have just descended like UFOs onto
the main floor of the venue, which happens to be a barn from
the 1800s. Except this is Los Angeles, and there are no barns
from the 1800s. So instead, every creaky floorboard, every
corroded piece of siding, and every decrepit roof shingle has
been sourced from deep in the countryside of southwest Iowa
to create the sense that guests are surrounded by rolling fields,
fragrant orchard blossoms, and fruiting trees. The reality being
that just outside the wooden walls of the coveted, three-year-
long-wait-list Oak Mill Barn stands honking, gridlocked traffic on the 405 and an accompanying smog alert.

As I continue to wait for my impromptu wedding date,
Chad, to come back from the bathroom, I robotically swipe
left on the first three guys who pop up on Bumble, another
dating app I'm on, then finally decide to message a guy who
looks like a bright-eyed Jason Bateman (you know, pre-*Ozark*)
and is a stockbroker, according to his profile. We end up
matching and he asks me for drinks. I vaguely accept. Welcome to dating in LA.

I've conducted some research that has shown that after the age of thirty, it becomes exponentially harder to find your future husband. What number constitutes *exponentially*? I'm not sure yet, but I'm working on narrowing in on that because generalities don't really cut it for me. Thinking through things logically like this centers me, calms me, and resets me—no matter what life throws my way. All that's to say, I'm officially in my last good year of dating (and my last year of not having to include a night serum in my skin care regimen), and I'm determined not to wind up with my dog, my roommate, and a few low-maintenance houseplants as my sole life partners.

"Sorry that took so long," says Chad, returning from the men's room twenty minutes after leaving. "Did you know the bathroom at this place is an actual outhouse? Thank god it was leg day at the gym—I had to squat over the pot. My quads are burning nice now."

Confession. I didn't just bring a date to the wedding, I brought a *blind* date.

No worries, though. Monica knows how serious I am about the path to Mr. Right and supports the fact that I go on my fair share of dates to get me there quicker. Plus, he isn't a total stranger; she knows him—or, she *met* him, rather. He attended her work event last week at the LA County Museum of Art and is supposedly this cute, single real estate something or other. Of course he tried to hit on her and, unlike most beautiful people in Los Angeles, Monica actually copped to being in a committed relationship with Danny. (Who doesn't like to brag they're marrying Mr. Galaxy himself?) So she did the next best thing and gave him her single coworker's Instagram handle and told him to slide into my DMs. It's a bold move on her part, but I appreciate her quick thinking and commitment to my cause, Operation: Reclassify My Marital Status.

Since Chad first messaged me a week ago, I've done my

homework on him. And I'm not talking about just your basic cyber stalking. I'm talking about procuring and sifting through real, bona fide data. It's essentially a version of what I'm paid to do for a living—track down all the "influencers," people with a lot of fans and followers on the internet, and match them to events we plan for our clients so they can post on social media and boost our clients' profiles.

Some may think my side-project software, the one that computes how much of a match *I* am with someone, is a bit...*much*, but I don't see it that way at all. I'm on the hunt for a man who is a true match for me—one who won't just up and leave in the blink of an eye. I left things up to fate once and look how that turned out. I'll be damned if I do it that way again.

While I studied up on Chad, I conducted a hefty "image search," yielding about a hundred photos of him that have been uploaded across a variety of social platforms over the years. In real life, I'm pleased to say he checks out. Chad is over six feet tall, tanned, and toned, with coiffed Zac Efron hair that's on the verge of being described as "a bit extra." From the shoulders up, he's an emoji. A walking, talking emoji. But as I step back and admire him in his expertly tailored suit, he looks like a contestant on *The Bachelor*. In retrospect, Chad is just the right amount of good-looking to complement my physical appearance, which can be described as a made-for-TV version of an otherwise good-looking actress.

"Something to drink, sir?" one of the caterers asks Chad.

"Yes. A spicy margarita. Unless... Wait. Do you make the margarita mix yourselves? Or is it, like, that sugary store-bought crap?"

Eek. I had forgotten my discovery that Chad is a bit of a wellness guru. I guess so is everyone in LA, but I can't help but be taken aback when I hear that there are people who actually care about the scientific makeup of margarita mix.

"Fuck it. Too many calories either way," Chad announces before giving the waitress a chance to answer his question. "I'll just take a whiskey."

"Splash of Coke?"

"God, no. So many empty calories."

With his drink order in, Chad rolls his neck around and pops bones I never knew existed. Then, one by one, the joints in his fingers. The sound makes me a bit queasy but I'm trying to focus on the positive, like his beautiful hazel eyes and the fact that cherry tomatoes and mini mozzarella balls with an injection of balsamic vinegar are the latest and greatest munchie to hit the floor.

Chad turns to me with a smile, his palm connecting with the small of my back. "Should we find our seats? What table are we at?"

Good question, I think to myself. *I'm* at table six. Chad is... on a fold-up chair we will have to ask a caterer to squeeze between me and Monica's great-aunt Sally? I kind of forgot to mention to him that I didn't really get an official okay to bring him tonight.

"Table six," I say pleasantly with a smile.

"Six is my lucky number. Well, that, and *nine*, if you know what I mean," Chad says with a wink accompanied by an actual thumbs-up.

The waitress comes back with his whiskey neat, and he proposes we clink our glasses in a toast to meeting up as we make our way to the table. Still not over the lingering effects of his immature, pervy *sixty-nine* joke, I reluctantly concede to do the cheers with the perpetual high-schooler.

"So, what did you think of Monica's event?" I say to break the ice as we take our seats at the luckily empty round table.

"Well, I don't really know what she does for a living, but she *is* fine as hell. I mean, that's why I hit on her last week at the LACMA. Sure, I saw the ring on her finger, but couldn't resist saying hi to a goddess like her. My god, that woman is something else."

I nod in agreement. Partly because, yes, Monica Hoang needs her own beauty column in *Marie Claire*, stat. And partly because I'm too shocked by his crass demeanor to really do or say anything else. Did I say Chad reminded me of a contestant on *The Bachelor*? I think I meant he reminds me of a guy who gets sent home on night one of *The Bachelor*.

"She said you're a real estate...attorney, was it?" I awkwardly segue. "What's your favorite neighborhood in Los Angeles?"

It sounds like I'm interviewing him for a job, which in a way, I am. But had I known the conversation was going to be like forcefully wringing out a damp rag, just hoping to squeeze out something semidecent, I would have never invited him to join me at the wedding. In fact, I likely wouldn't have gone through with a date, of any kind, at all. Conversation skills rank high on my list of preferred qualities in a mate. Looks like he's the exception to the rule that attorneys are good linguists, because my app sure as shit didn't predict this fail.

So how does my software work, then? Well, it's all about compatibility. My algorithm is programmed to know what I like and what I'm looking for in the long term. So to see if a guy is a match, I comb through his online profiles, enter the facts I find out about him, and generate a report that indicates how likely he is to be my future husband or how likely we would be to get a divorce, for example. One of the most helpful stats is how likely we are to go on a second date. I've determined that anyone scoring above 70 percent means that chances are good we'd go out again. And, well, a second date is the first step to marriage. You get the point. Anyone below a 70, I ignore and move on. Chad pulled a 74, which is a solid

C if you're using a high school grading system. Not stellar, but certainly passable with room for improvement.

As it's turning out, there's a lot of room for improvement.

"Huh? I'm not in real estate," he says with a confused look on his face.

"Oh, Monica said you were an attorney at Laird & Hutchinson?"

"Well, yes, that's the name of our firm. The Laird side is real estate. But they acquired Hutchinson a couple years ago, and that's the side of the practice I work on."

"What kind of law is Hutchinson?"

"We're the 'Life's too short, get a divorce!' guys. You've probably seen a few of our company's billboards."

Chad slides his business card my way, and as soon as I see the logo, I picture those billboards slathered all over the bus stop benches down Laurel Canyon Drive and feel physically ill. Not only because he's in the business of making divorce seem cheeky, but also because I'm wondering what other things I might have missed or gotten wrong about Chad. .

"Wait. So have *you* ever been divorced?" The question pops off my tongue involuntarily. As soon as the words come out, I remember he reserves the right to ask me the same question in return and immediately regret posing it. I'm not ready to explain the demise of my first marriage.

"Me? Nah. Never married."

Luckily, a server reappears to take our dinner order. But let it be known that if Chad had asked, I would have explained that I didn't give up on my life partner because I was frustrated he failed to load a dishwasher in any sort of methodical way. I didn't just get bored and say "screw it," chalking the whole thing up as just a starter marriage (google it, this is a thing now). In fact, if anyone abruptly left anyone, *he* abandoned *me* out of nowhere.

"Would you like the chicken and veggies or the short rib and scalloped potatoes?" the caterer asks me.

"Short rib and potatoes," I say, a game-time decision made entirely by my growling stomach.

At that, Chad looks at me like I rolled into the Vatican wearing a tube top. "You sure about that, Char? There are so many hidden carbs in potatoes," he whispers with a hint of disgust.

First off, *Char* is reserved for people with a little more tenure in my life, thankyouverymuch. And secondly—

"Yes, I'm sure. An extra scoop of potatoes if possible," I say, loud enough for our waitress, who jots down the special instruction.

"Chicken for me. Extra veggies," my 74 percent match requests.

There it is. His wellness obsession flaring up again. I'm racking my brain for what to say next to a guy who screams "dead end" to me.

"Excuse me, hon. It's the firm. I've got to take this." Chad's waving his phone at me.

Hon?

He leaves the table to take his call by the hallway to the outhouses.

I spot the vision herself, Monica, in the chicest strapless Vera Wang ball gown to ever have existed and make my way over to her.

"Oh my god, Mon! You look amazing!" I squeal as I give the bride a hug. "I can't believe you're *married!*"

"Aww, thanks, Char. We're about to do speeches, so I can't chat long. Hey, did I see you brought a date?"

"Yeah, sorry. I hope you don't mind," I say, caught.

"It's all good. You're at the 'Work Table' and Zareen texted that she couldn't make it out of Palm Springs in time. Dust storm or something."

I was wondering why the table looked so empty.

"That sucks," I say about our boss missing her big day. "But the good news is, I brought that Chad guy."

"You did?! LACMA Chad? Where is that chiseled Greek god? Wait, can I say things like that now?" She flashes her shiny diamond band my way.

"Over there in the doorway on his phone."

She diverts her attention his way and a smile purses her ruby-red lips. She's seemingly so satisfied with her match-making abilities, she doesn't care that I amended her guest list.

"See? I told you he was hot," she says.

I'm not sure I'd call him hot. There's a bulging vein in his forehead and he looks like he's cross-examining an invisible Brad Pitt.

"He's better looking than me, that's for sure," I concede.

"That's not true, Charlotte. But my two cents? Take your hair down and put this on."

Monica pulls a bright red Chanel lipstick from her cleavage and jerks it my way like she's offering me a cigarette. I stare at the tube of lip lacquer with the same skepticism I would a shot of warm bottom-shelf tequila.

"Hurry up, put it on. You ought to play up that whole Zooey Deschanel thing you've got going on. A bold lip is going to work wonders on you."

I sweep the lipstick across my mouth and rub my lips together while handing the tube back to Monica. My lips feel creamy and smooth, although I wonder how much of the red stuff is stuck to my teeth.

"Now, if you'll excuse me, it looks like Danny needs me for a toast."

Monica tucks the lipstick back where it came from and scurries away amid the whir of clinking champagne glasses. The crowd is demanding that the newlyweds kiss, and I pick up my knife and flute to join the movement.

Monica's beaming. Well, she's always beaming. But today's glow is different. I remember what it felt like to get married. The wedding was the best day ever. Regardless of how things ended up for me, I'm thrilled for her and wish them the best.

"Sorry about that. My partner is trying to get some residual business from Gavin and Gwen," Chad says, rejoining me at the table.

"Rossdale and Stefani?"

He makes the *click* sound with his tongue again and points at me. I guessed right, I suppose.

"Look, I know what you're thinking," says Chad. "How does a guy who makes a living divorcing people think he can be in a genuine relationship?"

"Actually, I was thinking about how good those cheesy potatoes are going to be."

"The truth is," he blazes on, "I see so much separation, I know *exactly* what it takes to have a serious relationship with someone."

"That's interesting," I say. "Kind of like that whole *you have to know dark to know light* concept."

"Exactly!"

My curiosity is piqued for the first time since spotting a giant gourmet cupcake tower near the dance floor.

"So then, tell me, what are the secrets to lasting relationship happiness?" I begin to pry.

He takes a sip of his whiskey before divulging. "First of all, prenups. Those are an absolute must. They just make people feel more secure in the marriage, knowing that if it all ends, they won't rob each other to death."

Fair enough. Although I did not have a prenup with my first husband and things still managed to work out pretty fairly in the end as far as assets went.

"Continue," I say.

"Then, a sex contract."

I nearly choke on the last few drops of my gin and tonic.

"A sex contract? What...what the hell even *is* that?"

"Relax. It's not that big of a deal. Just something that binds a couple to engage in regular intimacy. So many couples stop having sex after marriage, or it becomes like a chore that happens about as infrequently as a SoCal thunderstorm. For me, I need sex four times a week at minimum and I don't want that to stop just because I put a ring on it."

"What if your wife—"

"Isn't in the mood? I mean, of course we could work something into the contract that would excuse you for a few days if you're on your period or if someone close to you dies. Stuff like that."

And there it is: like malware, this date has been infected and is now crashing. Quickly.

"Okay, Chad. You know what? I'm not sure we're a good match here."

The fact: I'm 100 percent positive.

"How can you possibly know that? We haven't even danced together. Which, by the way, is a really good indication of how your sex life will be."

My appetite is officially gone.

"I just...know."

"Oh, come on. We were just getting to know each other," he bargains.

"I already know *plenty* about you, Chad. I think you should go."

"Go? The meal hasn't even come yet. I'm not going anywhere. And I want to know what you *think* you know about me."

The whites of his eyes are more pronounced than before and the vein in his forehead is pulsating at me like a blinking reflector on the back of a bicycle.

I should say nothing. I should thank him for his spontaneity in being my date to Monica's wedding, then guide him to the door before he turns into The Hulk.

But… I won't do that. Because he struck a nerve. He struck a few, actually. Most importantly, Chad asked a question I can't hold back on answering.

"For starters, you're telling me you're ready for a genuine relationship, but you openly admitted trying to swoop up a nearly married Monica. I'm not sure that screams 'genuine.' Secondly, never in a million years would I ever sign my name on a *sex contract*. What is this, *Fifty Shades of Grey*? Third, I researched the shit out of you, and while I admittedly flubbed your professional credentials—which, by the way, will *never* happen again—I know more about you than I should for a first date, *Chadwick Harold Johnston*. Based on who you follow and what you've liked on social media over the last eighteen months, it appears that you tried your hand at becoming an amateur fitness model but didn't qualify for the PowerBar open—whatever the hell that is—which is why you started working out like crazy and taking gym selfies every other day. Unfortunately, it didn't grow your following enough organically, so you started paying for Russian bots to like your posts. Sometime after that, you started dating a Norwegian supermodel who dumped you for an 'up-and-coming SoundCloud rapper'—talk about an ego blow—and that's when you switched your account to private. And only just recently, I'd say in the last three months—because that's how long it's been since your pics started getting more than eleven likes—did you go back to being public. My guess? So you could show off your thirteen-pound muscle gain in time for 'summer body season' in hopes that Nadia, your Norwegian ex, would somehow see it and want you back. But you're here. With me. So that didn't exactly go to plan, now, did it?"

"How…how do you know all this?"

I can't tell if he's horrified or impressed, but it doesn't matter.

"Not that you've asked any questions about *my* life, but let's just say I'm sort of a master of internet research."

"You're a freak and a stalker, that's what you are."

"And finally," I say, ignoring his dumb dig, "I don't need social media to know that last week, you snuck into one of our invite-only influencer events at the LACMA."

"I didn't *sneak in* to that event, okay? I *am* an influencer."

"The hell you are. You were never on the invite list because *I made* the invite list."

"Um, do you guys still want this?" A waiter has been hovering at the side of the table with the steaming veggies in one hand and a platter of gooey potatoes on the next.

"Yeah, she wants it."

I'm not surprised misogynistic Chad answers for me but am surprised, however, when he continues talking.

"She wants it *to go* so she can eat it in the privacy of her own home, where she stalks people on the internet like a lonely, pathetic creep. Speaking of stalkers, Char, I was on MySpace back in the day, if you're looking for something to dig up tonight."

I'm thankful that Monica and Danny are canoodling at the head table and see none of the scene we've just made. I'm even more thankful that Chad has taken the cue and decided to leave.

"You can just leave both on the table," I say to the waiter, never having been so happy to be alone with a double scoop of au gratin potatoes.

Chapter 2

"Dude. You're home early," my roommate, Casey, says. "How'd it go with Brad?"

"Chad," I say, handing her his business card. "And not good. Not good at all."

"Well, think of it this way. If you ever need a divorce…"

Her blasé response is the reminder I need to tread lightly on the marriage subject. I don't bring my first husband up to people who didn't know him. Casey didn't know him, and so now (or ever) is not the time to have that bridge-crossing conversation. I change the subject.

"Has Leno gone out?" I ask, bending down and letting my dog lick my face as I scratch his cute little French bulldog butt. Even though I'm emotionally drained from my botched date with Chad, there's something about my dog that instantly takes the edge off my mood, no matter what.

"Yup, I took him out about an hour ago."

I tap my Apple Watch. It's only 9:00 p.m. This is the earliest I've been home on a Saturday night in a long time, but what can I say? When your date leaves before the bread basket has made its way around the dinner table, you're just not in the mood to stick around for the Chicken Dance with strangers.

"Wait a sec. Is that a dark lipstick I spy on you? I like it, Char!"

I promptly wipe my fingers over my lips in an effort to dismantle the final remnants of Monica's all-for-nothing vampy red lipstick that can be seen from space. The red stain on my fingertips is a reminder that I wasted effort on a guy who probably only agreed to go to a wedding with me to see if I know how to twerk. For the record, I don't.

"Thanks for taking Leno out, Casey. I owe you."

"Consider us even. I borrowed your car to get a tattoo earlier."

I'm not in the apartment but two minutes before Casey reminds me for the hundredth time how she couldn't be more different from me. For starters, she's extremely scatterbrained and is addicted to Netflix and tattoos. Meanwhile, I'm über-focused, task-oriented, and haven't had time to watch a show for leisure in about five years, and the only tattoo I have is the small one that needs to be removed. Other than that, she's a wee bit Goth, totally brash, and I'm fairly certain her gauged ears are only the start of many body modifications for her. Yes, I found Casey on Craigslist. And, yes, she's the real-life Janis from *Mean Girls*.

"I burned my damn ass when I got in and sat down on that leather seat. Holy greenhouse effect, Batman," she goes on to say.

I've said it before and I'll say it again: an all-black car in Southern California is completely, utterly impractical. But then again, it's a BMW 7 Series sedan. And it became mine after my marriage ended and there are no monthly payments on it, so who cares if it scorches your thighs every time you sit down in it?

"Is this for me?" I ask of a medium-sized brown box lobbed against the wall.

"Yup. The doorman said there was a package for you, so I snagged it on my way back up."

I breathe easier knowing the hard drive I ordered so my computer can handle combing through more stats has arrived, which means my plans for the rest of the night are baked. I thought about messaging the Bateman look-alike for a nightcap, but how can I go on a date with Mr. Right if I don't know for a fact that he could be just that? Statistics so far have shown me I will likely need to date upward of a hundred men before finding my ideal match. Chad was Lucky Sixty-Eight for me. Seeing how that crashed and burned, I've got some serious work to do with vetting my remaining guys, and pseudo Bateman is no exception.

As I set my purse down on the counter, I see two tickets for the Catalina Singles Cruise. I've heard of this event before, a dinner cruise that companies and organizations pay big bucks to sponsor twice a year. Basically a ferry takes a bunch of yuppie singles out to Catalina Island and back. I've never heard of any guests getting married, but like all cruises, the entertainment and all-inclusive drink packages make it worth it, I guess.

"Where did these come from?" I ask Casey as I hold the tickets up and dangle them back and forth, as if they are a scandalous pair of panties.

"Oh. Those. I won them in a silent auction at my brother's high school football fund-raiser."

"You *won* them? I can't believe *you'd* bid on a singles cruise." A dating environment wherein large bodies of surrounding water could potentially cause her solid black eyeliner to run down her face doesn't sound like it'd be Casey's thing. That's not me being mean either; that's me looking out for her signature Alice-Cooper-esque makeup.

"I sure as hell didn't bid on those. I'm not *that* desperate to find a man. I'm not *you*." As you could probably tell, we have a mutually snarky relationship, as proved by her cutting clapback. "But my mom threw my name into the hat to be funny and now look what's sitting on our counter."

"And the reason you haven't put them down the garbage disposal yet is...?"

"Because I thought it would be fun for us to go," she says matter-of-factly.

"You thought it would be *what*?" I nearly choke on the string cheese snack I've helped myself to. "Are you feeling okay, Casey? Is the tattoo ink seeping into your bloodstream by chance?"

Casey gets up from the couch to refill her cup of ice water. She's wearing a size XL Slayer T-shirt as a dress with a choke chain and Dr. Martens combat boots. The cool thing about Los Angeles is that one man's freak show is another's fashion icon.

"Yeah, why not? The tickets are good for free booze, food, and boys. Sounds right up your alley, to be honest, Char."

"Hmm, let me think about that. Speed dating, Sperry's, and endless SoCo Limes. Forget about my dating habits, Casey. I'm not sure you're going to find anyone even remotely interesting to you at this thing. But the good news is I bet you could flip those on Craigslist for a pretty penny."

I pick up my phone and check my work email. On Mondays, TIF caters in a casual lunch as a little "thanks for not calling in sick and giving yourself a three-day weekend" perk. The "Free Meal Monday" menu gets posted over the weekend in time for everyone to submit an order. This time, I see that it's Chipotle. While I've been known to house an entire bag of chips and guac myself, I haven't had their food in almost five years and it's a streak I'm vowing not to break come Monday.

"I'm not flipping anything," Casey says, snatching my

phone from my hands as I respond to the email with *Nothing for me.* "Pay attention, lady: we're going on the stupid cruise next week because I registered us about an hour ago and we're not exempt from the hundred-dollar cancellation fee if you back out. So put it on your calendar and get your red lipstick ready, girlfriend. We're going."

I wait for the noise of ice crushing from the freezer door to stop so she can clearly hear my reply: "No, thank you."

Casey and I don't hang out much. Read: *at all.* I mean, of course I see her around the apartment every single day, but she's not the kind of girl you spill all your dirty secrets to or with whom you'd go to the movies and see the latest Nicholas Sparks tearjerker. I'm frankly a little surprised, albeit flattered, she took the initiative to choose *me* as her plus-one to the singles cruise.

"Oh, come on. It'll be fun, Char. Quit thinking of it in terms of all the guys who *won't* be our future husbands, and instead, think of all the people we can make fun of! How about if I put it like this: I've run it through my Asshole Algorithm and statistics show we'll have solid material for at least six months."

Along with poking fun at me, she gives me puppy dog eyes that make me wonder if this is it. Is this the moment she and I finally hang out together? Our lease is set to renew in a few months. Maybe a good faith gesture wouldn't hurt to ensure she re-signs?

"Fine," I concede to her pathetically lovable stare. "I'll go."

"Yessss!" She high-fives me. Instant regret sinks in. "So, what's in the box?"

"That? Just a hard drive."

I almost forgot about the delivery sitting just feet away, although Leno sure has not. My little tan-and-white Frenchie with the jingly collar has been sniffing the box incessantly for the last ten minutes. I take a quick fuzzy photo with my iPhone and send it to my mom, Jean, aka Jean Rosen, aka The Jeaner, who is back in New York. Since I have yet to procure grandkids for her, she's transferred the entirety of her Jewish grandmother obsessive tendencies to my dog instead. I'm sure she will love this picture of Leno investigating a package like a bomb-sniffing dog.

"Well, then, that hard drive is made of solid gold. Have you picked it up? That box weighs about thirty pounds give or take. Trust me. The elevator was out of order, so I carried it up myself with Leno on the leash. Most cardio I've done in a decade. Man, I really need to quit smoking cigs."

I walk over to the box, kicking off my high heels along the way, and tilt it toward me. I, too, am shocked by its weight. Something doesn't quite scream "two terabytes" about this über-heavy delivery, so I bend down to read the return label. It says,

Hancock Insurance
832 Wilson Lane
Pala, CA 92001

Hancock Insurance doesn't sound like they broker external hard drives. And come to think of it, why is this box not slathered in blue-and-white Amazon Prime shipping tape?

But even more jarring than the mysterious info on the return label is that when I look closer, I see that the package is addressed to "Charlotte Austin." That name hasn't auto-populated the shipping fields for my online orders since I was married to Decker, and there's no way I accidentally entered that name.

"Hey, can you hand me scissors from the junk drawer?"

Casey instead pulls a switchblade from her bra and cocks

it open with the flick of her finger. They must not happen often, but I can tell she lives for moments like this.

I roll my eyes and quickly slice through the clear mailing tape. When I open the flaps, I find a bunch of packing peanuts and underneath all that padding a solid metal box with two identical keys taped near the handle. The box is locked at the hinge.

"What is it?" Casey asks, champing at the bit.

"I literally have no idea. It's not the hard drive, I'll tell you that much."

"Ooh! Maybe it's a time capsule. Open it and save it for me. I might be able to use it at an upcoming exhibit."

Casey is the curator of a monthly oddities expo in Los Angeles. We've lived together for almost five years and I've never been to her show. It's on my to-do list, right after checking off dates sixty-nine, seventy, and seventy-one. Suffice to say, she gets a little googly-eyed over things like gloves made for people with six fingers, sunken pirate treasure, bearded ladies, and—apparently—mail-order time capsules.

I peel off the keys from the side of the metal box. They look no bigger or sturdier than those I used to keep my diary locked up when I was a teenager. Regardless, they are a perfect fit into the lock, and with a quarter turn to the left, the hinge pops open.

I recognize what's inside immediately and let go, allowing the box to gently fall back onto the pile of packing peanuts.

I take a few steps back toward the kitchen.

"What is it?" Casey asks again.

There's an open bottle of wine on the counter. It's not mine. I don't know what kind it is. Or who it came from. Or how long it's been sitting there. In fact, it could be balsamic vinegar, for all I know. Nevertheless, I pop off the cork and chug a quarter of it.

"Jesus, Charlotte. You look like you've seen a dead person."
She's not far off.

"What the hell is in there?" Casey pries with more intensity.

"It's an urn," I say, wiping the wine from my lips with the back of my hand and taking one more pull for good measure.

"Oh, sweet! I can definitely use that in my show."

Except she can't.

"My dead husband is in it."

Casey closes her eyes and shakes her head, as if she's trying to tune out some bad music. "Excuse *me*? Wait. What? You were *married*? To *who*? Back the train up, lady."

"Hand me your knife again." I deflect her questioning because I've located a large envelope in the packaging, which I imagine is there to explain. Casey ceases fire and hands her blade to me.

I cut the envelope open and rip out its contents so quickly, it gives me an immediate paper cut on the tip of my pointer finger. I draw my finger to my lip and suck on the salty blood as I unfold a typed letter with my other hand.

"Need help, Char? A Band-Aid maybe?"

I shake my head no as I begin to read the letter. Again, it's addressed to a name I haven't gone by in almost five years.

Dear Mrs. Austin,
We regret to inform you that the mausoleum in Pala, California, was destroyed in a devastating wildfire on May the 20th of this year.

When the mausoleum identified itself as being in the path of the fires, all urns were evacuated to a safe place. Rest assured, your loved one(s) is still intact, although the Pala Mausoleum is no more.

Hancock Insurance is the company handling the insurance claim filed by the mausoleum. At this time, the owners have declined to rebuild and will be considered permanently closed. As such, we are returning all urns to the documented next of kin.

Your couriered package includes a locked, fireproof capsule. You may access the capsule with the attached set of keys to find the original urn.

The choice of where and when you rehome your loved one's ashes is entirely your own. We are terribly sorry for any inconvenience this may cause and thus grief counselors will be available for up to three complimentary sessions during the next two weeks. Again, this will be offered at no charge to you and we urge you to take advantage of the support during what we can only imagine will be a difficult time. Please call the 800 number listed on our website for more information.

Sincerely,

Robert Hancock

President, Hancock Insurance

It reads as formal as a court summons, but this letter is a casual confirmation that Decker is in this box.

Decker is in our apartment.

"It's him," I say with certainty and a hint of defeat. I've worked hard to keep this a secret and to keep it in my past. Now it's neither of those.

"I don't know what to do in this situation," Casey says. "But I think we should figure it out somewhere not here. Somewhere that serves beer."

She grabs my car keys for the second time today and pulls me out the door.

Chapter 3

I don't want to be here. *Here* being perched on a wobbly bar stool in a neighborhood drinking hole wearing the same toothpaste-laden dress I had on at Monica's wedding. But when your brain suddenly functions as well as a waterlogged sock, there's no fending off your roommate from dragging you out to discuss the untimely return of the most unexpected delivery.

It is evident that my pushback reflexes are experiencing a delay. They did the same thing when this was all going down, when everyone and their mother—specifically Decker's mother—were trying to tell me what to do. For now, I'm just hoping any piece of therapist advice that I've managed to catalog over the years bubbles up. My brain feels like a white noise machine and I need something to cut through the deafening sound of a silent shock.

"Ladies, what are we drinking this evening?" asks a chummy bartender as he puts down two Pabst Blue Ribbon cardboard coasters.

Focus on what you can control is the grief-healing mantra that finally rises to the surface. So, I take some ownership and order a double bourbon and ginger. As the bartender makes my drink, I wedge my hands firmly between my butt and the bar stool. If I don't take them out of frame, eagle-eyed Casey—the same girl who spotted my crimson lip like she was solving *Where's Waldo?*—will for sure notice they are trembling, and I don't want to be asked if I'm okay right now. I don't *know* if I'm okay right now.

"Well, you'd think a mausoleum, of all places, would be built with just a tad more protection against flames, *amiright?* I mean, aren't they setting dead bodies on fire there every single day? How did they not safeguard the place?"

I've done a really good job masking this from everyone. Hiding the fact that I was ever married. Hiding the fact that I am a widow. Now the curtain has fallen. All because I thought my stupid hard drive was in that box. I should have insisted on a little privacy upon seeing *Austin* written on the *To* line. Instead, I rushed to open it. I involved Curious Casey. I have no one to blame but myself.

"A mausoleum is different from a crematorium," I say, as if I'm reciting a sentence off a Wikipedia page. I bring my palm up to my mouth. Mundane as it was, I'm surprised by my ability to even utter words right now.

"Ohhhh, that's right. The crematorium is where they set the dead bodies on fire, isn't it? And a mausoleum is just a place where the urn stays. Like a graveyard but for urns, right?"

"Something like that," I mutter.

I hate that I am familiar with the nuances of these things. Girls my age, they know the difference between highlighter and bronzer. Not the difference between a mausoleum and a crematorium. And of all the things I feel right now, I'm embarrassed that I'm somehow still able to feel jealousy. Jealousy that it's just so blatantly clear that I'm not a part of the *girls who don't need to know this kind of stuff* camp anymore.

"Where's Pala again? Like a hundred miles from here?"

I nod my head yes. I know she's probably wondering how he wound up there. This is Los Angeles. I'm not saying mausoleums should be as frequent as cold-pressed juice shops, but you'd think there'd be a slightly more convenient option than a place a hundred miles away that's best known for its casinos and crypts. And there was. It's just that *convenience* never mattered as much as *coveted* to his mom, the Austin family matriarch.

"You've never heard of the Pala Mausoleum?" I ask Casey. "I thought you would have..."

Before I even finish the sentence, Casey has already executed a Google search on her iPhone. Over her shoulder, I see the photo of the place pop right up and my head feels like it has taken a hit of helium, like it's not even connected to my body anymore.

"Is this it?" She has no idea how the mere photo of it— the chevron marble flooring with flecks of real gold in it, the dreamy high ceilings, the massive flower display of award-winning hydrangeas smack-dab in the center of the lobby— carves an instant pit in my stomach like someone is hollowing out a pumpkin.

"Yeah, that's it."

"Well, I guess this reclaimed wood beaming didn't fare so well for them, huh? Bet that thing was covered in lacquer and the first to go up in flames. The good news? He's safe with us now."

Casey taps my shoulder twice in consolation, and it's like she's activated a sensor on a faucet. A few tears drip from my eyes.

"Hey, relax. Just breathe, okay? *Breathe.*"

It's a simple request. But what she doesn't realize is that the air was sucked out of the room the moment I found out Decker was gone and it never really came back. Ask any widow and they'll confirm the ability to take a deep breath doesn't quite regenerate back to the way it was before. *Just breathing* is a little harder for me, no matter how many years have passed.

"Sorry, I'm not sure what to say. I like to think I have all the answers," Casey says. "But I'm still just wrapping my head around the fact you were even married. I mean, you've been a widow for *five* years and I never even knew."

The way she explains it, it's like she's offended that I kept her in the dark. But I kept everyone in the dark and it's not like I hid some scandalous, dangerous criminal past from her. I just neglected to tell her the ins and outs of my marital status. Why? Because when I met her, I didn't know the formula for making my own self feel better. I'm not sure I really do now. And therefore I couldn't just pretend it into existence around someone I hardly even knew.

"Did anyone else know?" she asks.

"Not really. Mostly just my parents and some people I've met at support groups."

Sure, there are a few mutual friends from back in the Decker days who also obviously know I'm a widow now, but I don't mention them. One girl messaged me a month after he died and said she couldn't talk to me anymore because it just made her sad and want to emotionally eat more. Being told I was a liability to her ideal weight range put a bad taste in my mouth. The others? They all faded away once they realized inviting the widow to stuff like bachelorette parties and book clubs was kind of a buzzkill. But it's all good. Because I used to think, *Since Decker's gone, do these people still like me?* Now I think, *Do I even like them?*

"I mean, I get it. We don't talk about our periods, so why

would you tell me about your love life? I guess I'm just mad at myself for not picking up on it. I'm usually sups intuitive like that. Hey, is that what this is for?"

Casey grabs my wrist, plucks it out from under my bum, and twists it so that the inside of my arm is facing up. She moves the band of my Apple Watch up an inch, exposing my *D* tattoo. I nod my head to confirm. I got the tattoo after Decker proposed. After I knew we'd be together permanently. Or so I thought.

"Well, for what it's worth, you've done a good job," she says.

I look up at her, surprised. "Of what?"

"Hiding it. Now that I know, I can't say that I could look back on the last five years of living with you and think *Aha! That explains it!* So, I've got to hand it to you, kid. You definitely don't act like a widow."

I had one, too. A widow stereotype. But I've been to enough support groups not to be shocked when I see a fellow widow in her twenties. To Casey, it feels like a widow should be an older woman. Not necessarily an *old woman*, just someone... older than me and old enough to have had time to earn that label. I picture someone my mom's age who seems like she's carrying emotional baggage, not someone who has yet to celebrate her thirtieth birthday.

"Well, I am. The package sitting on our kitchen floor confirms it."

"In case you were wondering if I'd be cool with it, I am," she says. "You can keep him at our place as long as you want. In fact, I think it's rad that you get to have a death do-over of sorts."

"A what?"

"You know, like a second chance at dealing with his death. Think of one thing that bothers you about how it all went down, and change it."

Casey polishes off the rest of her Guinness, lets out an audible belch, and heads to the bathroom. She couldn't be more Courtney Love if she tried, down to the wiry bob that's styled with god-only-knows-what goop.

There are a million things that bother me about Decker's death. Starting with the fact that he died at all. We were married less than a year. Yes, I've been a widow for much longer than I ever was a wife.

Also, I didn't even know he wanted to be cremated. I was twenty-five years old when he died; he was twenty-seven. It wasn't something we'd had the chance to discuss yet over a bottle of pinot noir and all-you-can-eat sushi. Unfortunately, "not knowing" or "never discussed it" weren't valid excuses, and it opened the door for Debbie Austin—my Know-It-All mother-in-law—to swoop in, take over, and decide Decker was going to Pala.

The buzz of an incoming text message lights up my Apple Watch. It's my mom.

Sorry, was sleeping. Give my grand dog a squeeze! PS what's in the box, J.Crew sale?

It hits me that the box I thought had a hard drive in it—the one I photographed and sent to my mother while trying to score some mom-points—actually contained the ashes of her former son-in-law. Right now, Jean Rosen thinks I splurged on a J.Crew summer sale and I'm fine with letting her believe that's the case. This whole situation isn't something I can explain in a text. Not to my mother. Not to his mother. But I know I'll have to fill both of them in eventually.

Night, Char. I love you, she sends next.

I turn the phone to black and get a little squeamish. "I love you"s at the end of a conversation, especially ones via text, gut me. My mom could get hit by a city bus crossing the street tomorrow morning and our last conversation would have been about a faux J.Crew delivery, but take it from someone who actually has experience doling out famous last words: you don't always get what you want in that department.

Casey props herself back up onto the bar stool that's about six inches too high for her five-foot-nothing fragile frame. She smells a bit like cigarettes, which leads me to believe her bathroom break turned into a smoke break, but I'm not judging. I could go for a drag right now myself.

"Okay, so you know I was going to eventually have to ask this. How did Decker die?"

Chapter 4

Back at the apartment, Casey and I brush our teeth. Our routines overlap like this in our one-bathroom, single-vanity apartment most days of the week, but we make do. Although the layout of this place is mildly inconvenient, neither of us is willing to suggest moving elsewhere. Because this one—this tiny one—is home.

"So, yeah," I say, spitting into the sink. "That's the story."

"Damn, that's fucking crazy," she says, mouth full of toothpaste, waiting for her turn.

"Hence—" I wipe my chin "—why his mother would say…"

Like I said, there are a million things that bother me about Decker's death. Especially the fact…

"…that you killed him." Casey completes my thought, wiping her wet, leftover toothpaste from her lips with *my* bath towel.

Bingo.

"You going to be alright tonight?"

I nod.

"Just one thing," I say. "I know this was a lot of information tonight. And that it was a huge surprise. But please promise not to treat me any differently now that you know it all? Just...continue to be normal around me."

She holds up two scout's honor fingers and states, "I, Casey Kevdale, hereby promise not to treat you any differently now that I know you are a widow."

She drops her fingers.

"But," she goes on, "I do hope you realize that *being normal* is not exactly in my repertoire." Casey peels down her bottom lip, exposing that new tattoo she got earlier in the night. It's a crow sitting on a telephone wire on the inside of her mouth. "Sleep well, Rosen," she says before shutting the door to her bedroom, a subtle reminder that I am Charlotte Rosen now—not Charlotte Austin. Despite what that box in the kitchen says.

I close the door to my bedroom and invite Leno up on the mattress. Decker didn't let him sleep in the bed—he said it was a "bad habit" dog owners get into—but I haven't let Leno sleep anywhere besides the bed since his death. Decker and I obviously never got the chance to have kids, but with Leno, we had started a family. The reason I wanted Leno close to me after Decker died is the same reason I want him near me now—grunts, snorts, snores, and all—it's the closest thing to having Decker still share my pillow and steal all the covers. It's the only living, breathing thing that connects me to the man I happily married.

I unhook Leno's collar and drape it on the bedside table. His name tag clinks against the base of my dim little lamp, the inscription on the shiny metal tag reminding me that whatever is left of the man who was so smitten with the legendary host that he vowed to name his firstborn—or dog—"Leno" is just feet away from me.

It's been nearly five years. I want to sit with him. I want to be close to him. I want to do all this with no (Casey) questions asked.

Once I hear my roommate steadily snoring for five minutes, I peel my covers off and tiptoe out of my room using the flashlight on my phone for guidance. I make my way über-quietly to the kitchen and sit cross-legged on the floor next to the box, peel back the flaps of the cardboard for the second time tonight, and pause. It's been a while since Decker and I were in the same room and I'm not really sure how to act around him.

I pick up the glassy ceramic urn and it is cold to the touch. It's not a traditional-looking "urn," this shiny, grayish-blue jar that his mom picked out from an artist from Argentina. As I shift it from one hand to the other and give it a three-sixty, it dawns on me that maybe another wealthy woman purchased this same ceramic art and is using it as a dog treat container in Bel Air. Crazy how what's one woman's urn is another woman's cookie jar.

"Hi," I whisper.

And that's when they hit again, the tears.

I miss him. I've always missed him.

I miss our life together. I miss watching him scramble to do his taxes the night before they were due because he insisted that paying an accountant to do them was a waste of money even though he wasn't good at math. I miss us taking turns throwing Leno's tennis ball for an hour at the park while sipping rosé on a grass-stained blanket that smelled like mold no matter how many times we washed it. I miss grilling grocery store butcher counter steaks to a perfect medium rare and talking about how our neighbor two doors down might actually be a high-end hooker. I miss so much about my life back then, my old life.

I can't help but draw my finger—fresh paper cut and all—to the urn's inscription and run it lightly back and forth, feeling the shape of each and every letter.

Debbie facilitated the cremation. That's what she said he wanted. So Debbie picked the mausoleum. And Debbie ordered the custom urn. But I got to choose what this little nameplate was going to have on it. This was my part of the process to own.

I was shocked that Debbie came to me, albeit in an email, for my buy-in. I was simply told it needed to be under thirty characters per line, three lines max.

I don't know why she outsourced this task to me. Maybe her conscience couldn't possibly be okay with her not consulting his wife on at least *one* thing on the list of death to-dos. But instead of dissecting the semantics, I decided to reply to her email as quickly as possible so I could delete it out of my inbox just as swiftly as it had pinged in. Short and sweet, just like our marriage, is what I went with: Decker's full name, his date of birth, and the date he died. While it may not have been the most colorful arrangement of words, at least it fell well within the character limit, unlike my other idea—THIS NEVER SHOULD HAVE HAPPENED.

I shift my legs and kneel to the side, my thigh pressing against the cold tile of the kitchen floor. I sat just like this in his hospital room next to his bed when I was too tired to stand. As Debbie paced back and forth telling me exactly how things were going to go after I told the doctor to stop resuscitation efforts. I don't remember the exact things she said; all I know is it sounded like the white noise I heard earlier at the bar tonight. Muffled musings drowned out by the sound of a monitor flatlining.

After he died, it wasn't exactly like planning a wedding—even though you call some of the same types of vendors (flowers, caterers, etc.), it's expensive, and there's a lot to organize. And I wouldn't go as far as saying Debbie *enjoyed* making Decker's arrangements, but she certainly plowed through them in a way that seemed like she was worried about what others would think if she chose an ill-fashioned urn or just a run-of-the-mill mausoleum for her one and only son.

I take my finger off the engraving and realize then that it has gone tingly. In fact, all my fingers have. Like pins and needles poking and prodding my extremities.

No, no, no, I say to myself, refusing to go there right now. *There* being fetal position on the floor where Casey will eventually find me when she gets up to refill her water, probe me with questions, and vow never to leave me alone again. AKA: the thing I've wanted to avoid since day one with her as my roommate.

Though I'm not there yet, the last bad episode I had, I was in the grocery store getting lunch meat for the week. Just out of nowhere, I suddenly couldn't breathe. I've never been on an airplane when oxygen masks had to descend, but I imagine what I felt is similar to that: a change in cabin pressure followed by pure panic. I ditched the roast beef and cheese on a shelf in the chip aisle and ran out the exit, where I proceeded to sit on the curb and tuck my head between my knees. I rocked back and forth, ignoring all the people who asked me if I was okay. Eventually I got back in my car, popped one of my prescribed emergency pills, and the little black spots I was seeing started to go away. Once the meds fully kicked in, it was off I went to pick up my dry cleaning. A relief? Sure. I had errands to run. But scary to think the pills made it feel like my panic attack never happened; like it wasn't real.

I lay the urn back on the packing peanuts for the moment and grab my purse off the counter. I haven't tapped into my "emergency stash" in years because I've been good—really good—since the grocery store meltdown. But today, my world has changed. I'm scared I won't be able to stay glued together much longer. So I unzip the hidden pocket in my purse and pull out the last two now-expired antidepressants to my name and wash them down with the wine on the counter from earlier in the night. My tongue puckers and I wipe my wine-stained lips with a dishrag.

When he realizes I'm no longer in bed, Leno groggily emerges from the doorway of my room. He trots his way over and takes a seat by me. As I pet him, I feel like I'm ascending on an airplane, weightless with the white noise of the engine whirring in the background. I have found smooth air; I feel calmer. I am under control.

"Should we go to bed, little buddy?" I whisper while petting him softly.

Before retreating to the bedroom, I stare once more at the urn, still not over the fact *he's in there.*

"How about you, Decker? Do you want to go to bed?" Without much hesitation or thought, I grab the urn and carry it to my room. I set it next to Leno's collar on the nightstand. He sniffs it as if it's a new toy. I shoo him away so he doesn't knock it over.

It's not going to stay here permanently. I just want to see what it feels like. What it feels like to get ready for bed with my husband in the same room as me for the first time in five years. To experience a routine that we should have been enjoying together all this time.

Feeling like the medicine is kicking in, I do one more task before climbing into bed.

I locate the USC lacrosse hoodie. The things I have of Decker's are starting to get sparse, but I still have a couple of his worn-out USC hoodies in my sweatshirt drawer for easy access. Even after college, the lacrosse hoodie was a regular part of his wardrobe. I would steal it from him when I wanted to relax on the couch in something baggy and comfy. It's soft and worn out, and even though I've washed it several times since he's passed, I'm convinced it still smells like him if I just close my eyes and inhale hard enough. When I wear it, it feels like I'm putting on a hug from him. And that's what I want right now as I throw it on over my head and shimmy my arms through the too-big sleeves. I want a hug from Decker.

"Well, good night, babe. See you tomorrow," I say as I turn off the bedside lamp. I kiss my *D* tattoo and touch it to the urn. In this moment, I'm glad I never had it removed.

I know it could be the pills talking, because this is by far the strangest conversation I've had with a guy recently, but I suddenly don't feel anxious.

In fact, I feel married. Or something.

Chapter 5

I pop in my earbuds, leash up Leno, and make a quick left at the corner toward a neighborhood coffee shop with a dog-friendly walk-up window. But just then, like the way your mind spins thinking about whether or not you left your flat iron plugged in, I second-guess if I locked the door to my apartment. Involuntarily, I tighten up Leno's retractable leash and head home.

In the lobby, I obsessively press the up button for the elevator three times in quick succession. While waiting, I visualize how easy it would be for thieves to jack my computer, my *one* pair of ill-fitting-but-stylish Louboutins, even the fifty-five-inch flat screen TV. But what if they take the urn?

Dings from faraway floors indicate the morning church-going rush is clogging up the shaft. So I scoop up Leno like he's a frozen grocery store turkey and head straight for the stairwell. There's no choice but to take them two at a time. I need to get back to my apartment.

Once at the fifth floor, I fling myself into the hallway and erupt in an all-out sprint to apartment 518. Leno must be getting whiplash. I grab the handle and it flies open with ease. I left it unlocked just as I had feared. Except once I'm inside, nothing seems to be missing. There aren't thieves robbing the place. There's just one man sitting there.

"Hey, honey. Can you please tell my mom I'm back and I'm okay?" Decker says from the couch while watching SportsCenter.

At the mere sound of his voice, soft-spoken and genuine, I spring up in my bed and put my hand to my chest to calm my heavy breathing.

I reach for a glass of water on my nightstand that I don't remember getting and chug the room-temperature liquid.

The door to my bedroom is cracked open and Leno isn't in my bed anymore, which means he's probably sitting in the foyer in front of the door, his way of letting me know he's ready to go outside for a morning potty walk. But I'm not ready for anything other than a triple-shot latte and an Advil or two. I toss my sweaty covers off, put on a robe over Decker's USC sweatshirt, and head toward the Keurig in the kitchen.

"Morning, Char. What's good?" Casey is eating a plate of scrambled eggs at the kitchen counter.

I rub my eyes and realize I never took my contacts out last night. I'm sure I look like a bloodshot mess. Good thing Casey doesn't care how I look. Or that I just borrowed her fork and shoveled a scoop of her breakfast into my mouth.

"Coffee. Now," I say with my mouth full of rubbery eggs.

"The Keurig is tits up again. We need a new one. But I brewed a regular pot over there. Help yourself. Are you okay?"

I pour a generous serving of blond roast into a mug monogrammed with the letter *C* on it. Casey's mom got us a set of four for a housewarming gift when we signed our lease five Octobers ago. It's cute how we can both use them interchangeably since our first names start with the same letter, but it's clear Casey uses them most often from her plum-colored lipstick, a shade she says is called "Black Eye," which has permanently stained the tan ceramic rims.

"I've been better."

"Well, I'm sure the middle-of-the-night wine chaser probably wasn't the best choice," she says, nodding in the direction of the empty bottle on the counter.

"I'll replace your wine, I promise."

"Can you get me a bottle of rosé when you do? I'm not basic enough to buy a bottle myself, but I'm really in the mood for it. By the way, what are you up to today? Some friends from the expo are going to the beach if you—"

"Can't," I say, holding my hand up to signal she should save her breath. Since my little escapade into the kitchen led to a full-blown fucked-up dream, I've come to realize that this normal day of rest is going to be anything but. "I've got a lot on my plate."

"Hey, I was wondering, can I see a picture of him?"

Of all the questions Casey has asked so far since Decker's return, this one hits me the hardest.

"A picture?"

"Yeah. I'm curious what the guy who did it for you looked like."

If I do this, if I show her a picture of Decker, it'll be the most vulnerable I've been with anyone who isn't family, a therapist, or a stranger from a support group. But I've lived with Casey for five years, and if anything, she's been the constant in my life since Decker's death. Always there to offer a pick-me-up bottle of wine (which I normally accept) or funky new eye shadow to try (which I normally decline). I should meet her in the middle.

A warmth washes over me—perhaps because I've just slowly shut the fridge door like it was made of a thin, fragile sheet of glass—like the way you pull thick covers over your cold shoulder at night. It feels comfortable. It feels safe. Hell, I just saw him in my dream. Maybe seeing him on my screen won't feel as foreign. What's there to be afraid of?

"Okay. Gimme a sec," I say, pulling my phone out of the pocket of my robe.

I pause, briefly, thinking how to navigate the ask. I could visit his Facebook page. It's still there, along with all the photos of him, us, and everything in between. But I don't go to that anymore. Not after I mistakenly decided to read through all the messages people left him on his wall after he died, then again on his birthday. They wrote these things to him as if he were still alive, as if he could read them. I guess it was sweet. But to the one person who wished more than anyone that Decker was still alive, it wasn't sweet. It was scary. I'm not going to let my heart get tricked like that again.

So instead I choose to show her a photo of the two of us in Punta Cana that I keep in my "favorites" folder on my phone. We went there one time on a whim—a quick Friday through Monday getaway. We weren't living together yet, so getting an email from him in the middle of my workday saying he booked the Travelzoo deal turned me into that cliché lunatic you see in public cheesing at their phone. On the last day of our vacation, after two too many margaritas in, he convinced me to rent a Jet Ski. Decker drove fast—really fast—and I…I held on for dear life and screamed bloody murder, white-knuckling him from behind. Admittedly I was having an absolute blast, and at one point he took his cell phone out of its plastic bag and we fired off a few quick selfies on the open water. When I look at him in that picture, a few crow's-feet surrounding his smiling bright blue eyes, I am reminded of all the ease with which he navigated this complex world. His worries capped at appreciating the moment and doing things that scared him so he could learn and grow.

"Holy shit, he's hot," Casey exclaims after I tilt the phone her way. "Wait. Is that kosher to say about a dead guy?"

"Yes, it's fine." I sort of smile as I watch Casey awkwardly navigate what is *kosher* or not in a situation like this. Ironically, that is the same conundrum I have faced since he died. I may be a widow, but I don't have the rule book. In fact, I'm pretty sure there isn't one.

And, yes. Decker is—well, was—hot. He was a six-foot-three lacrosse player. All in all just your healthy Cali-boy who liked french fries in his burritos and occasionally called in sick for a surf day when the waves were just right. I remember thinking, *They don't make them like this in NYC.*

I'm already ready for a refill of my coffee when my eye catches a dish towel draped on top of the stove.

"Why is the towel like this?" I ask as I look over to the oven.

"Like what?" Casey responds.

"Crumpled on top of the stove. Did you do that? Did you put it there like that?"

When Decker used to wash his hands at the kitchen sink, he would use the decorative dish towels I threaded through the handle of the oven to dry them off, but never put the towel back on the handle. Instead, he'd leave the expensive Anthropologie linens I was gifted at my bridal shower just strewn about the top of the stove. Not only a fire hazard, but his most signature, lovingly annoying habit. It is truly as if someone has broken in here. Someone I once knew—was married to, actually.

"No. Not that I know of. Why? Is something wrong?"

Upon closer inspection, I see there's a brush of red lipstick, along with some wine, right through the middle of it. It matches the color Monica had me swipe on at her wedding mixed with a bit of pinot noir. I'm the culprit—and I must be losing my mind, thinking this was some kind of a sign that he's back and he wanted my attention.

I thread the cloth through the handle, where it belongs.

Chapter 6

On my way into The Influencer Firm, an incoming call rings through my car speakers and I answer with a click of a button on the steering wheel. Sure, it may burn your thighs, but I have to give credit to a car that makes it this easy to pick up my mom's call.

I have a standing Sunday morning phone call with The Jeaner, something we've been doing since I moved out west after graduating college. But I admittedly missed her call yesterday. I was too busy nursing an ugly hangover that left me with little more energy than that required to lie in bed and avoid any conversation about the recent turn of events. It's a horrible thing to slice your own flesh and blood's incoming call, especially when it's from a woman who has always understood what you're going through, had your back, and supported you.

"Hi, Mom," I say through the echoey Bluetooth in my car.

"Hi, honey. How are you? We're thinking of painting your

room. What do you think about a nice shade of lilac?" She cuts right to it.

It doesn't matter what I think of *a nice shade of lilac*. My parents still live in the Brooklyn apartment I grew up in, and every time I go back to visit, nothing about the place has changed. My room still has the same twin mattress I slept on as a teenager, the hot-pink-corded landline, and faded boy band posters taped over the closet door. Despite acting like they intend to modernize it—or even just repaint it—I know that what they're really hoping is that one day I will find myself living with them again and they can pride themselves on having not touched a thing in my old bedroom. As if they are preserving an exhibit for the Smithsonian. I don't know how to break it to them, but if I didn't move home, if I didn't come crying to Mommy and Daddy after my husband died, then why would I now? I'm already over the hard part. Aren't I?

"Lilac sounds great," I say.

"I'm not sure. That room doesn't get a lot of sunlight. Could end up being very dark. Anyhow, what's new with you? How's your love life?" Unlike the boy band posters in my room, Jean's "mom antics" and thick New York accent have not faded one bit.

"Nothing new, really," I say with a hard swallow. "Sorry I missed your call yesterday."

"That's quite alright. Were ya on another date?"

I love the way my mom says "ya" instead of "you" when she wants to sprinkle a little extra sugar on things.

"No, I was just sleeping, actually. Things have been...kind of *crazy* around here," I say, merging into the middle lane as if that's the one that'll allow me to go faster than seven miles per hour.

"You're not overexerting yourself, I hope?"

Since Decker died, my mom has never stopped oscillating

between *what if* and *who's next*. Telling her things are crazy concerns her, and I get it. She wants to make sure I'm not raising my blood pressure or doing anything that might cause me to have a stroke out of nowhere. That outcome sounds extreme and she sounds overbearing, both of which actually describe my mother perfectly, but once you watch your daughter lose her otherwise-healthy husband that way, the instinct kicks in and doesn't really go away. At least it hasn't for Jean. So I cut her some slack and insist that I'm fine.

"Everything's good. I've just been putting in some longer hours at work recently. It's kind of like how it is in New York, except us LA peeps can't all jet off to the Hamptons on the weekends, you know?"

"Oh, bless it," she mutters, one of her famous Jean Rosen sayings.

In hindsight, blaming my exhaustion on "LA things" was probably not the right move. I don't want her to be sad. She didn't take it well when I decided to move to Los Angeles three weeks after graduating from NYU, and she still hasn't fully accepted that I moved to a place that doesn't sell pizza by the slice on every street corner. I know I'm not the first native New Yorker to up and move three thousand miles away from celebrated carbs and public transportation for some bullshit "job in entertainment" on the West Coast, but I could bet Jean Rosen took it the hardest.

I never had it in me to direct or produce, which is why I didn't go to school for that kind of a thing. But I knew I'd be good at coordinating all the back-of-house happenings like…rounding up the production assistants, constantly walkie-talkie ing with the crew about stuff, overseeing craft services, helping with casting, things like that. I didn't know if that role had a real name, or if it even existed in Hollywood, but an NYU alum who also happened to be an Emmy-nominated set designer got me a gig working as a super low-level assistant to an assistant at a big studio in Hollywood. Couple the minimum wage pay with the cheap sublet I found on Craigslist, and the twenty-two-year-old me was all-in on the whole Los Angeles experience. I just needed to pack my bags and officially switch my wardrobe over to something that could be described as less "big city" and more "boho chic." I had no idea that a month after my move, I'd end up meeting the man who would become my husband while on the job.

The studio I was working at was filming a reality show about plastic surgery. I wasn't as good at social media as I am now, but I found some guy on Instagram named Brian Jackson who was an intern at a surgeon's office. He geotagged the clinic in all of his posts and hashtagged every upload with #ABoobJobIsTheBestJob. I DM'd Brian to ask if he'd want to be part of the segment, and a week later, Decker was the guy who gave his good-looking boob-guy friend a ride to the studio for the taping. That left Decker and me alone to talk in the greenroom.

While chatting, I learned that Decker was a teacher, off for the summer, and had plans to drive up to Tahoe with his buddy right after the shoot. I don't know what it was, but we just clicked. Instantly. So we exchanged numbers and texted his whole way up. When the flirting reached a critical mass, he decided to come back solo a day early and take me out for sushi. And the rest, as they say, was history.

Considering how worried my mom got at the thought of a busy weekend, I decide now is not the time to slip into conversation the arrival of Decker's urn. So I hurry to end the conversation and cap it with a promise that I will call her after work one night this week.

"Sounds good. You know what? I'm going to ship you matzo. You can make some matzo ball soup. I don't want you getting sick. That'd really put a damper on your dating life, wouldn't it?"

She wants grandchildren. I get it.

An intern whizzes by me with an aromatic barbacoa burrito bowl. She plops down at the desk across from mine—Monica's. I guess while she's out on her honeymoon, a girl named Marigold is guarding her inbox. Marigold's proximity to me is, at best, a necessary annoyance considering I have zero in common with the girl whose "fun fact" at our last team meeting was that she's distant cousins with Justin Bieber and gets mistaken for a young Uma Thurman "at least once a week."

Regardless, her fresh meal triggers a battle of scents. In one corner, there's the smell of heavily seasoned meat and cilantro. My mouth wants to water. My stomach wants to growl. I haven't eaten yet today and a flavorful lunch, a free one at that, *should* sound good. But in the other corner, all I can smell is the sterile odor of a hospital room clinging to my nostrils as if my nose hairs were dipped in patina.

"You're staring, Charlotte. Want some before I dump half a bottle of hot sauce on it?" Marigold asks.

I'm staring because that's the last meal I was supposed to eat with my husband, you dipshit.

"No, thanks," I say. "I'm good."

"I read in *Cosmo* that sriracha speeds up your metabolism. So you can pretty much eat whatever you want, as long as you drench it in this first," she explains as she proceeds to douse her burrito bowl in the reddish-orange sauce.

I put my headphones on and scoot my chair closer to my computer screen to mask the serious eye roll I'm directing toward Marigold. Antisocial as it may seem to block her out of my most basic senses, I just can't help it. I'm no longer interested in conversing with a girl who has little-to-no life experience and a pumpkin-spiced latte tattooed on her ankle.

As I look to my right, I notice that the rest of the intern pod resembles a United Airlines call center on the busiest travel day of the year. I know there's no shortage of Botox in LA, so how everyone's faces look so scrunched and frantic right now is beyond me.

I peel my headphones off and get Marigold's attention by tapping the back of her computer monitor with a pen. As much as I can't stand engaging with her, I'd like to know—

"Why are the rest of the interns on the phone right now?"

She puts her hand over her mouth and holds up the "one second" finger as she finishes chewing. There is a single shred of lettuce, half-covered in her purple lipstick, hanging from her mouth.

"Voyager just emailed Zareen. Three of their top execs are going to be in town this week and want to do an impromptu dinner before they catch their red-eye out of LAX. She's got us trying to secure dinner resos at BOA. If we get in, it's going to be a total schmooze-fest with these guys. Wining and dining at its finest." Marigold stuffs another spoonful of saucy rice and beans in her mouth, pushing the lipstick-covered shred of lettuce back in her mouth. I wonder how much makeup she eats in a given year.

I don't know enough about the difficulty of securing last-minute reservations at hot new Los Angeles restaurants, but I do know whoever scores this reservation is getting a job *and* a signing bonus. There hasn't been a Zareen-issued, seemingly impossible task these interns haven't been able to tick off their lists so far this summer, and my money is on the girl who currently has the receiver up to one ear and a finger plugging the other closed, as if she's receiving very specific hostage instructions.

Voyager is the fastest-growing organic athletic shoe company in North America. It makes sense they'd want to team up with a firm in Southern California—the land of vegans and yogis—to make their all-natural shoes much cooler than I'm managing to describe them. And because Voyager initiated tomorrow's meeting, I'm assuming the likelihood they'll hire us is set to skyrocket. If I were to guess, they're going to sign a contract in the twenty-four to forty-eight hours after the dinner. By my count, the biggest deal of my tenure at TIF is totally happening and I should probably tell Zareen what my statistics are showing.

"No, no, no. 9:30 p.m. is *way* too late," says Zareen. "Keep trying for something earlier. Get creative if you have to. Pull out all the stops. Make something up. Where's Marigold? Can't she tell them it's for Justin Bieber? *Do something*, okay?"

Zareen, who's hovering over an intern's desk with her fire-engine-red readers resting on the bridge of her nose, normally doesn't talk to our trendy-named interns—Marigold, Scotland, Bentley, etc.—like this, nor does she encourage anyone here to "make something up," but I've worked with her long enough to know she's just edgy about Voyager.

"Can we chat?" I say softly, saving the intern from the wrath of a stressed-out boss.

"Follow me to my office, please." She swoops her short salt-and-pepper hair to the side. She's certainly rocking a *The Devil Wears Prada* look today.

She stomps the heels of her Christian Louboutin pumps into the hardwood floor all the way back to her desk, and I question whether our distressed wood floors came like this, or if they were hammered over time by Zareen's four-inch heels.

She sits down, takes off her glasses, and mumbles under her breath as she checks her iPhone.

"Yoo-hoo," I say, knocking my knuckle on her door to remind her of my existence.

"Charlotte, dear. Come in, come in," she responds rather warmly given the tense situation. I may not be the cutest, spunkiest, most well-dressed employee, but as I take a seat in the purple velvet chair across from her sprawling black walnut desk, I'm reminded how satisfying it feels to be on this woman's good side—and that's a quality very few people who work here possess.

"So… Voyager?" I say with a hint of excitement in my voice.

"Yes. Voyager. The execs are in town for a running conference and want to do an early working dinner before they get on their flight home tomorrow," she says. "So, we're going to pitch how great The Influencer Firm is one final time and we're going to do that over a few plates of tender filet mignon and expensive bottles of wine."

"Are you sure these people even eat meat? None of their shoes are made of real leather, you know. That's their shtick."

"I thought about that, but I had Scotland comb through their personal Instagram accounts. All of them posted photos of barbecuing beef burgers over Memorial Day. Go figure. I think we'll be good giving them a little reprieve from the monotony of the vegan day-to-day."

I give her a nod. She's got a point.

"Anyhow, I predict that with full bellies, and with a little wine buzz, the Voyager crew will go on to sign the contract after the check drops. Which, by the way, we will pick up with our American Express Black Card so they know our company has some serious capital behind it. What do you think?"

"I think it sounds like a grand slam," I say, making a mental note that my boss has referred to *wine buzz* as a legitimate business-closing tactic. "Who's all going since Monica's on her honeymoon?"

"Funny you ask. I begged and pleaded with Monica to come

back. She thankfully obliged when I mentioned the words *Christmas Bonus*, so I'm paying for her to fly home ASAP on a red-eye. When the meeting is over, she can go back to Turks and Caicos and rejoin Danny for the rest of the week. She and I will take the lead on the dinner," Zareen confirms.

I can't believe Monica has to interrupt her honeymoon for this surprise dinner, but she is exactly who needs to be on the guest list if Zareen really wants to clinch the business. I nod my head in approval and agreement. They'll land this, no problem.

"Oh, and *you*," she says with a pointed delay.

"Excuse me?"

"There's probably a 50 percent chance we're going to get this account," she says.

"I think it's closer to 90 percent, actually." I quickly interject my calculation.

"Well, then, 40 more percent of a reason you need to be there. You see, a big part of if they sign with us is going to come down to what we can show them insofar as reporting and analytics. They've stressed that from the very beginning. And that is all you, girlfriend. That's your wheelhouse and no one else's."

Her words reassure me my job is secure even with all the minions proving their worth by Insta-Stalking our potential clients' holiday barbecues. But still, I don't want to be at the dinner if I don't have to. I'm not a schmooze-fest kind of girl and, even though work is a welcome distraction, it doesn't change the fact that there's something in my apartment that kind of needs some serious attention.

"Why don't you just tell them whatever they want, I can do?" I suggest it flippantly, but I mean it. I've yet to encounter a script I couldn't run, a problem I couldn't solve, a code I couldn't crack. True, I may have come to Los Angeles to work in show business, but I'm a Numbers Queen now.

Zareen gets up from behind her desk, walks over to me, and puts her hands on my shoulders from behind. Her perfectly manicured fingernails tap me like she's fanning piano keys. A B C D, A B C D.

"Telling them that some faceless, nameless employee can do 'whatever they want' is not enough. I need you to walk them through how you do what you do. I need that Charlotte Rosen razzle-dazzle."

That's a thing?

"You want me to explain my whole reporting strategy to them? They aren't going to understand if I get that granular," I say, trying to pass the buck.

She steamrolls on: "So show them; don't tell them. This isn't about explaining the nuts and bolts, Charlotte. I just want them to see firsthand what the woman behind the data looks like. I want them to know we don't just use a third-party software, we don't just outsource it to a foreign country. No, we have our very own Bethenny Frankel of the influencer space sitting right here in our office!" She taps the top of her custom-built desk twice with her pointer finger and her dangly jewelry clanks together like percussion.

The Bethenny Frankel of the influencer space? I'm not so sure that's the best way to describe what I do, but I'm happy to take it as the compliment I think she means it to be.

Zareen resumes circling around me like a shark. Following her with my eyes as she moves side to side makes my vertigo flare up.

"I have no doubt that you're going to help us bring home this business," she says, giving my shoulders another squeeze to drive home the point. "And when they sign, you know what that means."

She's hinting at opening a New York City office, a second headquarters located near Voyager's offices so we can slowly but surely take over the East Coast influencer world. She probably thinks I'm open to relocating since that's where I'm from; I could be closer to my family. But being closer to my family means I couldn't hack it in LA after all. It means that room they've been preserving might actually be needed. Besides, is there a professional way to tell your boss that if you didn't choose to go home after your husband she never knew existed died, then what other motivating factor—personal, professional, or otherwise—could there be for a cross-country move at this point?

"Or I guess I could also have our Marigold come to the dinner in your place if you can't make it. This may be a good opportunity for her to show me exactly what she has in mind come the fall when I'm ready to staff up."

"Marigold is interested in account management," I announce as if I've ever talked to the girl longer than thirty seconds.

"Is she? Because I heard she's taken a liking to analyzing your reports in her spare time. Even tried her hand at making an influencer list for a small event last week. Wasn't half-bad, actually."

This is news to me. And whether there's any truth to this or Zareen is just trying to ruffle my feathers, the thought of someone else encroaching on *my* safe place is enough to make me concede. Knowing how much our office resembles a *Real World* house right now ("seven interns, picked to work in an office for the summer"), I can't risk Zareen thinking I'm not a team player. If something goes wrong at the dinner tomorrow, Zareen will need me to step in and save it.

"Fine. Just know I'm ordering a side of ketchup with my steak, though."

★ ★ ★

In the ladies' room, I hear a gaggle of high-pitched girls, the interns, enter, and I quickly activate the sensor on the flusher so they know they are not alone.

I wait until I hear all of the other stalls lock shut before I vacate mine. I even debate not washing my hands so I can scurry out of the restroom and back to my desk to avoid any and all possible contact with these plebes. But research suggests I'm 35 percent more likely to catch a common cold from a public restroom if I don't at least run my hands under hot water for fifteen seconds. Knowing I've got the Voyager dinner tomorrow, I can't exactly afford to stay at home for a week straight, despite the fact that a box of soup-ready matzo is probably already on its way. So, I rinse fast and grab some paper towels—but not before overhearing a bit of their conversation.

"Did you hear? *Charlotte* is going to the dinner," one says.

"That's not fair. Marigold should be going."

"Thank you," Marigold says. "I agree."

"Yeah, you're way more personable. And stylish. I can't stand that giant purse Charlotte carries everywhere," another responds through the stalls.

I'm not going to go so far as to say that I thought these girls *liked* me, but I definitely didn't think they had it out for me. Nor did I realize my bag was such a controversy. I want to not care what they say about me, and normally I wouldn't. But the truth is, I came to work today thinking this was a safe place. Clearly, it's not. And worse, I can't stop listening.

"At least it's a Birkin," someone else defends.

"No, it's a *FIRKIN*. You know, a *fake* Birkin," Marigold chimes in.

(Audible gasps.)

Marigold is correct in her assessment of authentication. But it's not my fault. This is LA and the purse you carry dictates how your server will attend to your table, how much whip you'll get on your latte, and so much more. I wasn't about to drop fifteen grand on a bag, so I went down to—

"Chinatown sells them. Vendors carry knockoffs like hers on every corner. I've seen that exact one a million times."

I storm out of the bathroom before the girls can see with their own eyes that the subject of their catty conversation was just feet away the whole time. Sure, that'd be vindicating, but I don't want vindication right now. I want privacy.

I settle back down in my desk chair and it feels like I'm floating on a raft in the middle of the sea. I'm safe enough on this thing, for now, but I don't know what to do next. I don't know whether I'm supposed to wait to be rescued, or if I'm supposed to save myself in this situation. I've never felt like this since taking this job. My to-do list has always been a great neutralizer, but it's not showing up as the lighthouse I need it to be right now.

Marigold sits back down across from me, wakes up her monitor, and lets out a huff as she reads an email.

"What's wrong?" I ask, thinking something bad has just bombed Monica's inbox.

"I left my Louis Vuitton in our hotel in Punta Cana last week. And now the manager just wrote that the housekeepers never saw it. That purse was, like, three thousand dollars. I *loved* that purse."

Marigold starts crying and leaves her desk for the intern pod, where she will undoubtedly be comforted by others who actually believe a missing Louis Vuitton purse is the most impossible loss one can experience.

Decker has been gone so long. I'm used to life without him by now. But regardless of how much time passes, this morning it feels like the walls I've managed to build up over the years are crumbling.

Chapter 7

In the privacy of my car, I put my Apple Watch up to my mouth to tell it to make a call, but I get stage fright and nothing comes out. So I fish for my phone and do things the old-fashioned way. I scroll to the contacts listed under the letter *D*.

Debbie Austin comes up first. I click her name and the phone gives me the option to call, text, or FaceTime. Before pulling out of my TIF parking spot, I briefly contemplate if calling to say I'm coming over is even necessary. Perhaps Decker's return is something I can just type in a lengthy but eloquent text message? I even begin to compose one. But then I think back to Decker's face in my dream. I know it was just that, a dream, but the way he looked at me when he asked me to tell his mom he's back and he's okay tells me this is not meant for an iMessage. If this really is a death do-over, per Casey, then I have some responsibility to woman-up and do the hard things I couldn't before. I can't let him down. So I take a deep breath and hit the little phone icon.

It rings once. Maybe she's gardening and doesn't have her phone handy.

It rings twice. Maybe this isn't even her number anymore.

It rings three times. Maybe she will pick up and this will go shockingly well.

It rings a fourth time. And right when I think it's going to go to voice mail, she answers.

"Well, well, well. It's not every day I see *Charlotte Rosen* pop up on my phone. How are you, dear?"

To anyone else, that might be a cordial, warm hello. To me, it's Debbie Austin subtly reminding me that after Decker died, she immediately edited me back to my maiden name in her contacts list. Even though I had yet to legally change it back, I simply wasn't considered an Austin anymore.

"I'm doing good. I mean, well. How about you, Debbie?" I say, trying my hand at being proper and polite to a woman I know hates me. A woman I haven't spoken to on the phone in years.

"We're lovely. Kurt and I just returned from a long weekend in Laguna," she starts off. "I know Orange County can be a little seedy these days thanks to that trashy reality show on Bravo, but I still think the beaches there are the best on the coast."

Does she not realize she could easily star on that trashy reality show on Bravo? I digress.

"Now Kurt's jetted off again," she continues. "Attending some big dental conference in Tokyo. He's gone for ten days. I was going to go with him, but I'm expecting a shipment of blue roses any day now. Have you heard of those? They are the rarest of all roses; the scent is spectacular. I've been on the wait list for three years now. I can't believe it's finally my turn."

Something about the tone of her voice tells me I've interrupted her whilst reading *Vanity Fair* and enjoying a mimosa by her pool. I need to get on with this call because hearing about luxury roses is not what I have in mind right now. Soon she will realize that there is another *shipment* to discuss.

"Wow, a blue rose? Very cool. You'll have to Instagram those." I pull the phone away from my ear and mouth a *what?* to my own self. Did I really just say that?

"Look, I know you said Kurt is out of town, but are you home by chance? Can I pop by real quick? I wanted to chat with you about something and it's probably best we speak in person." Before she can needle me, I clarify: "It's about Decker."

My words feel like they are coming out in chunks, like a clogged-up pasta maker spewing out ill-shaped rigatoni noodles.

"If this is about his alumni fraternity event coming up, we will not be attending this year. But we *will* pledge a generous donation in Decker's name. Might you consider doing the same?"

"No, that's not actually it," I say, wishing our affairs were about something as simple as a frat event. "So, is it okay if I come by over my lunch and we talk?"

She takes her sweet time answering, and all I can think is if this woman comes back with a response that in turn strong-arms me into telling her over the phone that her son's ashes have been returned, I will officially be scheduling an MRI because I apparently have no backbone.

She lets out a breathy "I suppose that's fine. However, I do have guests coming over at 2:30, so we'll need to keep our engagement rather limited."

"That works for me," I say, noting that keeping the conversation short and sweet is about the first thing we have agreed on in five years. "I'm already on my way. I'll be there in fifteen minutes."

★ ★ ★

I have actually not been inside the Austins' mansion since before Decker passed away. Even when I would try to bring over flowers or a Tupperware of fudge brownies in the weeks and months that followed, I only got as far as the front door. Debbie and Kurt had never done a particularly good job of making me feel like "their house was my house" during our shared time of grief. Even the memorial service was held at the Beverly Hilton instead of their home, which makes me believe they didn't want the girl who was easiest to blame their son's death on standing under their roof for the foreseeable future.

All that is okay, though, because the only thing that matters now is that they haven't updated their keyless entry code, which I memorized when Decker and I lived here for the month between our apartment lease ending and the closing of our house purchase. So instead of ringing the doorbell and painfully waiting for Debbie to let me in today, my fingers robotically enter 9-8-9-8. It's not very cryptic, but it is very Decker. Nine was always his lacrosse jersey number, even since he was a little kid. And eight is the day in March he was born.

The glass door makes a quiet buzzing sound as it unlatches automatically. If she's offended that I've let myself in, so be it. This will be the last time I come over. I head straight toward the kitchen, where I know I will find either Debbie or her housekeeper, Sandra, who will undoubtedly take me to Debbie, wherever she may be. As I turn the corner from the foyer into the open kitchen-living area, I am greeted by the matriarch herself without so much as a hi, hello, how are you.

"I saw you coming up the driveway," Debbie says, manning the stovetop while looking at a high-def security monitor that's framed into the nearby refrigerator. She pinches the screen with her thumb and her index finger to zoom in on my car. "And I also see that Decker's BMW is still running. That's good. Is that a scratch on the bumper?"

At that, I remember just how obsessed the Austins were with not just keeping up with the Joneses, but being the Joneses. This house has always been wired to the nines with all sorts of leading technology and still is. I wonder if she saw me adjust my underwear under my skirt as I headed up their brick walkway.

On the counter, two floral teacups are set out to accept the tea Debbie is pouring from a futuristic-looking teapot.

"Thanks for having me over so last minute," I say as pleasantly as possible, although I'm sure she can hear the waves of nervousness in my voice.

"It's certainly a good thing this pot can boil water in thirty seconds or else I would have been ill-prepared for your surprise visit." She gestures toward the space-age electronic teakettle. "You look…healthy. Dressed nice today, at least."

"Thanks," I say with a brow so furrowed, I'm going to need to look up a Groupon for Botox later. It's a backhanded compliment. Granted, the last time she saw me I looked like a version of myself that was battling West Nile, but it sounds now like she can't believe there's come a day that I've stopped exclusively wearing sweatpants and actually started washing my hair.

"Alexa," Debbie announces. Who's that? Did she fire Sandra? "Set a reminder to change the front door key code."

"Okay, Debbie. Reminder set," her in-home robot says back.

Oh, *that* Alexa. While I would need Casey to confirm, this certainly feels like an episode of *Black Mirror*.

"Let's take a seat in the living room, shall we?" Debbie blows on her cup of tea and leads the way. I follow her to a velvet sofa and find a place across from her in a matching tufted wingback chair. We are separated by a marble coffee table that I'm sure cost ten times my monthly rent.

The Sharon Stone look-alike takes a sip of her tea and just stares at me, a relaxed smirk on her face. She's always so irritatingly composed, but I try not to let that distract me. I take a deep breath, ensure that my legs are crossed in a way that won't betray my lady-parts, and lean in toward her as a gesture of warmth. At least that's what it said to do in the book *Lean In*.

"So?" she says. I guess that's my cue to begin.

"I'm not sure if you heard on the news or what, but there was a wildfire in Pala recently and the mausoleum was in the path of destruction."

"What?!" Her eyes widen and she sets her teacup on the table with a clank. "I did not hear such a thing. Why didn't their Death Concierge contact me? They're supposed to contact me should anything come up regarding the urn."

Death Concierge?

"Relax, relax. The urn is in good shape. It was sent back to me this weekend with a note from the insurance company who is handling the damage claim filed by the mausoleum. It's totally fine."

"Oh my god," she exclaims as she draws her palm to her mouth like it's magnetized to her lip. "How...when did you get it?"

"It was delivered to me Saturday night."

"That must have been a mistake. You weren't supposed to get that."

I'm pretty sure I was.

"My name was on the package. *Just* my name," I clarify.

"And you're only telling me *now*? Why didn't you call me immediately?"

It's been less than forty-eight hours. I want to ask *what's the big deal*, but I have a feeling it will be met with contention. So I take the high road.

"I'm sorry. I was trying to process the fact that his remains just appeared at my door seemingly out of nowhere. But now I'm slowly coming to terms with the shock of it all and I will figure this whole thing out, I promise. I just wanted to come by and let you know, in person, that—" My words snag like a hangnail on a chenille sweater. I blank on how to finish this sentence. But then the dream I had of Decker flashes into my mind and I choose his words over anything I could come up with. "—that he's back and he's okay."

"No need to figure anything out. I will take this off your plate, Charlotte. Where is he? Your apartment? I'll send Sandra right now to pick him up. You can get back to things at the studio."

"I don't work at the studio anymore. I'm a software developer at The Influencer Firm."

I get specific about my employment because out of the corner of my eye, I spot a copy of the most recent *Forbes* on the top of a stack of magazines. Though I'm sure the subscription belongs to Kurt, should anyone happen to flip it open to the table of contents, they'll see the shout-out *Forbes* gave TIF. Debbie was always vocal with her disdain toward people who migrated to LA for a "career in showbiz." Maybe knowing her former daughter-in-law now has a legit job at the latest and greatest "Company to Watch" will give me a bit of a long-overdue edge.

"MY SON," she says, using her baritone voice, "who I thought was peacefully resting in Pala this whole time, has been—I don't know—rolling around in your trunk? Tossed into your purse? I mean, where are you even keeping him?"

So much for the edge.

"In my apartment," I quick-fire back.

"With that freak roommate of yours? She's probably going to turn his ashes into a circus exhibit when you're not looking."

I try not to linger on that hurtful remark. I may not hang with Casey all the time (or really at all before the urn came back, to be precise), but she definitely doesn't deserve to be the target of Debbie Austin's rage right now.

"He was on my nightstand all night, Debbie. He's been right next to me this whole time until I went to work." I leave out the part where he stayed at home while Casey dragged me to the bar Saturday night.

"I don't care if you kept him in your bank vault. Anywhere besides Pala, where I thought he was, where I put him on purpose, is unacceptable for any length of time. For one minute, Charlotte, try to think about *me* in this situation. Imagine not knowing where the ashes of your only child are. It's a little unsettling, isn't it?"

I don't appreciate the accusations she's throwing at me, her news source on all this. If she was so concerned, she should have set up a Google alert for the Pala Mausoleum and she would have been the first to know. I've done so since Decker's return and I've already gotten news hits. In fact, there's even a farmers' market there later this week and proceeds will go to fire damage relief efforts. So there.

"Again, I'm sorry, Debbie. But he's safe and the urn is obviously fine, so please try to calm down."

"Calm down? I'm glad that he's managed to make it this far, Charlotte. Really, I am. But I think it's pretty clear that he should stay here with his mother and father."

I know I mentioned Debbie is an irritatingly composed person, which she is. Until she isn't. This quick-to-boil demeanor has always thrown me for a loop. She can make any situation unnecessarily tense and difficult, skewing my ability to think clearly. She got like this in the hospital, too, which is how he wound up in Pala in the first place. I can't let her take control again.

"Debbie, I can assure you that Decker's remains were not just banging around in the back of my trunk like a two-liter of Diet Coke, okay? This situation, though unexpected, isn't going to just be some sort of afterthought for me. In fact, it's been my *only* thought since it showed up at my door."

"Good god, I feel like we're back in the hospital again, Charlotte, arguing about semantics."

That makes two of us.

In an attempt to keep my composure and stay focused on the point of the visit, I reenter the conversation using information only—data has been, and forever will be, my strong point. I made it that way since the day I knew we lost Decker for good.

"I understand that he was your only son, but I'm his wife. And I need some time to think about the right thing to do with these ashes. Next of kin doesn't just go away when he passes, Debbie."

"You *were*," she says point-blank and seemingly out of nowhere as she stares out the window at her glistening saltwater pool.

"*Were* what?" I say.

Her eyes gaze back at me. They seem to have darkened to more a midnight blue in the last few seconds.

"You *were* his wife five years ago. Your marriage to our son ended when his life did. Now, I think it's lovely that you've had the opportunity to spend a night with his remains, but I strongly suggest that you leave the urn—the urn that I had handmade specially for Decker by a master ceramicist in the hills of Argentina—with me. Letting me handle this again is the decent thing to do."

"Because letting *me* handle it would be a disaster?"

"No, because I'm the one woman who will *always* place him at the center of her heart. You, you can get another husband.

I can't have another son. What happens when you move on, Charlotte? When Decker becomes nothing but a memory, a distant one at that? Do you think my son will ever just be *a distant memory* to me?"

I don't know what she expects from me right now. Decker is a core part of me. Why is this woman punishing me for something that I cannot change? Stick to the facts, I remind myself.

"Debbie, you chose to put him in Pala and now…that place doesn't exist anymore. Considering you had no idea about that, I highly doubt you have a backup plan just locked in and ready to go. And neither do I. So we're even there. But let's not forget there's a legal reason Decker was sent to my address and not yours."

Just then Sandra, the housekeeper, enters the room, a sea of children standing behind her in bathing suits and goggles.

"Excuse me, Mrs. Austin? The pool party is here," she announces.

I check the time on my Apple Watch. It's 2:30 p.m. exactly. Is this the company she was expecting? A gaggle of preteens who want to swim in the neighbor's pool?

"Take them around the back, please. All of them. I don't want anyone cutting through the house. I just had the carpets steam cleaned with filtered eucalyptus water."

"Yes, ma'am," Sandra says as she leaves the room.

"And tell them no diving!" Debbie shouts. "I don't need a lawsuit on my hands when someone breaks their neck on the bottom of the shallow end."

"Who are all these kids?"

"Kurt and I volunteer our pool for the neighborhood to enjoy on Mondays in the summer while school's out," she says.

That's way too noble for Debbie, so I figure one of these kids' parents must be her ticket to skipping the membership line at the SoHo House or something.

"It's time for you to go, Charlotte," Debbie says as she propels herself off the velvet seat cushion and begins walking back toward the kitchen. "I'm sending Sandra to get the urn."

I am momentarily distracted by little kids cannonballing into the water just outside. So much so that I almost miss her casual declaration.

"No, you're not, Debbie," I say, trying my best not to sound combative.

She stops in her tracks and slowly turns back around. Debbie's gaze shifts ever so slightly to me and our eyes connect. Her expression screams, *You bitch.*

As if I needed another reason, that look is my cue to leave. I stand up and straighten out my skirt. On my way to the door, I just about steamroll a stringy tween.

"Jesus Christ," I mutter under my breath, startled.

"Do you have any pool noodles?" the squeaky-voiced boy says.

Debbie rushes to put her hands on his wet shoulders and face him back toward the pool like a round of Pin the Tail on the Donkey.

"No wet feet on the shag rug, please!"

I watch her interact with the boy—all stiff and rigid—and on the way out think to myself how it was probably a good thing Decker and I didn't get around to having children.

"Oh, Charlotte. I wanted to ask. Does it ever haunt you?" Debbie says before I clear the living room.

I don't turn around because I don't want to see the look on her face accompanying her callous tone.

"Does *what* ever haunt me?" I say, my eyes locked on their freshly steam-cleaned flooring.

"All the damage you did to our family the day *you* decided to yank our son off life support?"

Chapter 8

'm not sure which was more brutal to wake up to this morning: a stream of texts from Debbie Austin asking if I've "changed my mind about the urn" and if I "want to come over and talk again"? Or my boss, Zareen, begging me to bypass the office and instead attend an influencer event by myself at a new gym in West Hollywood.

As far as Debbie is concerned, it's clear she is suffering from what I learned in therapy is called a "Rage Hangover." It's when you do things and say things you normally wouldn't and otherwise fly off the handle in a moment of emotional desperation, but then eventually calm down and realize you were being, for a lack of better words, *an ass* about stuff. People don't often apologize in their rage hangovers, so much as they just act all nicey-nicey after in an effort to convince everyone involved they should just silently agree to sweep things under the rug. For the record, I'm not sweeping shit.

That last comment about pulling the plug was a low blow, and she knows it. As the sole name on the DNR, it took a lot for me to come to the conclusion that simply having a desire to keep someone alive isn't enough to make them stay alive and experience any sort of quality of life when their chance at such is less than 1 percent. It wasn't back then and it certainly isn't now. Which is why it stings to know she's hanging the power of attorney over my head like I actually got away with murdering him or something.

So as a thank-you for reminding me of the part I played in his death, I simply responded to Debbie that I can't text right now because I'm working a very important client event at West Hollywood's new hot-cycle studio, WeHot. The more I name-drop, the more I'm convinced she'll put two and two together with that *Forbes* article and realize for once that I'm a smart and capable woman who can handle rehoming her husband's urn.

It sounds like the name of a menopause research center, but WeHot is actually a place that combines hot yoga with spin class. Not at all my style, but there's definitely a market for it here in LA, and frankly, I'm surprised it took this long for someone to invent it. I figure that if my services are needed and Casey is at home keeping watch on the urn (she's either off Tuesdays or doesn't start work until the sun goes down— I'm not entirely sure of her schedule/circadian rhythm), then being here on official Influencer Firm business is actually the perfect distraction for the fact I've got an issue at home that would just make the most fascinating *Today* show segment. So I take the opportunity to embrace my work and lean in— or pedal out?—of the saddle, whatever empowering slogan makes sense for this situation.

Normally a programmer like me wouldn't even have to come to a client event like this, let alone try the product first-hand, but since Monica is on her honeymoon, we are a little short-staffed on the client services front. I've been on board at

The Influencer Firm the longest, which means when it comes to sending me or one of the new summer interns, there really is only one option as to who's truly qualified enough to make the locker room area of this trendy boutique her office for the morning. And that's me.

Our client list is growing like a weed thanks to that cheeky little write-up in *Forbes*. For the first time in company history, I have a feeling my boss is going to cast a few full-time offers out into the intern pool at the end of August. Even more so if—I mean, *when*—we land the Voyager account.

Given the fact I've been pressed to consider stats and make decisions a few times in my life, I can't help but look at everything with an analytical eye. And now that the dinner is officially on the books, I'm estimating there's a 90 percent chance that the company who is putting sustainable shoes on the map will come on board in the next 2.3 weeks.

Two point three weeks, eh? Even though work helps me put Decker out of mind for the moment, I can't help but think: Will the ashes of my dead husband still be sitting in my house in 2.3 weeks? What aha moment could I possibly have about this thing in the next 2.3 weeks? Time. Is. Ticking.

"Are you okay? Can I get you a cold towel or something?"

"Everything's fine," I tell Gemma, our client who's caught me skipping out of the spin class extra early. "I just needed to grab my computer and run a quick script on the social media engagement going on inside the room."

I hope that my über-flushed cheeks don't completely contradict the very chill excuse I just gave for abandoning my spin bike.

"What was your name again?" she asks in a semicondescending way.

"Charlotte."

"Do you think there will be stats generating already, Charlotte? The class just started seven minutes ago." Gemma taps her Apple Watch and flashes the time my way. It's a techy move on her part—probably to counter the social media jargon I was just throwing down—but I have one of those fancy watches, too. I've been on the wearables train ever since these things were available for preorder, so I'm not all that impressed. I tap mine to bring it into frame as well. Except mine is showing another new Tinder message first instead of the time.

Despite Gemma's concern, this is what I do for a living. And for the record, posts have been accruing since @PrettyNFun007 uploaded a mirror selfie this morning with the caption Heading to @WeHotLA to get my sweat on! and therefore—

"Stats are coming in, yes. Now I need to make sure everyone's Snapchatting like they're supposed to be," I confidently say back to her. "I'm sure your account executive, Monica, told you before she left for her honeymoon that impressions are *everything* if you want WeHot to take off. After all, that's what you're paying The Influencer Firm to do, right?"

I shoot her a little wink, then bury myself back into my screen. A subtle reminder of the hefty price she has paid to be popular on social media is exactly what I needed to put a pin in that judgmental stare of hers. Now if I can just get her to leave me entirely to my devices, that would be the icing on this half-baked, kill-her-with-kindness cake.

"Well, let me know if you need anything. I'm going to sanitize the bathrooms." Gemma places an iced-lavender waffle weave towel on the bench next to me. I wonder for a moment if I'm supposed to wring it out and drink the flavored water that it's soaked in like it's some kind of Starbucks specialty drink. She whips her perfect Ariana-Grande-esque ponytail around and heads back to the front desk. Not a single inch of her body jiggles, especially not her fake double Ds. That's the difference between a New York girl like myself and an LA chick like Gemma. My closet has Spanx, hers does not.

While it obviously can't hurt to check my reports this early on, I'll admit that I ghosted that spin bike simply because I was over it. That, and…exercise still freaks me out. I know a spin bike isn't a race, but since driving the heart rate up is how Decker had a stroke, I guess The Jeaner isn't the only one who is oscillating between *what if* and *who's next*.

That said, Gemma's question is valid. If I was that quick to leave the sauna-like group exercise class, will there be others who jump ship in the near future, too?

The answer is simple: no. There won't be. That room is full of young twentysomethings who are *way* too worried about sweating off the fried goat cheese balls they ordered from SUR this weekend. By no means would anyone in there take workout cues from *me*—a pushing-thirty exercise hack who lasted a mere five minutes in the saddle before slumping over the handlebars.

Finally, it's just me and my computer and the SoCal sun pouring through the windows of WeHot, which heats up the smell inside like dinner simmering on the stove. Only the ingredients in this stew are Chanel No. 5 and kitschy Instagram handles. I remind myself (not for the first time in the past twenty minutes) how this client is paying a cool twenty-five grand for my company—for the company I work for, rather—to be here.

I find myself with too many tabs open on my laptop and distracted by one in particular. Well, two, to be honest. The Google search results for "los angeles mausoleums" that I haven't yet gone through and an old Match.com tab from a few days ago. The Match.com tab is blinking with a new message from William, a thirty-four-year-old artist from the Atwater Village neighborhood, who just messaged me.

His "dating headline" says, Could U B the 1? Out of habit, I start to copy and paste some of William's data into my compatibility algorithm, but I notice someone walking toward the locker room area and tilt my screen down. The last thing I need is Gemma to see in the reflection of the floor-to-ceiling mirrors that I'm surfing the dating web.

I hear a familiar voice behind me. "Hello, Charlotte."

I look up and right into the face of Brian Jackson. The Zack Morris of every friend group he'll ever be in. His coolness is the reason that I instantly cast him for the plastic surgery segment all those years ago. It's also how he got that bomb internship in the first place, how he was featured in *Luxe LA*'s "40 Under 40" issue (I know this because Monica wasn't the only person I recognized in those pages), and it's also now the reason he's able to waltz into *my* work *completely* unannounced after not really seeing each other or speaking to one another for the last *four and a half years*. All the while, he makes it seem like he's just casually stopping by a birthday party that I invited him to.

But alas, this isn't a party and I sure as hell didn't invite him here. In fact, as he stands in front of me holding a cup of coffee and examining an ink stain on his mint-green scrubs waiting for me to acknowledge him, it's quite clear he's not here for the hot-spin class dubbed "Gaga Glow."

"It's been a while," he says nonchalantly. "Since—"

"Since that time I saw you at Whole Foods," I respond, keeping my voice factual.

"Really? That long? Wow. Come to think of it, you're right. Good memory, Char."

Brian and I don't really keep in touch anymore. Like I said, the last time I saw him was more than four years ago in the hot bar buffet line at the Whole Foods on Sunset Boulevard.

He was filling up a container with some barbecue chicken around lunchtime while I was packing a to-go pint of mac 'n' cheese just opposite him. There was no avoiding him when our hands went for the same serving spoon, so we exchanged casual pleasantries and I made sure to hide in the bathroom for the next fifteen minutes just to make sure we wouldn't have a second run-in at the express checkout line.

"So, how are you? What are you up to?" he continues with a jovial smile.

"I'm running stats at the moment," I say, staying focused on my screen and avoiding contact with his bourbon-colored eyes. "For my job."

"Where are you working these days?"

"The Influencer Firm." I hope he can tell by my curt tone that I'm not interested in conversation right now.

"That's cool. What do they do?"

Evidently not.

I surrender and shut my computer screen completely. There's no way I can concentrate on anything other than taking off my spin cleats. I bend down to do so, but they don't budge. Perhaps I should have afforded myself a quick Google search regarding how to eject these first, because I am seriously struggling and my feet are starting to get claustrophobic.

"Need a hand with those?"

Before I can answer, Brian sets his coffee on the bench next to me and kneels. He unclips the godforsaken spin cleats with the ease of a high school stud unhooking a bra.

"Thanks. Blood flow," I say with relief as I rub and bend my toes through my socks.

"Try rolling your ankle from side to side and tapping your foot like you're pumping a brake pedal."

I shoot him a furrowed look.

"Sorry. Doctor speak. That said, your spin shoes are now off. Suffice to say you're not going to do this class with me?"

"*You're* here for Gaga Glow?" Never in a million years...

"That's the name of the class?" He lets out a bit of a laugh. "God, no. I'm just kidding. I'm not quite sure I'm the demographic for a class called *Gaga Glow*."

You're not. The demo is metropolitan women ages eighteen to twenty-seven, I think to myself.

"But I am here because Debbie called me. She told me about Decker."

I nod like I knew it. But the truth is, no matter how much I want to say that I indeed *fucking knew it*, I definitely didn't. The last thing I expected Debbie to do was rope Brian into this and turn him into her little messenger when she saw I wasn't taking her nicey-nicey bait.

I'm not annoyed because she disturbed Brian from his busy life of prepping women getting a new rack at the surgeon's office, but rather because she's just taken her "doesn't think I can handle this urn thing" to a whole new level. If I wasn't so Debbie'd out right now, I'd dial her for the second time in twenty-four hours and call her ass out. But I know Debbie Austin. My effort would be futile anyway. She's a villain whose superpower is making inappropriate, rash decisions. I can't penetrate that, no matter how fueled I am to confront her.

"Well," I begin. "I appreciate her calling in the reinforcements, but I can assure you—and her—that I'm fine and everything is under control. So, thank you for your visit, but you can get back to work now."

"Relax, Rosen. My rounds at Cedars don't start till noon. I'm in no rush this fine morning."

"Cedars? As in... Sinai?" I ask.

Brian peels open his black Members Only jacket and looks down at his chest pocket. My eyes follow his down to the script font. The hospital's name is clear as day, along with Chief Resident right underneath it.

"Try to ignore the ink stain," he suggests. "My pen exploded earlier, but have no fear. I'm the proud owner of a Turbo Washer 6000. It'll rinse it out of these scrubs before tomorrow's shift, no problem."

"And what about that spit-up just below your pocket? Will your spiffy washer get that, too?"

"Did I get vomited on again? Damn, Pediatrics can be brutal." Brian licks his thumb and tries to wipe it off. Gross.

"Pediatrics? I thought you were working with the *Real Housewives of Beverly Hills*, prepping them for breast augmentation surgeries, last time we saw each other?" I chase the dig with a sip of piping hot coffee—*his* piping hot coffee. The one he placed on the bench next to me before unhooking my shoes. Oops.

"Come on, Charlotte. Cut me some slack. The internship with the plastic surgery office was years ago," he says. "And you're welcome for the coffee. It's good, right? Alfred's makes a killer honey-chai latte."

So he's a children's doctor now? At the same hospital where Decker died? I try not to think too far into all of that.

"So, just curious, but what did Debbie tell you? Besides my exact location, I see."

He gestures to the bench. "May I?" I nod and he takes a seat next to me. "So, Debbie. Yeah, she just told me about the fire and how Decker was returned to you, and then she just suggested that maybe I...see if you need a hand with anything and told me you were at a place called WeHot. I googled it and now I'm here."

"Thank you, Captain Obvious. Let's be clear: you came straight here, while I'm working an event for a client, and thought this would be a good time and place to come talk to me? Why didn't you just call if you wanted to know if I need any help? Which I don't, by the way."

"Why didn't I *call*? Really?"

Fair enough. I forgot that Brian stopped trying to reach me after about six months of my ignoring his calls and texts. My grief was—is—a complicated thing. And of all the people who I didn't know how to be my newly widowed self around, Brian, Decker's best friend and reason for us ever meeting, was at the top of the list. I took away his drinking buddy, his lacrosse teammate, his frat brother. Besides that guilt, how can you be a flailing emotional mess around Mr. Joe Cool? He was going to be over Decker dying long before I'd ever be. It was too painful then to pretend I was fine around him, and I'd never bothered to see if things had changed on that front. Why would I? My life has shaken out pretty okay since paring down my involvement with the Austins and those closest to us as a couple. New home, new roommate, new career, new everything worked out for me.

"Okay, I get it. But, for the last time, I don't need your help."

"I never said that you did." Brian puts his hands up like I'm about to shoot.

"I know. Sorry. I just… I want everyone to understand that I'll figure this Decker thing out myself…just like I'll figure out how to get these influencers to stop spelling WeHot with two *T*s. *Shit!*"

At that, my eye jets over to a TV monitor mounted in the locker room area featuring a livestream of Tweets from the influencers. I'm mortified to see that @AvocadoToast1997 is just one of many who haven't bothered to absorb the spelling of the name of the place they've been invited to take free classes at for the next six months.

"Well, this isn't good," I mutter to myself as I wedge back open my computer.

"What happened? And what exactly do you do for a living again? Gaga Glow is *work* for you?"

"I write code," I say, feverishly typing away.

"Okay, yeah, sure. You write code. How about one more time, but in English, please?"

"I'm a Numbers Queen. I stalk people on the internet who I think would like to go to events like *Gaga* freaking *Glow* and then I design custom reports to show the client how much they all talked about how much they loved it. But right now, my metrics are getting shot to hell because apparently no one knows how to spell. Now, if you'll excuse me, I need to adjust my code so those cute little typos you see on that giant screen count toward the overall impressions." Hell if I'm losing credit for curating a successful invite list because these '90s bitches legitimately think *hot* has two *t*'s. "Here. Can you plug in my adapter? My computer's about to die. The outlet is by your foot." I hand Brian my computer cord like I'm handing him shock paddles.

"Power is officially flowing, Numbers Queen."

Monica was the first person to call me the Numbers Queen. It was our first year working together and I was able to prove to one of her beer clients in a matter of clicks that they were the most tagged and Tweeted brand on the internet during the Super Bowl. It sounds maddening, but that's just how I think—exclusively in numbers. That's just how life has been since Decker died—data, then decisions.

How did I get to the point I was able to code a custom report in under five minutes? Let's just say I've come a long way since being so depressed I couldn't manage to do things like pick up the phone and text my friends back. When that was my norm, it also meant I couldn't manage to pick myself up off the floor, put clothes on, and go to work a lot of the time either. Turns out people don't have a lot of patience or understanding for that kind of thing—for never responding to texts and habitually not showing up to work. So I lost a bunch of friends and also my movie studio job. For a lot of people, that pretty much defines their whole reason for being in Hollywood—a circle of good-enough friends and a low-paying job in entertainment. That's why I came out here. But my whole reason for being in LA changed overnight when I met Decker Austin. Suddenly, my reason for being here was a tall blond guy who played lacrosse, told nerdy jokes, and looked good in every flannel button-down J.Crew ever made.

I pulled myself together after about six months, right around the time Brian finally left me alone, actually. A coding school offering accelerated classes had recently opened in Los Angeles, and I kept seeing their ads slathered all over the city. So one wine-infused night, I took that as "a sign"—something I'd never do normally—and enrolled myself in a beginner's level class. Every time I entered keystrokes on the back end that made something on the front end happen—a picture move to the left, text bigger, etc.—I felt a rush of endorphins. Being able to control a cause and elicit a specific effect was comforting. The more technical the task, the more I could block out the grim realities of my personal life. So I kept going and re-enrolling until I learned everything that school had to offer in a mere matter of months. It was the first time since losing Decker that I felt alive and excited, and I knew this was the path for me. Not another job in show business. Not moving back in with my parents in New York City. And four years later at TIF, I can honestly say that my work has been more rewarding than I could have ever imagined. Plus, in a round-about way, it's how I got my groove back in the dating world.

Just then, my Apple Watch lights up with an incoming text.

"Crap, it's Zareen," I say to Brian like he knows who that is. "I need to respond."

"Take your time," he says as he gets up to take a closer look at the artwork—a spray-painted abstract portrait of Kim Kardashian doing a push-up. At least that's what I think it is.

How is it going? her text reads.

Even though Zareen is pretty chill as far as bosses go, everyone at TIF has been a little edgy knowing that we are so close to potentially securing the Voyager account, and Zareen, the big boss lady, has been feeling it the most.

Gaga Glow = HUGE hit, I message back.

Sure, the all-caps is a bit on the exaggerated side considering I only experienced the room for mere minutes and the influencers can't spell, but the event *is* a hit. The list of attendees I curated could not have been more spot-on for this early-morning, sneak-peek gym class.

Awesome! Did everyone show up?

The room is packed. Casting was my strong point at the studio, and I've found myself carrying that skill here. After all, I coded the list-finding software so that it would automatically dismiss anyone who Tweeted about drinking on a Monday night in the last six months. Why? Because those people—and their hangovers—aren't reliable attendees. We couldn't trust them to pull themselves together in time for a brutal Tuesday morning sweat session. We couldn't let our client down like that.

It's a full house, I fire off with sheer confidence.

Brava! she sends back. Feel free to head home after and I'll see U @ BOA.

I let the excitement of a job well done sink in. While the algorithms never steer me wrong, that doesn't mean it's any less validating when I see upward of thirteen thousand social media impressions in the first fifteen minutes of the class. It's just proof for Gemma that burning calories to Lady Gaga's greatest hits while glow sticks hanging from the ceiling change colors to the beat of the music is something worth bragging about online. That translates to job security for me. And *that* translates to the ability to continue using my TIF chops to develop my side-project dating app.

Gaga Glow dismisses while I finish texting Zareen. One by one, the girls emerge like extras from a Lululemon commercial, steamrolling Brian out of their way. If they just stopped for a minute, they'd realize he's the most Instagrammable piece of eye candy they'll see all day, but instead they are dripping sweat onto the screens of their phones while uploading the selfies they took with the instructor. It's all so obnoxious and perfect I just want to clap my hands and throw confetti.

"Is the class over?" Brian asks.

"Yup," I say.

"And is the crisis averted?"

"Yup."

"Well, then… Remember it's WeHot with one *t*—ONE *T*!" Brian shouts to the crowd, his voice lost in the din of whispered plans to grab kale salads from Whole Foods and take "Outfit of the Day" pics in front of the new Restoration Hardware on Sunset Boulevard.

"Thanks, but that's not necessary. They're already Snapchatting the rolled ice cream food truck that's parked across the street," I explain as I pack my computer bag up.

"Kids these days. Well, look, it sounds like you don't need my help with the whole Decker thing."

"That is correct," I confirm.

"And that's fine. But I do have a request. Can I…come over and see him? Or if that's too forward, me coming to your place, can you bring him to a coffee shop? I have to admit I didn't make it up to Pala much, and before he goes away again to wherever you decide, I'd love to—"

"I get it," I say, cutting him off before I embark on another strange conversation with a man, dead, alive, or otherwise. "But I have to get to my office and run some reports now. So how about I get back to you on that, okay?"

He says nothing. Instead he offers me a closed-mouth smile. "What?" I say.

"Will you, though? *Will you* get back to me? You've played keep away with me for the last four years."

"Four and a half. But I promise," I assure him. "I will text you."

Brian comes in to hug me, a move I'm not expecting. I think it's meant to be comforting, cordial, but I know it can't be. And he should know that, too.

Chapter 9

Casey agrees to take Leno out for me as I head into the bathroom to get ready for the big Voyager dinner. I start with a liquid concealer. As I dab it just above my cheekbones to cancel out the purple-green hues that have occupied that space since turning twenty-nine, I notice my left eye is twitching. It's not an all-out tic, more of just a flutter—like a flickering fluorescent light bulb that needs to be changed. In the past, this was something my eye did only when I was overly caffeinated or underrested. It used to happen a lot while working my studio job. Coffee was its own food group there and the hours were long, coupled with the fact that when I was off the clock, I was with Decker, and we had a habit of staying up late on "school nights" (which was every night; he was a high school history teacher) just talking, watching movies, thrilled to be in each other's company. Anyone who has ever been in love knows what that restless, giddy phase is like. It's a phase where time stops mattering. Wide awake still at two o'clock in the morning? Who cares, let's stay up. Let's continue to answer hypothetical would-you-rather questions, watch me struggle to do the too-hard *New York Times* crossword puzzle my mom sent me, and make out until the birds start chirping. That's just...how we rolled.

"Relax, babe. The eye twitch is just your thing," he'd say as I'd hold down my cheek, trying to get it to stop. "It matches the way you crinkle your nose when you're stuck on a cross-word clue." *God, I haven't done an* NYT *crossword puzzle in years*, I think to myself as I move on to bronzer, blush, eye shadow, and finally end the application with a sweep of jet-black lengthening mascara.

Sorry to bother u, but have u thought any more about me seeing D?

The text from Brian triggers an eye roll. He's not being a bother, but he is right. I did completely zone out on following up on his cavalier request to hang with the ashes of my dead husband, his best friend.

I've got a super important client meeting tonight. Can I get back 2 u tmrw?

Sure. Good luck tonight.

I appreciate Brian's understanding as I slip into navy-blue cigarette pants with a side zipper and toss on a crisp white button-down shirt. I take my hair down from the messy bun held together for the last six hours by a ballpoint Bic pen and a little leftover sweat from my five minutes on the spin bike. There's a visible crease where the pen was, but the volume is good and the overall style has somehow managed to go from "blah" to "beach waves," which rest nicely on my shoulders. I take one final look in the mirror, proud of how I've cobbled myself together once again.

"Duuuuuude," Casey says, barreling back into the apartment with a panting Leno. "Denise is at our apartment."

"Who?" I say, packing my Birkin (okay, Firkin) with a nude-colored lip gloss.

"Darlene? Donna? Oh, whatevs. Decker's ma."

"*Debbie* is here?"

"Yeah, I think so. Some wine-wasted middle-aged woman tailed this Grubhub deliveryman but the front desk guy intercepted her. When he asked who she was here to see, I overheard her saying, 'My son, Decker Austin.' Doorman said the name wasn't on the residence list and he'd have to call the police if she didn't leave."

"You've got to be kidding me," I exclaim, setting my bag down and marching to the door.

"Relax," Casey says, grabbing my arm. "She's gone. The doorman ended up escorting her out. It was harmless and sad more than anything."

Harmless? I doubt it. Clearly Debbie came to my place after Brian failed at doing her dirty work. This lady is the definition of desperate. Not to mention, a trespasser.

"Well, did she see you? Did she see the dog?"

"Nah, Leno and I hid by the elevators like little secret agents. It was so cool."

"What do you think she wanted?"

"Considering she didn't drop *your* name or bother calling, I think she's after the urn, TBH."

My brain jumbles like a piece of bad code causing all my text to turn into Greek letters. Let me get this straight: my former mother-in-law just reenacted a scene from *The Walking Dead*, and would have banged down the door of my apartment to steal back the ashes of her dead son if it wasn't for our building security guy? What if he was in the bathroom? Taking a smoke break? Thank god he was there to hold down the fort. Debbie's heist-like antics certainly make me realize the urn isn't so safe at my house after all.

I'm glad Casey has resolved that this all was a pathetic display of shock for Debbie, but it doesn't change the fact that I feel utterly violated. Who's to say Debbie won't come back when it's a different doorman's shift and pose as my sweet mother who just wants the spare key to our place for five minutes so she can leave behind "a surprise bouquet of flowers" or some other seemingly innocent scheme to gain entry into my unit so she can steal the urn? Who's to say she won't come back and make it all the way up to my front door? I won't let it happen. Not on my (Apple) watch. I guess I'll need to make room in my bag for more than just lip gloss tonight, because Decker's coming with me to BOA.

This BOA place is nice, albeit kind of dark and pretty crowded at 6:00 p.m. for a city full of people who don't like to dine until after 9:00 p.m. But that's okay because I believe those things—dark and crowded—are helping to take the attention off the fact that I've sausaged myself into cigarette pants that suddenly feel two sizes too small.

And that I have Decker's urn in my purse.

I'll admit that it feels inappropriate to have brought Decker along to something like this, but what other choice did I have, given Debbie's stop-at-nothing antics? I try not to think too much about the fact that Decker in my bag makes us a party of seven and glance down at my watch. This dinner will be over relatively soon, and once it is, I'll head straight back to my place, where I will put Decker back on my nightstand or the kitchen counter. Then tomorrow, I'll take time over my lunch break to hunker down and pick up on my mausoleum research. I'll even book a conference room later in the afternoon to make some calls in private. I will put this task first, I promise myself.

A waitress zips by and swaps out Zareen's lipstick-stained water glass with a fresh one. I like their attention to detail here. I admire and I appreciate it.

That said, I must give the interns major kudos not only for having the balls to shit-talk me behind my back in the bathroom of a small office building, but also for securing the early reservation Zareen was eyeing at the most coveted restaurant in Beverly Hills. We've been here an hour already and every seat is filled. I'm not sure how a simple steak house can be the hottest ticket in town—usually that's a title reserved for places with celebrity chefs that serve twenty-course meals, one of which is simply a marinara-flavored vapor that you inhale. But for what it's worth, we've cruised through our entrées already and the meat was broiled to a perfect medium rare and the spinach was sautéed in some sort of garlic-butter nirvana. Not to mention, James Van Der Beek has been sitting at the table next to us all night and it's taking everything in me not to walk over there and ask for a selfie with Mr. *Dawson's Creek* himself.

The waitress is pouring my third glass of pinot noir. The pours are heavy, too. You can tell she's trying to move through the expensive bottles to bring up the overall tab for our table— oldest server trick in the book. Zareen secures a moment of eye contact with me and makes a subtle "easy on the wine" motion with her hand. The same one my driver's ed instructor would make as I approached a stop sign with a little too much heat.

To no one's surprise, the dinner thus far has been largely the Monica-and-Zareen Show. Zareen has an enchanting spirit about her, which is only exemplified by her raspy smoker's voice (even though she doesn't smoke) and heaps of dangly gold jewelry that clink together when she makes hand gestures. She is also wearing a silk caftan that looks more like an ornate rug, a piece of clothing that is fascinating in and of itself. Looking at her is accepting that I'll never be the type of woman who can pull off a caftan as "business casual" attire.

Then there's Monica, who is not only a vision of beauty—especially with her fresh Turks and Caicos tan and overall marital bliss—but also a smooth talker who is currently charming the pants off the Voyager guys. It could also be her form-fitting red bodycon dress that has captured their attention, but who cares. They are eating out of the palm of her hand, which will no doubt make my job easier when it's my turn to take the floor.

The Voyager team is comprised of three men who are considering working with us largely for our ability to target women in the influencer marketing space. I forgot their names as soon as they said them, which is a personality flaw of mine. Strangely, I find it difficult to retain the names of people who I haven't first met (read: stalked) online. Associating a profile picture with a username is the only way I can remember names these days. It's kind of like the way I learned Spanish vocab words with flash cards back in high school. Regardless, I've since dubbed the gentlemen in our company this evening as Eyebrows, Loafers, and Bald, and resolve that when they send a follow-up thank-you-for-dinner email on their way to the airport tonight, I'll learn their names then.

"Okay, everyone," says Zareen. "In the interest of time, why don't we move on to our reporting capabilities now, shall we? I don't want any missed flights on my watch!" She taps her wrist to bring her gold Rolex into frame, a true power move.

"Sounds fantastic," says a buzzed Loafers.

"Charlotte, do you have Decker with you?" Zareen nonchalantly asks in front of everyone.

I wipe my face with my napkin as my stomach drops into

the seat of my burgundy leather dining chair. How does she know about Decker? And that I have him in my bag?

"What was that?" I ask, clearing my throat.

"Do you have the deck...or is it with Monica?"

She said Deck-OR. She said Deck-OR, I repeat in my head as I attempt to safely bring my heart rate down.

"Oh, right. Yes, I have it," I confirm. "I've actually loaded the presentation onto these iPads so that everyone may individually view it in the palms of their hands."

At that, I dig into my Birkin for our five spare office tablets. I didn't tell Zareen I was doing this, but when your boss kindly asks for razzle-dazzle, you bring it. Her eyes light up, knowing that I've just introduced a new element of cool to the table. The fact that everyone will be able to view the slides on a personal handheld device as I control the presentation from my iPhone should bring our clinch percentage into the high 90s.

As I reach around for the iPads, I can't help but acknowledge that Decker is in the same bag. Right next to the thousands of dollars of technology, in a fake Birkin from Chinatown, in the swankiest restaurant on this side of the canyon.

"Ready?" I ask after handing the last iPad over to Zareen.

"Wow, a digital presentation? I'm already impressed," says Eyebrows as he elbows Bald.

"The iPads are a nice touch, right?" Bald volleys.

"They make it so easy to follow along," chimes in a subtly sales-y Monica.

"How do we get it to start?" asks a tech-challenged Loafers.

"Just swipe your finger across the bottom to activate the screen," I say, somewhat concerned that the screen might not respond to his greasy fingers.

"Aha! There we go! Would you look at that?" Bald nudges Loafers.

They are loving this. *Take that, Marigold.*

I look to Monica and Zareen, who gives me a confident nod that says, *Go get 'em, girl.*

"Okay, gentlemen. Slide one. As you can see, it all starts with our proprietary—"

"I'm so sorry to interrupt," our waitress says as she does a lap to refill our waters and wine. "But before you begin your presentation, can I get any desserts sent over to you this evening? I can put the order in immediately and then we can stay out of your way while you chat."

"Sure. One of everything is fine," Zareen answers for the table. She then inconspicuously hands our server the company's black AmEx card. Only I'm sitting close enough to hear her whisper: "Bring one more bottle of wine and tip yourself 30 percent. Don't drop a bill when you bring my card back. I want this to be smooth, you understand?" Her attention returns to the table and she gives me permission to start once again.

"As I was saying, our proprietary software is configured to understand your target demographic, which in this case we have already determined to be fitness-minded women ages eighteen to thirty-five. Because of our research, we can pitch to them in creative new ways that's never before been explored. For instance—"

"Excuse me, Charlotte," says Loafers. "Zareen mentioned you coded this program yourself. Is that correct?"

I'm not usually comfortable patting myself on the back like this, but I remember Zareen mentioning this was a key reason she wanted me here, to show off a bit. So I allow myself—or maybe the oaky red wine allows me—to soak up a bit of the spotlight.

"Yes. I designed the ins and outs of this program entirely on my own, which means I know it better than anyone else. So basically, if you want this program to do something special, I can code it to perform in that specific way and export the data you are looking for in whatever format you need—Excel, PDF, you name it."

"That is very, very compelling." Loafers' eyes light up. He looks like the kind of guy who likes spreadsheets.

I have to admit, I may not have my personal life together, but I feel like a boss right here, right now.

"Swipe to the left to advance to the next screen." I am a cruise ship director, riding my professional high.

About a minute later, the food runner comes back as promised with a speedy tray of desserts. But as he approaches the table, his foot gets stuck on the drop strap of my Birkin and he loses his footing. A plate with key lime pie tumbles off the tray, landing first on the outfit I'm wearing, and then onto my bag. The mason jar sundae topples next, knocking over Zareen's wine and Eyebrows' Moscow Mule as well.

I hardly notice the whipped cream that has splattered onto the lens of my Warby Parker tortoiseshell frames—I haven't been able to wear my contacts since sleeping in them the other night—as I bend down to wipe off my only-*looks*-expensive purse. That's when I notice the restaurant worker's foot has also somehow managed to dislodge the urn from my Birkin. Decker is not in my bag anymore. Where the hell did he go?

I push back in my chair and take a quick peek under the table, as though I'm attending to the mess of whipped cream as the waitstaff swarms over to the table to begin the cleanup process. I can see that the urn is halfway between me and Loafers. One ill-timed stretch from him and this thing is going to get lobbed over to James Van Der Beek. Fuck.

I surface back to the top of the table for air, dessert topping still smeared over my lenses, but who cares? I have officially lost my place in the presentation, and there's no way I can concentrate knowing this urn is floating around like a soccer ball just waiting to be kicked out of play under our table. Zareen notices I'm distracted by more than just the spilled desserts and pulls her second power move in five minutes.

"Oh dear, it looks like my tablet got bathed in pinot noir. Charlotte, do you have a moment to take a look at why this thing isn't working?"

Monica picks up on Zareen's distraction tactic and chimes in as well.

"Yes, gentlemen. Why don't we give the staff a moment to clean up over here a bit. Can I interest you in a port at the bar? Or perhaps a cigar from their case? I hear they have a lovely selection of rare organic Cubans."

With the four of them making their way to the bar, I scurry over to grab the urn, put it back in my bag, and lodge my bag tightly under my chair, wrapping the straps around the leg so as to avoid a repeat performance.

"Sorry about that, Zareen. Now, what's the matter with your iPad?" I ask as I finally wipe the schmutz off my lenses with a cloth napkin.

"Cut the shit, Charlotte. There's nothing the matter with my iPad. What's the matter with you, though? Are you feeling okay? What *was* that?" She puts the back of her hand to my head to feel for a fever.

Maybe I wasn't as graceful as I thought in retrieving the urn? She's on to me, and the thought that I may have blown this dinner—as well as my cover—causes my hands to start to tremble.

I quickly shove my hands behind my back. "Not now. Not now. Not now," I mumble to myself. The air...it's getting harder to breathe.

"What did you say? Speak up. I can't hear you, Charlotte. Speak up!"

"I'm sorry. I have to go," I tell Zareen as I stand up from the chair.

"What? No, no, no. Leaving is not an option, Charlotte." She pushes me back into my seat. "I can see Monica closing up the tab at the bar right now. You've got to pull it together and finish this presentation. Please. Give it five more minutes. Then you can go splash some water on your face in the bathroom or whatever you need to do."

"I need to go," I repeat.

"You can't. These guys are loving it. We're *so close* to securing this business."

I try to take a deep breath. "I'm sorry. I just can't. Tell Monica to finish the presentation. You have no idea how bad this will get if I don't go home."

"How bad *what* will get? What is happening with you, Charlotte? Just a moment ago you were army-crawling under the table. Now you suddenly have to head home? Please fill me in so that I can understand why your antics are sending this dinner to hell in a handbasket."

Zareen is my boss and I'm afraid she just might fire me right here, right now, if I leave with no viable explanation for my behavior tonight. So I close my eyes and brace for what is bound to be a rough landing.

"I was married to a man who died and his ashes are in my bag right now but they weren't two minutes ago. His urn fell out of my purse and rolled under the table and that feeling of losing him again hit me like a ton of bricks. Earlier today, his mom came to my apartment to try to steal the urn back. So, yeah. Everything is just sort of combusting right now and I feel like I can't breathe. God, I feel like I can't breathe!"

"Shhhh, relax. Relax, Charlotte." Zareen pulls me in to her side as she rubs my back with her hand, the sound of her jewelry clanking together like wind chimes. "In through your nose, out through your mouth."

I give that a try and compose myself enough to tell her, "I'm not doing okay right now. I'm sure I'll be fine tomorrow, or even just later tonight, but I can't stay here. I'm really sorry I ruined everything."

"It's okay." Zareen's tone softens. She sounds motherly. "Monica will finish the presentation. The slides are pretty self-explanatory, right? You sent her the deck this morning, so she has it on her phone, right?"

I nod my head yes. I sent Monica the slides in case my phone acted up. Not in case *I* did.

"Well, then, I'm confident Monica can handle this. She's an expert schmoozer and this will be—no pun intended—a piece of cake for her."

I smile at her, grateful for her understanding as I toss the bag over my shoulder and prepare to leave.

Zareen grabs my wrist. "Charlotte, thank you for your honesty tonight. But I need you to know that I'm putting you on a forced leave for two weeks. Don't worry—it'll still be paid."

"A *what*? Why?"

"I know we go way back, and I know you are struggling with something right now, but you can't conduct yourself like this at my company. You need to figure out whatever is going on in your personal life and get it together before coming back to the office."

"I said I'll be fine. I said I just needed a night to myself. Not *two weeks*, Zareen."

"I'm worried about you."

"And I'm worried about your company. If you put me on leave, who's going to run the programming then?"

"Marigold will do it," she says with so little hesitation, it's actually frightening.

I've been with Zareen for five years and suddenly she thinks some twenty-two-year-old who's been interning with us for a month and a half is a capable protégé? Moreover, that Marigold has what it takes to hold down the firm for more than half a day without instant messaging me some novice coding question? I'm offended. Maybe Zareen's the one who needs to take some time off and figure things out.

"So, you're replacing me with Marigold?"

"No need for dramatics. You're not being replaced. You need more than just a day, Charlotte. Maybe you can't see that right now, but if what you said is true, then those are serious issues and you need to—"

"If what I said was true? You don't believe me? You think I'm making this all up? Actually, don't answer that. I'll take the house arrest and see you in two weeks," I say and hightail it to the door.

Chapter 10

I cancel all of Leno's midday walks since it looks like I'm going to be home for the next two weeks and can actually do them myself for once. At least, that's what this note from Human Resources in my inbox is implying. The note, coupled with Zareen sending me straight to voice mail three times in a row and not answering a single text, call, or email this morning, also tells me she wasn't bluffing about this whole leave-of-absence thing.

The forced PTO makes me realize I haven't taken a single vacation day in the four-plus years I've worked at The Influencer Firm, and it feels so weird not to be getting ready to go into the office today. Instead, it's 8:30 a.m. and I'm troubleshooting the Keurig, which appears to be tits up again.

After pressing the brew button incessantly to no avail, I finally cave and decide to go to Alfred's. Frankly, I haven't been able to shake the honey-chai whatever whatever that Brian brought to WeHot, and if the coffee is ten dollars a cup, maybe I'll sip it slow enough to do all the urn research I've been intending. So I strap on a sports bra, throw on a short-sleeved shirt, slide into a pair of leggings, and complete the whole "fun-employed" look by leashing up my dog, throwing my hair in a messy bun, and tossing my computer—along with my husband's urn—into my bag.

Thankfully at this hour, it's not quite blazing hot just yet. But give it forty-five minutes and the sun combined with the smog will turn the wire chair I'm sitting on into a waffle iron. For now, I find a shady spot near a water bowl for Leno as I take the first sip of my latte. The caffeine hits me instantly, the way a sip of wine at happy hour takes the edge off a crazy day. Today, arguably, is going to be the craziest considering the morbid tabs I'm about to open.

Hey, how did last night go? Brian's text lights up my Apple Watch just as I'm typing the words *nearby mausoleum* into Google.

When I'd told Brian I'd get back to him today about visiting the urn, I hadn't thought I'd be in the shit with my work. But as tempted as I am to brush him off—again—I also realize there's a good chance I'm going to put this whole urn thing to bed today. I mean, I have to if I want to go back to work.

Realizing that this may be one of the last times I have the urn in my possession *and* can meet Brian somewhere neutral for him to see it (or whatever he wants to do with it), I decide to cave on his request.

If you want to see Decker, I'm at Alfred's having coffee rn on the back patio.

Moments later, the world's fastest texter who actually has a very important job writes back: Perfect timing! I have a break in rounds. I can be there in 15.

While I'm still alone, I attempt to pull up Brian's Facebook profile. But when I type in his name, it shows that I "unfollowed" him. In tech speak, that means we remained connected as Facebook friends, but under this setting, he never showed up in my feed.

I remember doing this because at the time, I hadn't wanted to see where he was gallivanting off to in his impeccably tailored Banana Republic short-sleeved button-downs, or what concerts he was checking in front-row at with other friends from the frat, or his next relationship conquest. All of that would have been proof that another person close to Decker was able to bounce back and live a normal life and that I... hadn't. I was still stuck in a constant state of being mad and angry and sad. Like a bad soundtrack on repeat.

There's also another reason I unfollowed him. A very specific reason. A reason that I'm hoping he's forgotten now that we'll be sitting face-to-face for the first time in years.

As I stare at his profile picture, his smiling face is like a shiny fishing lure drawing me in. Whether I'm ready for it or not, I'm curious for more. So, I uncheck the "unfollow" box and his profile comes into full, bright view like a surprise party.

On the top of his wall is a pinned post reminding everyone about a fraternity fund-raiser. Probably the one Debbie mentioned. I had forgotten for a minute just how much of a frat boy Brian really is and can't decide if it's admirable or sad that nearly a decade after graduation, he's still the social chairman of the group.

As I move on to look through his photos, I discover a gradual transition from his spiky-haired frat boy days. Even though he was already graduated, I remember a version of Brian Jackson who was still fond of beer bongs and layering pastel-colored polo shirts. One who couldn't say "Go Trojans!" without making a condom joke. But each passing picture shows a more polished version of him. He's a doctor now—a children's doctor. There's a photo of him crossing the stage at graduation, a photo of him dressed up as Superman standing next to his patient—an adorable Clark Kent, mind you—on Halloween, a photo of him with an X-ray of a broken arm, and so on and so forth. I have to admit I didn't really peg him as a guy who would be responsible enough to be in charge of kids' health, but good for him for growing up. Consider me officially impressed.

"Howdy, howdy," he says, forcing me to snap out of my digital stalking spree.

"Morning," I say in the most casual, I-wasn't-just-looking-at-every-single-Facebook-photo-of-you kind of way.

"Got to love Alfred's: where the lattes are overpriced by about a dollar per ounce and there's always a chance you'll see Leonardo DiCaprio playing cat's cradle with Jonah Hill on the back patio," Brian says, doctoring up his drink with a packet of Sugar in the Raw and a healthy dose of creamer. I think he's being facetious about the celebs, but I do afford myself a three-sixty-degree stretch in the event we might have an actual sighting.

"Thanks again for texting me," he says, reminding me why I invited him in the first place. I dig into my Birkin and put the urn on the table like it's a centerpiece.

"Ta-da."

"Oh, hey there, buddy," he says. I want to judge him for talking to an inanimate object, but realize it was only a few nights ago I found myself doing the same thing.

"So why are you here? Don't you have to be at work?"

"No..." I say, struggling to figure out what should come next.

"Oh, no. You didn't get *fired*?" He whispers that last word like my parents are at the table next to us.

"No, I did not get fired, thankyouverymuch. But I did get put on a forced leave, whatever that means."

"I think it means free vacation. What happened?" Brian asks as he lifts his circular black Ray-Ban sunglasses to the top of his head, pulling back his thick brown hair.

"Well, you know I had a big client dinner last night. There was a snafu and I got put on some sort of a paid leave."

"Tell me more about this snafu." Brian swirls his drink with a stirrer. The way he casually invites me to go on makes it seem like I was telling him about a bad haircut I just got or some great poke bowl I had for lunch—like *I* actually started this conversation.

Ordinarily, I would never repeat what happened at BOA. How could anyone understand or even believe something so ridiculous could happen? But Brian actually knows about my past, so I don't have to catch him up or censor myself.

"I brought the urn with me to the client dinner and it fell out of my bag midmeal. Caused a bit of a 'scene,' some might say."

"I guess that *is* a snafu, huh? I take it the big boss lady didn't know Decker was back?"

"She didn't know I was ever married. So, yeah. She wants me to take some time off to collect myself. Or, at least, that's the politically correct version of how the company is responding to what happened last night. And now here we are. They even blocked me from my work email and our Slack channel. I'm totally off the grid."

"And how does that feel?"

"Why? Are you my therapist now?" I ask, mentally noting that all that's missing are his clipboard and stethoscope.

"Sorry, sorry. Asking probing questions is just a pesky bedside habit. But look at it this way. Maybe it's not such a bad thing to take some time off and clear your plate a little bit, you know? I mean, how's it going with rehoming the urn and all?"

"I've got the Google search result for some five-story mausoleum breaking ground on Gower Street pulled up on my computer. Other than that, Debbie showed up at my apartment trying to steal it back last night."

"She *what*?"

"Yes. You heard that correctly. Casey said Debbie found her way into the lobby of our building and was harassing the doorman, wailing about Decker. In fact, that's what made me bring the urn to the dinner in the first place. If she wasn't so insanely invasive, maybe I could have actually felt comfortable leaving him behind for a few hours."

"Well, what did you think was going to happen?"

"What do you mean?"

"Like if she made her way to your apartment. Little five-foot-nothing, midsixties Debbie Austin was going to barrel your door down and tackle you for the urn?"

I can't tell if the question is rhetorical.

"I wouldn't sweat it, Char. Remember, grief works in mysterious ways. I'm sure it was just a little onetime flare-up."

Even though Brian's not one to judge, I honestly was expecting him to bandwagon hate on Mrs. Austin. But his response is actually rational.

"So, let's move forward. What can I do? How can I help? Surely there has to be something. What's one task related to this whole urn thing that you *don't* want to do? Like, at all. That's the one I'll take off your plate."

"You're about a day late and a dollar short. The part I didn't want to do was tell Debbie and clearly that's been checked off the list."

"Perfect! That's out of the way, then. What's next?"

Brian's always had an extreme go-getter mentality. Sometimes I look at how a guy like him—kind of loud, always eager, a little too in your face—could ever even be friends with a quiet, methodical, reserved guy like Decker. But they had a good dynamic. Someone had to buy the keg, someone had to pump it.

Brian looks at me wide-eyed in a way that indicates he won't take "No, thanks. I'm good" for an answer. While I want to—and insist that I will—do the heavy lifting myself, what's the harm in outsourcing the *cringeworthy* lifting?

"Call Robert Hancock," I say, as if he's Siri.

"Happy to. But who's that?"

I grab the letter the insurance agency sent with the urn and slide it across our bistro table. "I want you to ask them what they think I should do."

Brian is focused, like it's a med-school midterm, as he reads the letter over. I can bet that he wasn't expecting my task would be to call the urn people, and I'm waiting for him to put the paper down and explain to me how this is really something *I* should do. But after he finishes scanning, he promptly takes out his phone, dials the number, and says, "I'll put them on speaker."

"It's a stellar morning at Robert Hancock Insurance Brokers. My name is Kenya. How may I assist you?" The rep is very clearly reading a script because I can't imagine anything could be stellar about the job she has.

"Yes, hi," Brian says, then clears his throat. "I'm calling on behalf of my...client?" He looks at me and I shrug my shoulders. I have no clue where he is going with this.

"Yes, my client," he continues firmly. "Her name is Charlotte Rosen and her late husband's remains were delivered to her apartment last weekend."

"Yes, sir. This is in regards to the Pala Mausoleum fire, correct?"

"Yes, exactly. That's the one."

Was there another?

"How can I help you?" Kenya asks.

"Well, we… I mean *she*…was wondering where the best place to send them back to might be?"

At this point, I'm nervously chipping off my peach-colored gel manicure, which is leaving behind flakes on the ground all around me, including in the fur on Leno's back.

"I'm afraid I can't speak with you about this without the consent of Ms. Rosen herself."

"I'm here," I blurt out. "This is Charlotte speaking."

I spatter off my Social Security number and mother's maiden name and soon enough Kenya accepts my identity.

"Thank you for confirming, ma'am. It'd be my pleasure to connect you to a grief counselor at this time," she says. "As a reminder, they are standing by free of charge for your benefit for the next two weeks."

I grab the phone from Brian's hands and say loud and clearly: "I don't need a grief counselor."

Debatable, I know. But another agent standing by to read another flowery script won't be of any help to me. I need real advice. It's go time.

"Well, then, how may I assist you exactly?"

"I want to know where I'm supposed to put him now. Now that the mausoleum has been destroyed and I sort of thought this whole thing was a done deal five years ago, where *else* can he go?"

"Um, uh…" It is evident that Kenya is about to go off script for the first time in her career. "Ma'am, the mausoleum burned down. So where you store your husband's remains at this point is a personal decision. One that would be entirely up to you and your loved ones."

"So there's no backup mausoleum that you guys have a con- tract with or something like that?" Brian asks.

"No, there are no other mausoleums we are working with at this time. Just the complimentary grief counselors. Are you sure you don't want to be connected?"

"Yes," Brian and I say at the same time.

Kenya reads her exit script and the line fades to dark.

"Okay, so don't panic," Brian says in his signature casual tone. "This isn't a dead end. Besides, who says you have to figure this out right now? What about keeping him at your place for a while?"

"I don't know about that, Brian. I mean, he's in there. What- ever is left of Decker *is in there.*" I point to the urn to drive home the "this is weird" point. "It's not a vase of flowers, for crying out loud. These are *bone fragments.*"

"Okay, fair enough. I can respect the science going on in there. So, here's a thought: How about you—willingly, of course—return him to his mom?"

I want to spit my latte across the patio at the mere men- tion. While I know that solves the "not in my house" prob- lem, I'm not leaning in the "her house" direction either. The truth of the matter is if I could trust that Debbie would make a more practical decision with the urn this time around, then there'd be a chance I'd drive the thing back over to her place right now. But part of the whole reason I think Debbie chose to put Decker in Pala in the first place was so that she could pull some rank. It was a move that made it nearly impossible for me to spend time with him the way other widows can just visit a grave site with flowers anytime they want. The trek to Pala was just a cheeky little jaunt for her. She doesn't work a regular job and the Austins have a driver. A two-hour chauf- feured trip in a Wi-Fi-enabled Bentley was nothing for her. Clearly her visits must have tapered off in the recent past or she would have known what happened to the mausoleum before I told her. But visiting him frequently really only mattered in the beginning when she went to see him and I didn't, because it served as the proof she needed that she made the right choice, the best choice, and the only choice—after I made the impossible choice. I'm not going to let things play out like that again.

"He deserves more from me now," I tell Brian. "He deserves actual thought and effort and meaning *from me*. If I can't figure it out, then sure. I'll turn things over to Debbie. But I need a chance this time."

"I get it. Giving him to Debbie was just a thought in case that made things easier. It was dumb of me to suggest; I know you've already thought about that, and more importantly, I know you can handle this, Charlotte." He pauses. "You're the strongest person I know."

Brian reaches across the table and puts his right hand on my shoulder, and we hold eye contact until an alarm goes off on Brian's phone. He springs his hand away to silence the noise.

"Well, that's my cue. I've got to get to the hospital for rounds. Thanks for letting me visit and help a little bit with Project Decker. I like doing that kind of thing. Helping people." He smiles and points to the embroidery on his scrubs pocket. If I still worked for the studio, I would try my hardest to land him a walk-on role for some hospital drama. He'd be a great D-list McDreamy.

"And just remember...if shit hits the fan, I'm your guy. Call me, come over, whatever."

"I'll keep you posted," I say as I open the screen of my laptop back up.

Alone again at Alfred's, I afford myself the liberty of a Google search titled "what to do with your loved one's ashes." The top result is an article with fifty-two unique options. When I click the link, I am hopeful that something will trigger a solid next step.

Scrolling down the page, hope turns to confusion, then doubt, and then finally a little bit of nausea when I get to entry number forty-four: Sprinkle some ashes into your favorite jar of nail polish and wear your loved one on the tips of your fingers. And... I'm officially done here.

I spot a woman perching up an Open sign on the sidewalk outside a boutique across the street. The water bowl she sets down next tells me they're dog-friendly, and so I wake Leno from sunbathing, figuring I'll pop in on my way back to the apartment.

"Hi there," says the store attendant once I'm standing in the entryway. "Let me know if I can help you with anything."

Her bubbly greeting is a stark difference from what you get at most LA boutiques—a death stare followed by completely ignoring your existence when you ask for help. I smile back as I snake my way through the store, making sure Leno doesn't knock into a jewelry display.

What are you up to? The text from Casey lights up my wrist as I shuffle some striped T-shirts on a rack to the left in search of my size.

Nothing. Just shopping, I say back.

Oh.

Oh? The single-word answer makes me pause for a moment. Should I not be shopping? Is it not okay for me to do something banal right now? I got temporarily let go from my job and my husband's ashes need to go somewhere other than a bottle of OPI. I would think checking to see if these moto-style leggings come in my size would come with a little less judgment from Casey, of all people.

OK* Stupid autocorrect, she texts back before I get the chance to dissect her accidental word choice further. I breathe easier knowing it was just a typo. Was wondering if I left my keys at home. Nvm.

I respond that I'll check when I'm back. Meanwhile, I find the nice boutique owner and ask her about the leggings.

"Excuse me. Do you have these in a size medium?"

"Oh, I'm sorry. We don't do sizes here."

"What do you mean?" I ask.

"We don't believe women should be classified by smalls, mediums, and larges. So instead, we color code all of our inventory. You look like you'd be a purple. Look for things with purple tags. Those will fit you well. Or you could go for a tighter fit with a red tag, and a looser fit with a green tag."

Aside from this being one of *the* most LA things I have ever heard, I can't quite wrap my head around the system.

"Why don't you just make three different sections of the store and put all the same-sized clothes in each section. You can call them sections one, two, and three."

"We don't do sizes," she reminds me. "And we wouldn't want anyone to feel self-conscious about shopping in a section 'three.' The colors are neutral. They're arbitrary," she explains.

"Well, they're not arbitrary. Nothing is arbitrary if it's a system used over time. I know a purple fits me today. But if in six months I come back and all of a sudden I'm a green, I'll know what that means just the same: I gained ten pounds over the holidays."

The associate takes the leggings from my hands and re-racks them.

"With all due respect, I'm not sure Be Yourself is the right store for you. We tend to be a little more…free-thinking over here. But good luck with your search. I hope you find the fit you're looking for."

Not worrying about whether I'll have to fit my thighs into a green, purple, or red, I grab lunch at a honey-butter fried chicken place, splurging the extra dollar for a biscuit instead of a bun. The nice cashier with the septum piercing talked me into it, but I'm fine with the upsell because I can't remember the last time I had a flaky biscuit.

I find a spot for one at a communal picnic table on their patio. The whimsical red-and-white-striped umbrella doesn't have the breadth to go up against the midday sun and I can't wait to see the resulting suntan. I tuck Leno under the table like it's a makeshift doghouse. He lies down on the cool, shady cement.

A few minutes later, my tray arrives and I sink my teeth into the sandwich. I chew that first, dense bite slowly and wash it down with a sip of an ice-cold fountain drink. The warm, tangy buttermilk biscuit tastes like nostalgia. Even though I don't plan on telling the sous chef that his fifteen-dollar gourmet sandwich reminds me of McDonald's breakfast, I promise I mean it in the best of ways. I take another bite. It brings me back to simpler times—a drive-through, a combo meal, a thin wax paper wrapper with melted cheese stuck to it on the inside. I know this isn't that, but it doesn't stop me from heading back to the counter, pulling out another dollar, and hoping that's enough to cover an extra biscuit on the side.

Chapter 11

Brian takes a minute to answer the door the next day, which gives me some time to decide what I want to do with the second button on my denim chambray shirt *and* to soak in the fact that I'm standing in the hallway of his zonks-amaze condo building in downtown Los Angeles. Seriously, his monthly HOA fees here must be the same as my entire rent. Was that a framed and signed Annie Leibovitz in the lobby?

"Come on in," Brian says, wearing a weathered USC T-shirt and gray lounge shorts.

If you were to ask me this time last week, I'd say his brick-and-timber loft with soaring eighteen-foot ceilings is the last place I expected I would wind up this morning. But he told me to contact him if shit hit the fan and now I'm here, bright-eyed and bushy-tailed, at 8:00 a.m. on a Thursday morning.

"Sweet apartment," I say, walking in through his foyer, hoping that something slightly more astute will come out of my mouth next.

"Thanks. It's one of my dad's units, actually." At that, I

vaguely remember the Jacksons being hot-shot developers. "He finished the condo years ago and I convinced him to let me stay in it and use it as a study hall of sorts until he found suitable buyers. He agreed, moved on to the next project, and now I think he forgot about it, honestly. So don't tell anyone, okay? The doorman and I are finally on good terms since that time I— Actually, never mind."

I don't even want to know.

"Anyway, can I get you a coffee?" he asks.

"Please," I say.

"Cold brew okay for you?"

"Of course."

"Siri, brew my coffee," Brian announces. Nothing happens.

"Uh, Brian, I'm not sure iPhones can…"

"I know. It's a tech joke. Because you're a coder—get it? Never mind. Man, have my one-liners just tanked since becoming a doctor or what?"

He grabs two white ceramic mugs from his kitchen cabinet and sets them on a ledge that's nestled outside his refrigerator door. A couple of ice cubes hit the cups, and then a steady stream of cold brew starts flowing. The hidden built-in spout makes me wonder how much it cost him to transform his apartment into a literal Starbucks.

He slides a mug across his mammoth marble kitchen island.

"So what's going on, Char?"

"Well, you said to come by if shit hits the fan and, well, here," I say, handing him the Anthropologie towel that's normally draped through the handle of my oven.

"Is this a…housewarming gift?"

"Don't take this the wrong way, but I can't think of any occasion when I'd bring you a thirty-dollar linen as a gift. But I would bring a *stained* thirty-dollar linen as a…favor."

"I'm not sure I'm following you, Char. What's the emergency?"

"I was doing some laundry at home, and when I went to hang this back up, I noticed the mark didn't come out. This is one of my favorite towels and I'm not sure if the lipstick I borrowed from my friend the other night was actually red house paint, but I really don't want to see this stupid stripe every time I dry my hands at the sink."

Brian sets his coffee on the counter and takes the towel from my hand to give it a closer look. Then he stares at me.

"Please don't make me ask for it by name," I say.

"You want to use my Turbo Washer 6000, don't you?"

My eyes widen and I nod. Now he gets it.

"You have no idea how valuable I feel right now. I'll be right back."

Brian moves out of frame and a few moments later I hear his laundry machine filling with water. A wave of anxiety hits me like the rush coming from the faucet. Did I really just bring dirty laundry to Brian's house and call it an emergency? When I walked through his door, he probably thought the urn cracked, or Hancock Insurance was a fraud, or anything other than the fact that one of my Decker-era relics had a nasty stain my dollar-store detergent couldn't handle. But the truth is, to me, that *is* an emergency. Right now, I just need one thing, one familiar thing, to stay as I remember it.

"It'll be about a half hour. Shall we sit?" Brian returns and gestures toward his living room. A giant burgundy leather Chesterton couch awaits us. It feels like a cloud swallowing me whole as I take a seat. I let my body sink into the comfortable cushions and sip slowly on the refreshing cold brew; the caffeine is like a lifeline, warding off the start of a subtle headache.

"Thanks for doing a load on the fly," I say.

"No problem. I'm confident that lipstick will come out. I had this white shirt once, and all over the collar—"

"Okay, you know what? I think I'm good," I say, interrupting him. "You can spare me the story about the time you got some girl's makeup off your clothes."

"I was actually going to tell you about the time my nephew gave me a hug while in the midst of a torrential nosebleed. It looked like my shoulder had been dip-dyed in a vat of red food coloring."

"Oh," I say, embarrassed. I can feel my cheeks turning the same shade of red as the lipstick stain.

"Came out crisp and clean like I bought it off the shelf at Banana Republic that very day. Moral of the story: in the Turbo Washer we trust." He clinks his mug against mine in a pseudo cheers movement.

I'm not used to things other than my work being a neutralizer in my life, but his calming force is appreciated.

"Hey, can you help me with this, Char?" Brian hovers over a folded corner of a newspaper that's resting on his coffee table.

"You get the *New York Times*?" I ask.

"Yeah, only on Sundays, though. I like to know how the East Coast sees the world these days."

Perhaps he should take over my standing calls with The Jeaner, in that case.

"Don't judge. I'm a little backed up on my puzzles, as you can see." He points to a stack of at least ten more papers folded up in the corner of the living room, then diverts his attention back to the twelve-across. "*Therefore?* What the hell kind of a clue is that?"

"How many letters is it?" I ask.

"Four."

"And clues on the down?"

"Not yet."

el my forehead crinkle, the way it always does when ainst an ambiguous *NYT* crossword clue.

"Try *ergo*," I say.

"*E-R-G-O,*" he says as he inputs each letter with a black ballpoint pen. "Actually, yeah. That works. Thanks, smartie."

He sets the pen down and I watch him take a sip of his coffee. I've become remarkably comfortable in Brian's presence since first worrying what he'd think of me bringing a dish towel over. But now he feels like a friend right now, *my* friend, and not just a guy who knew Decker—who knew me with Decker—and has to be nice by association.

"So, what's on your agenda today?" he asks.

I tap the time on my watch, then slide over to my calendar app, which is of course blank due to my forced leave.

"After the wash, I'm thinking of driving up to Pala, actually. I got a Google alert that said there's a weeklong farmers' market going on. Proceeds go to rebuilding the farms that got damaged in the fire. Maybe I'll run into other people like me there and we can brainstorm what to do with our urns. Or maybe we can just pool our money and go in on some crypts at that new mega-mausoleum on Gower," I joke.

"Sounds fun. Want company? I could go for some vine-ripe tomatoes or a fresh fruit pie. Think they'll have either of those?"

Vine-ripe tomatoes or fruit pie? Are we shooting a pilot for HGTV?

"Don't you have to work?"

"Yeah, but not till tonight. Let's go. I can drive the Tesla."

"Tesla?"

"Graduation present." He shrugs. "It gets forty-six miles to the gallon. What do you think?"

Between the job with kids and the concern for fuel efficiency, *I think* this is a much different Brian than the guy who hollered at chicks from his doorless Wrangler years ago. Who is this guy who suddenly cares more about miles per gallon than who's bringing the Jell-O shots to the party?

Just then, there's a chime from the laundry room. I'm reminded of the fact that his washer is doing something that no prescribed anxiety medication can do for me, which leaves little room to protest agreeing to make him my impromptu Pala wingman. I consider the urn safe while locked in my car, which is parked in a guest spot in Brian's gated garage, and take him up on his offer—*after* he puts the Anthro linen in the dryer.

I want to say that riding shotgun in Brian's Tesla will never get old, but I also don't want to make a habit of this. I must admit, however, that when cruising down the 405 in a rare "light traffic" moment in LA, there are few other cars I'd rather be in. The scent coming out of the air-conditioning vents can be customized, for crying out loud. Today, Brian is pumping through the scent of "freshly baked waffle cones."

"For as high-tech as this car is, you'd think Elon Musk would have invented an app that would massage your shoulders while you drive," Brian says as he sits back in his seat, runs both fingers through his hair, and lets autopilot take the wheel.

"I'll work on that one. Right after I solve the world's dating crises."

"What do you mean?"

"I'm working on a dating app."

"I didn't know that. What's it going to be like, Tinder 2.0?"

Immediately I regret mentioning my little side project, which, by the way, is never going to get off the ground considering I haven't even touched my programs in almost a week.

"It's just something stupid I'm messing around with right now," I say.

"Oh, come on, Char. Tell me more. I'll tell you the secret to extracting a macaroni noodle from a nostril."

I crinkle my face, *New York Times* crossword puzzle style, and give him a look that says, *No, thanks. I'm good.* But his willingness to trade insider industry knowledge is a nice way of showing me he cares what I have to say, even if it's over his head. Or worse, even if he thinks it's stupid. Either way, I humor him.

"Well, you know what I do for a living?"

"Yeah, matching the popular internet people to your client events, right?"

"Close enough. My app functions kind of like that. But instead of it showing compatibility between a business and an influencer, it outlines the compatibility between a potential suitor and…myself."

I didn't have an elevator pitch prepared, clearly.

"Wow, that's pretty sweet. Can I try it?" he asks. "Curious how I'd pair with Jennifer Lawrence."

"*She's* your celeb crush? I pegged you for, I don't know, a young Pamela Anderson or maybe the nanny Jude Law cheated with?"

"What do you think of me, Charlotte Rosen? I've come a long way since flirting with your mom at your wedding. Although I think she was kind of into it." He looks at me and winks.

"Well, regardless, you can't try it. It's only in beta version. There are a few kinks in the code at the moment."

"So what's the endgame with it?"

"Endgame?"

"Yeah, like, are you just going to finish it and upload it to the App Store, or…?"

The question gives me pause. I know I will need to eventually quit The Influencer Firm and focus full-time on developing this thing if I want to sell the technology across the globe and take over the world. Even though I love what I do and have a great boss, TIF is not my endgame so much as a stepping-stone, which sounds harsh, I know. Like I'm using the setup Zareen has given me as part of my *nine-to-five*—superfast internet connection speeds, a giant monitor, tuition reimbursement for special coding classes, etc.—so that I can spend my *five-to-nine* grooming my not-so-casual efforts for finding a future mate and securing a lifetime of financial freedom while I'm at it. For now, though, I'm in no rush to shake things up.

"I don't really know. I guess I'm hoping I meet some tech investor down the road who will back it and turn it into the next Match.com."

He holds up his right hand for a high five.

"Come on —don't leave me hanging." I oblige and touch my palm to his. "There ya go, Champ. I'll be the first to subscribe. I can use all the dating help I can get."

The conversation stays in this sort of light and airy territory. Brian's an easy man to talk to, and when he asks questions about my hopes and my dreams, and deems my answers high-five-worthy, it makes me feel casual and cool. He's a lot kinder and more genuine than I anticipated this second go-round.

The farmers' market is mostly just wine and olive oil from Temecula and booths to sign up for a Winnebago giveaway sweepstakes. Such is what you get from a tiny town known for its proximity to wine country, a casino, and (formerly) a fancy mausoleum. Regardless, Brian and I still take this as an opportunity to soak up the SoCal sun and saunter down Pala's one main road.

"Olive oil lip balm or olive oil hand soap?" he asks, holding up two goodies from one of the vendor booths. "Screw it—I'll get both."

"Hey, can we pop into this bar real quick?" I say. "I've got to pee."

Brian ushers me inside and we make our way to the back. The restroom turns out to be a single-person unisex setup. I go to turn the handle, but it's locked. The bathroom is occupied.

"Oh, sorry. My buddy is in there," says a guy wearing an excessively low-cut heather-gray V-neck. "He should be out any second, though."

"Thanks," I say with a smile as I stand back and wait my turn next to Brian.

Moments later, there's a knock from *inside* the bathroom and the V-neck guy next to us sets down his Rolling Rock on the bar and springs toward the door to open it. Out comes another good-looking guy, same age. He is in a wheelchair.

"You all good to go there, Steve?" Rolling Rock says.

"Yup. Sorry that took so long. There was no railing, so I couldn't balance myself on—"

"No worries, man. Game hasn't even started yet. Let's get you a brewski, shall we?"

I can't help but notice a slight resemblance between the man in the wheelchair and, well, Decker. Blond hair, blue eyes, with the quintessential Cali-cool vibe. Steve smiles at me before he rolls away and says, "It's all yours."

There's an air-conditioning vent blowing directly over the sink as I wash my hands with a lemon-scented soap. The cold air feels good after walking up and down the rows of vendors under the midday sun, although it's not blowing hard enough to dry the sweat that's pooled on my upper lip. As I ball up some toilet paper to blot my skin, there's a knock at the bathroom door.

Opening the door, I am prepared to see an impatient barfly or Brian checking on me, but instead it is Steve, the man in the wheelchair. I'm taken aback again by his familiar facial features, especially his baby blue eyes, and put my hand to my chest.

"I'm so sorry. I didn't mean to startle you. Did I leave my hat in there by chance?"

I prop open the door with the heel of my Converse to let in a little more light, and sure enough, I spy a five-panel cap on the floor.

"Oh yeah, looks like it," I say as I do a version of downward dog to grab the hat. I see that USC is embroidered on it before handing it back. He flashes a subtle smile and I flash one back before he leaves to rejoin his friend at the bar.

I spot Brian, who has made himself rather comfortable on a bar stool sipping what looks like a Shirley Temple. "Gee, did I really take that long in the bathroom?" I say when I reach him.

"Sorry, couldn't resist peeping at this game. And the ninety-nine-cent Shirley Temples. Want one?"

"No, thanks."

"I can safely say this is the first time I've picked a farmers' market over watching a baseball game. It's Dodgers versus Yankees. A Coast-to-Coast Classic is about as exciting as it gets for the MLB."

"We can stay and watch if you want," I suggest.

"Nah, let's boogie. Shall we go?"

From across the bar, I see Steve and his V-neck-clad friend enjoying the baseball game and splitting a bucket of beer. I can't help but wonder more about Steve. Is this the best it's been for him? Or the worst? Is this wheelchair thing just a necessary inconvenience due to a recent ACL surgery? Or is he completely paralyzed from the waist down? If Decker somehow could have survived his accident, could this—in time—have been him and…Brian?

For an early one-year anniversary gift, which is supposed to be paper-themed, I bought Decker entry into a race called

The Mad Men Mudder. It was featured in *Men's Journal* as one of the best courses "for guys with serious balls." Even though that descriptor was my cue to sit this one out, he was so stoked that I registered him—and even more stoked that Brian was able to get a bib, too, before the race sold it. Decker didn't train much, didn't need to. An athlete his whole life, he would have no problem running three miles in thick mud, crawling through a thousand feet of sludge, and biking a rugged trail, all while dressed in a suit and dress shoes like a character from the TV show *Mad Men*. If I were to be concerned about anyone making it out of the race with their limbs intact, it would have been Brian, who at that time was still rocking a bit of a beer gut Dad-Bod.

On August first, the morning of the race, Decker kissed me goodbye just like he always did before going somewhere—work, the grocery store, out with his friends. A minute later, he came back in—he'd left his Clif Bar and banana on the kitchen counter—and gave me another kiss.

Then he returned once more. "What'd you forget this time?" I asked, amused by his forgetfulness.

"Nothing," he said. "Just wanted one more kiss for good luck."

I texted him shortly after because I forgot to ask what time he thought he'd be done. Noonish, he said. I volleyed with: Lunch after? He replied back: Chipotle. And my craving for a burrito bowl instantly kicked in.

Alone in the house that morning, I treated myself to a Postmates delivery of a McDonald's breakfast sandwich on a biscuit and noshed on it mindlessly as I read all the latest celebrity gossip on TMZ. A controversial outfit Beyoncé wore to an awards show, a feud between teenage rappers, the details of a celeb's tumultuous divorce—this was the kind of stuff Decker would make fun of me for caring about. So I enjoyed my guilty pleasures by myself, wiping my buttery fingers on my plaid Old Navy pajama pants in between blog posts.

When I finally read what felt like every gossip article on the internet, I checked my phone and saw several missed calls and texts. None were from Decker, but all of them were about him. They ranged from "Have you heard from Decker?" to "Did you hear what happened to Decker?" to "Cedars-Sinai. ICU. Now." My phone had accidentally been on silent.

Before I could figure out my next move, there was knocking at the door. When I opened it, Brian—donned in pristine race attire, not a speck of dirt on him—put his hands on my shoulders and told me the worst thing had happened. Moments after the starting bell, Decker had collapsed twenty feet from the line and was rushed, unresponsive, to the hospital.

Flash forward a week and Dr. Brandt was asking me: "What do you want to do here, Mrs. Austin?"

"Why are you asking *me* that?" I said as I paced the width of the hospital room, which was exactly nine footsteps.

"Well, I'm afraid we've come to that point and you're the next of kin, Mrs. Austin," he said, glancing at his chart. His face looked like the chubby old bald white guys from the vintage game *Guess Who?*

Next of kin. Three simple words I never thought would rise to the top of the list of adjectives that accurately described me. But somehow there I was, standing next to a trauma doctor I'd only met a few days before, being told that my husband of less than a year was unconscious and unable to specify his DNR wishes, which was medical speak for: *He's not going to make it without this machine and you can't take it home with you, so now what?*

We discussed it as a group—me, my parents, Decker's parents, the medical team—ad nauseam. But the more we talked about it, the more confused and stuck I became about the whole situation. What were we waiting for? A miracle? The doctor told us Decker wasn't going to make it. Was I the only one who had heard him?

"What are the chances he'll go back to being the way he was, that everything will end up being fine even if it takes months? Years. Whatever." I begged Dr. Brandt to get real with me one last time.

I could smell my own breath at this point—it stank of vending machine coffee and Fritos.

"All of our tests show less than 1 percent."

What is less than one? I asked myself. Zero. What is zero? Nothing. How had my husband—*my everything*—turned into *nothing*?

What was less than 1 percent of Decker? Was it a man I would love? Was it a man who would want to be alive? That's when it hit me: everything that made Decker *Decker* was gone.

Miracles were off the table; I had come to accept that. So I looked at it like a math problem instead, heartless as it sounds. That was the moment I became a technically minded woman. That was the moment I was finally able to say: "Okay, Doctor. Let's call it."

"Char? Should we go?" Brian asks again, waving at me to zone back in.

"Yeah, sorry. Let's roll."

As we saunter down the main road, I can't shake seeing those two guys watching the game. At the risk of sounding crazy, maybe even a little creepy, I ask: "Did you see that guy at the bar? The one in the wheelchair?"

"The one who was in the bathroom before you?"

"Yeah, him."

"Sure. What about him?"

"I know this is going to sound weird, but he looked like Decker, didn't he? Same vibe and all."

"I mean, I guess. Similar hair color."

"What if...what if Decker could have ended up like that had I just given him more time to heal?"

"Ended up like what exactly?" Brian asks.

"You know, like, that guy. Remarkably okay and normal considering the circumstances. I mean, that dude was just out with his friend—and that friend could have been *you*. They were just watching baseball, sharing a bucket of beer, hanging at the bar. Total dude stuff. What if Decker could have recovered like that and *I* never gave him the chance to? God, I never should have signed him up for that race."

"Hey, let's not panic here, okay? The stroke he had could have happened while he was taking a shower or playing video games on the couch. Instead, it happened at the start of a race. That's how these things work. It's sad and it's scary, but at the end of the day, it was a heart defect no one knew he had. You couldn't have controlled what happened next."

"Yeah, but—"

"His body wasn't made of steel, Charlotte. Look, I'm not trying to be insensitive here, but he had an irreparable brain injury and internal bleeding. I may be in the medical field now, but even a Joe Schmoe off the street would know that's a lot of trauma. So if you're wondering, I'd say you made the right choice, you made the *only* choice. And to be honest, I'm glad it fell on someone strong enough to make it. Hell, I don't know if I could have done the same thing then."

"Thanks. I hope you don't feel like you have to just say that, though."

It's not that I think Brian is appeasing me so that I don't start to cry or get too emotional while we have a hundred-mile car ride back to the city on our hands. I just want to be sure he's not walking on eggshells unnecessarily. Plenty of people have told me over the years that I did the right thing simply

132 • EMILY BELDEN

because they thought voicing any alternate opinion would upset me. The thing is, I was already upset.

He pivots his body toward me and sets down the olive oil this-or-that.

"You asked me a loaded question and now I gave you a loaded answer. We both know the chance that Decker would have ended up like the guy you saw at the bar was less than 1 percent. Have you forgotten what Dr. Brandt told you that day?"

How could I ever?

"Take it from me—Dr. Josef R. Brandt is one of the best trauma doctors in the country," he continues on. "I've read a million of his medical journals and seen him speak dozens of times. I don't think he was bluffing when he gave you those recovery odds."

Brian moves his arm to around my shoulder and pulls me in for a hug. I can feel his fingers swirl through the kink in my hair left from last night's rubber band. Then I swear, though I can't be sure, he sweetly kisses the top of my head.

"Stop spiraling, Char. Listen. I know I haven't been there to remind you over these last five years, but no part of what happened to him is your fault. It was just a bad accident. That's all it was. Decker was a healthy guy. There's no reason for this to have happened to him. You had nothing to do with it. You were just the only one brave enough to do the right thing with him in the end, and that's the bottom line."

I didn't intend to get emotional because of his answer. I just wanted his friendly medical opinion. But the times that I'm ever physically in the proximity of people who have my back and support my decision 100 percent are so few and far between that my eyes well up a bit. I wipe at them before a full-blown tear can transpire and trickle down my cheek, but I think Brian's already on to me. And so, just like I'm sure he does with his youngest patients before jabbing them in the arm with a shot, he goes into distraction mode to help me feel better.

"Hey, let's check this booth out," he says, grabbing my hand and pulling me toward a face painting station. "I want to do it."

"Really? Don't you think we're a little old for this?"

"Maybe. But I also think the kids I see tonight during rounds would absolutely love it if their doctor has a face painted like a leopard. How much is it?" he asks the vendor.

"Ten dollars a face."

"Sold." He hands the vendor a crisp twenty. "I'll take the leopard, please."

"One for your girlfriend, too?" the vendor asks.

"Oh, no, I'm not his—"

"Sure, she'll take one, too. Pick out an animal, Char. Go on."

Brian plops down in a chair and closes his eyes before I can protest this ridiculousness. I'm a grown woman with grown woman problems to solve.

"What'll it be?" the artist asks.

Fuck it. The proceeds go to fire damage relief, right?

"I'll take a panda," I say as an artist gets to work on my zoo animal makeover.

"Oh yeah, my kids are going to love this," Brian says, looking at his progress in a hand mirror.

"How did you get into pediatrics anyway?" I ask as his face painter continues drawing black spots all over his cheeks. "I thought you were on track for...something else."

"Well, hello there, Diane Sawyer. Let's see. I guess I just decided that working in a cosmetic plastic surgeon's office can get kind of redundant, you know? It's either a nose job or a boob job on any given day."

I wasn't going to say.

"And I wanted to be challenged more than that. What's more challenging than a little kid who isn't feeling well and can't describe what's the matter? So I fast-tracked my schooling in that direction."

"So the last four and a half years or so for you have been…"

"Until I landed residency at Cedars? School, school, and more school—with a side of bartending, dumpster diving for copper wire, and the occasional selling my blood, plasma, and bone marrow stints."

"Selling your *bone marrow*?"

"Yeah, you never know when you're going to need a little extra cash."

The face painters scold us for talking too much. All of our facial movements are smudging the little details they're trying to get right. As we quiet down, I think about what Brian just said. I thought his parents paid for his school, car, and condo, so what was he doing scrounging for money?

Regardless of his finances, I had no idea that he threw himself into the field like this. Forget about not having time to party or go out with girls, it doesn't even sound like he's had time for himself. Is that even healthy? Why is he so averse to slowing down at all? Probably for the same reasons I am… Life is a little scary when you have to sit one-on-one with it for any length of time.

A girl—more specifically, a cute girl with an even cuter blunt bob that I could never pull off—enters the tent and commends Brian on his bold choice.

"Hi, my friends and I saw you from across the street and I just wanted to say…leopard looks good on you."

"Ha, thanks," he says with a smirk. "I know it's silly but I work with kids in a hospital; my patients will get a kick out of it later."

I don't get it. How can he still be *this* cool with animal print goop all over his face?

"Oh, so you're a doctor? I'm Alexis," she says, extending a hand.

"Ready, Bri?" I say. "I know you have to get to work and I just realized I left my keys at your place." I toss that last part in as a little extra ammo. How threatened can Blondie be by a girl wearing a panda mask if I don't say something that makes her wonder if maybe I spent the night at Brian's place? And who cares if she does think that? I'm being protective, not jealous. I don't want him getting trapped by some gold digger chick wearing a flower crown.

"Enjoy the market, Alexis," he says, pulling out a few singles to tip the face painters. "Let's head back. Think you left something else of yours at my place, too," he says to me with a smile.

I know he's talking about the urn, but the inflection in his voice matched mine, and so I breathe a little easier knowing we were on the same page just now.

I'm drinking a Diet Coke and putting away the rest of my laundry from earlier when a knock at my door tells me I have a delivery: the matzo from my mom has arrived—and for what it's worth, so has my hard drive. Upon opening the matzo package, with no help from Casey's switchblade this time, I immediately help myself to a big, crackly square and slather on chunky peanut butter I found on Casey's side of the pantry.

Two bites in and I'm transported to my favorite Brooklyn bodega, Hadleigh's, where I imagine putting box after box in a red grocery store basket before checking out with the friendly cashier named Eli. The simple treat tastes like home. Just like bagels and lox, they don't make matzo like this in LA. In fact, I don't think they make matzo *at all* in LA. It is while

I'm basking in this unleavened daydream that Brian Jackson's name pops up on my iPhone.

"I thought you had rounds tonight," I say. As I stand up, matzo crumbs fall from my crotch and Leno is there to vacuum them up with his mouth.

"I'm on my way to work now, stalker. Listen, hey, I know it's last minute, but how about accompanying me to a Dodgers game tomorrow night? I've got some decent seats behind home plate if you're into that kind of a thing."

To be honest, I'm not sure if I am, but I'm willing to find out.

"Sure," I say as I thread my freshly Turbo-laundered Anthropologie linen back through the handle of the oven where it belongs.

Chapter 12

I baked a marble cake.

I saw the recipe on Facebook when I woke up this morning; one of my mom's friends shared it to her wall. It looked easy enough and then I remembered reading somewhere that baking decreases stress and anxiety levels by 35 percent because it puts your head and your hands somewhere else. Given my current life status, I let the baking bug bite me. Though it required an Instacart delivery, two additional trips to Trader Joe's, and hand-stirring three sticks of butter and six eggs because I put my quintessential wedding-registered KitchenAid in the Goodwill pile years ago, the real challenge was making the layers of melted, bittersweet chocolate look like intricate marble veins by using the tip of a steak knife to fan it out. Even though it's probably more a Pinterest fail than anything else, I pulled it off and now our apartment smells heavenly. Like Magnolia Bakery.

After using a spatula to lick the batter off every square inch of my mixing bowl, it's now time to get ready for the Dodgers game with Brian. Admittedly, I have no idea how to pull off a sporty yet cute style, but that's exactly the look I'm going for tonight. So I text Casey for fashion advice, knowing full well that whatever she says is likely going to involve...

Ripped jeans.

OK. What else? I write back.

Just then, her mug shows up on the screen of my phone. She's for whatever reason FaceTiming me. This is a first.

"Sorry, I'm in the middle of setting up a vintage electric chair at one of my booths. I can't text right now," she explains. "So you're going to a baseball game, Rosen?"

"Yeah, with a friend."

"OOOoooooooOoohh," she says. I don't have an annoying little sister. But if I did, I imagine she'd be just like Casey. "Maybe you can bring this *friend* to my expo after? Weird surroundings are perfect for lifting the awkwardness of a first date, just saying."

"It's not a date," I say, polishing off one of her LaCroixes. "It's just an old friend who had behind-home-plate seats he didn't want to waste."

"Behind home plate? Got news for you, Charlotte. You don't just invite some random girl you *aren't* trying to hook up with to take that seat. You take a client, your best dude friend, or a girl you're trying to impress. Hate to be the bearer of good news, but he's trying to impress you, my wonderful widow friend."

"Relax, Casey. It was a last-minute invite. Now, can we get back to the original question? What do I wear? I need to hurry up and get ready. He'll be here in a half hour."

"*And* he's picking you up? Christ. Throw on an oversized jersey, put your hair in a loose ponytail, and go with nude-colored makeup. No eyeliner. It's humid tonight. It'll smudge."

I'm shocked that she's advising against eyeliner, something she will likely have tattooed on her body next. I'm also somewhat stalled. I mentally scan my closet and know for a fact I don't own a Dodgers jersey and neither does she. But then I realize I know—or knew, rather—someone who does.

"Thanks, girl. Can you pop Leno out when you're home? It's gonna be a late night and I don't want him to pee on the floor."

"Late night? OOooooOOh," she says again.

I roll my eyes and tell her bye as I hang up while she's still teasing me.

On the top shelf of my closet, I spot the moving box labeled "Decker's Stuff." It's next to a few large suitcases, some winter clothes I haven't needed since moving to California, and the box for last year's Christmas present from my parents, an Instant Pot.

It's hard to believe there's just one left. *One* box is what I've pared the Decker collection down to. Everything else I've managed to slowly but surely take to Goodwill over the years. That's never a fun trip. It feels like I'm shedding a layer of skin each time I pull into the drop-off line, not knowing what'll be left of me without retaining tangible memorabilia of his. But it is a necessary errand, especially if you don't want to explain to a guy you have over why you have a shelf full of men's clothes in your closet.

When I place the box on the floor, a poof of dust flies off the lid. A curious Leno trots by and sneezes. I push him away as I dig around for the old Dodgers jersey I know is in here. I kept it because it was signed by their pitcher and I was told it'd be worth something someday. But it was never my intention to sell the jersey for a few hundred bucks. This thing is already priceless to me simply because it belonged to Decker.

I finally find the jersey under a bunch of his life insurance policy papers and lift it out of the box. I unfold it out and, of course, smell it. There's nothing lingering on this one, though I had hoped that there was.

The jersey is absolutely perfect for tonight, albeit a little wrinkled and big (hey, she said oversized, right?).

Howdy, partner. I'm downstairs whenever you're ready, says the text from Brian.

Give me just a sec to lock up. Be right there, I respond as I quickly shove the rogue policy stuff back in the box, toss the jersey on, and throw my hair into a casual ponytail just like Casey instructed. I may or may not have nailed sporty-yet-cute, but I am dressed for a drama-free night at the ballpark.

Outside my apartment building, I spot the only parked car with its flashers on about twenty yards up the block. Brian rolls down the window and greets me with a smile and a wave. I greet him with a slice of cake wrapped loosely in tinfoil.

Brian is also wearing a Dodgers jersey, except his is "away" and mine is "home," so the colors are opposite. His uniform is completed with a baseball cap, and he has managed to nail sporty-yet-cute way more than me, even with Casey's fashion direction. He could not look more boy-next-door if he tried.

"Buckle up, Sporty Spice," he says.

"Don't let the jersey fool you," I preface. "I know nothing about baseball. How many periods are there again? Four?"

"Innings. And nine."

"How was work?" I ask as Brian noshes on a bite of marble cake.

"Good. Really good, actually. I only amputated three legs today and treated one case of the bubonic plague."

"I didn't know people still get the plague."

"Yeah, they don't. I'm kidding. Just a few sinus infections and a sprained ankle. I was trying to zhuzh it up for you a bit. Everyone always thinks my work is so interesting. But really, my job is really just hanging out with a bunch of kids who blow their noses on me and cry when the blood pressure cuff gets too tight. Occasionally we get an emergency or two, but it's nothing like the episodes of *ER* said it would be. You'd be surprised what some of these LA moms think warrants a trip to the hospital. Still, I wouldn't change a thing. I love me some snot-nosed kids any day of the week."

Fifteen minutes later, we arrive at Dodger Stadium. Brian makes three loops around the jam-packed parking lot before finding an open spot that doesn't totally scream "door-dings galore." The car turns off on its own and the seat belts retract automatically like a ride at Six Flags has just come to the end, proof that I'm never getting over the novelty of this vehicle from the future.

"Hey, Char? Slight suggestion. You might want to leave the beach tote in the car," he says as I sling my Birkin over my shoulder.

"This is not a beach tote. This is a Birkin," I say to him, leaving out the part about it being a Chinatown fake as if the statement would carry the same weight to him as it would with the interns.

"That's great. It's really nice, and big, and all. But Dodger Stadium has a strict no-bag policy. Sorry, I guess I should have mentioned that earlier. They'll confiscate that thing at the gate."

I brought the urn in case Debbie the thief scaled the sides of my apartment building while Casey and I both aren't home tonight, not to have it sit locked in a car that screams "please, smash my Tesla windows because I have money, and if you look hard enough, there's a Birkin and a set of golf clubs in here."

"Everything okay?" he asks as I rub my hands together and stare into space.

"Yeah, it's just that…"

"You've got the urn with you and you don't want to leave it in the car in this giant stadium parking lot. I totally get it."

There aren't words to describe how embarrassed I am to be caught toting around the ashes of my dead husband like I'm trying to smuggle my own snacks into a movie theater. Bringing him to Alfred's was fine. I passed that off like I was simply making good on Brian's request to visit the urn before I take it away for good. And when we went to Pala for the farmers' market, he was locked in my trunk in Brian's building's secure gated garage. But now I'm just a deer in the headlights, unsure of my next move.

"How about this: we lock Decker in the trunk, I turn on the security system that's linked to my phone, and we drop the car off with the valet instead. I'll tip the guy a twenty right off the bat for safekeeping. Any funny business, and my phone will light up. We can leave right away. Do you feel okay about that, Char?"

It's been a really long time since anyone—guy, girl, co-worker, family member, you name it—has stopped to ask: What is Charlotte missing? What does Charlotte need? And right now, Brian has identified the thing that's causing me would-be crippling anxiety and proposed a solution.

"I'm good with that."

I'm no sports aficionado, but I will say it's a perfect night for a baseball game. The sun is setting in the kind of way that turns the whole sky into a field of pink-and-orange cotton candy. The sticky summer air is transitioning into something that's finally warm and comfortable, and there's a glow in the night that will make everyone look their personal best, even under the bright stadium lights. This is the kind of night that needs no Snapchat filter.

"Okay. Not going to lie, that was awesome," I say of John Legend being the special seventh inning stretch singer.

"You're telling me. I'm just glad I didn't end up dumping the tickets on StubHub," Brian says. "To be honest, I was a little on the fence about asking you to come with me. I mean, the daytime farmers' market excursion slash potential urn reconnaissance mission is one thing. But a just-for-fun ball game is another. You know, I'm still not over the death stare you shot me when I showed up at Wet Hot the other day."

"First off, it's *We*Hot. One *t*," I correct him.

"Whatever. You know what I mean."

"Secondly, if we're being honest here, you walked in and I didn't know what was going on or whose idea it was. Then when I learned Debbie was behind it, I was upset she felt the need to send for backup. It wasn't that it was *you* per se. It was more just the fact that she sank to a new depth to show me she didn't think I could handle the urn. Don't take it personally, okay?"

Even I surprise myself with my rational assessment of his impromptu reentry into my life.

When he doesn't answer, I decide to show my gratitude. "Regardless, I owe you a thanks for inviting me to the game. It's a beautiful night and I've never had seats this good to anything in my life."

"Cheers to that," he says, smashing his beer against mine. A splash lands in the tray full of loaded nachos. "So I have to be honest about something."

"You wanted the jumbo soft pretzel instead of the nachos?" I jokingly ask, snagging the chip with the most cheese.

"You weren't my first choice to take to the game tonight."

"Gee. Thanks."

"Wait—that came out wrong. What I mean is…there was

a girl, a nurse I work with, Bella, who I was dating. Actually, I wouldn't even call it dating. More like just—"

"Spit it out, Jackson."

"She's a huge Dodgers fan, and for her birthday I was going to surprise her with these seats, but I found out from someone in Internal Medicine that she's sleeping with some guy in Radiology and I just… I prefer things to be a little simpler than that. So I ditched that plan and ended up asking you instead."

Brian's explanation comes out a mile a minute. He needs to take a breath. Eat a chip. Relax.

"Well, I'm not so sure things on my end are any more simple than a love triangle at Cedars, but I do appreciate the ask. And these nachos. Here, this is a good one."

I grab a chip with extra jalapeño and ground beef on it and put it up to his mouth, the equivalent of giving Leno a chew toy so he doesn't destroy a pair of my shoes. Redirection at its finest.

"I just want you to know, I'm glad that I asked you. And that you said yes," he tells me as he crunches down the chip. The redirection may not be working so well, but at least there's a clear compliment in there. "It's just nice to have a no-pressure night out, you know? I can be myself and not worry if—"

"—you have nacho cheese dripping down your chin?"

Brian wipes his mouth with his arm.

"I see how it is. Me trying to be serious and you making fun of me. It's starting to feel a bit like old times, isn't it?" he says.

Just then, the stranger sitting behind us shakes Brian's shoulder. "Dude, kiss her, bro!"

Kiss me? Who is this guy who was eavesdropping on our conversation? Sure, it was on the warm and fuzzy side, but we weren't flirting and we are certainly not a couple.

The rest of the fans in our section then let out a loud scream and jump out of their seats, waving and pointing at the jumbotron. I look over that way, and sure enough, the ballpark's "Kiss Cam" has set its focus on the two of us.

"Kiss! Kiss! Kiss!" the crowd behind us starts to chant.

We stare at each other for a second and I can feel the pressure from the crowd mounting behind us. My mind flashes back to a different night with Brian, and I start to grow nervous, heat spreading across my neck. We're not getting out of this. Before I know it, Brian has planted a kiss on my cheek and is pulling away. It was like getting a flu shot—the prick is over and a Band-Aid is already being pressed onto my skin.

The quick peck, in neutral facial territory, turns out to be the perfect solution to the mounting pressure to kiss in front of an audience. Why hadn't I thought of it? I'm not even sure it lasted long enough to have made it on the screen before the cameraman moved on to the next unassuming couple, but as far as section 101 A, rows 1 through 5, is concerned, they're pleased. A sea of high fives descends on us as someone throws pistachio shells in the air like confetti.

Brian leans back in his seat and looks at the sky. He takes his cap off, briefly, and runs his hands through his dark hair while letting out what I imagine is a sigh of relief. Relief that an impromptu kiss on the cheek, with his friend's widow, in front of thousands, went as well as possible.

Or, at least, better than the first time we kissed.

"Sorry, had to," he says, gesturing to the drunk guy behind us.

Do not read into this, do not read into this, do not read into this.

As we take a sip of our beers, a helicopter whizzes over the open-air stadium.

"You ever been in a helicopter, Char?"

"Nope. You?"

"Yeah, with Decker in high school. Twice, actually."

"Are you sure we're talking about the same Decker? That

kid had hated heights ever since he fell off the monkey bars in elementary school. Why the hell were you guys in a helicopter?"

"It was our senior year of high school and it was for some bullshit 'Beginning Photography' class."

"God love him, but Decker didn't have a creative bone in his body. Can't see him excitedly taking a *photography* class just for the fun of it."

"Well, it was an easy two credits and we both needed them for graduation. Happy?"

"See? I knew there was another motive," I say, tapping myself on the back.

"Do you want to hear the story or not, Miss Know-It-All? *Anyway*, we came up with this idea for our final project to go up in a helicopter and take some aerial shots of the 405. His mom helped us charter the private chopper. Decker took photos during the day and I captured the same spot at night. And then we picked the best shots and framed them side by side—mine and his—so you could see the juxtaposition based on time of day. It was a cool little joint project. We both got an A on it and enough credits to get our diplomas. Did you not see that giant print of the 405 I have hanging above my mantel? That's the project. Remind me to point it out the next time you come over."

I pause over his use of the phrase *the next time you come over*. Even in this newfound friend zone, I'm not making it a habit to wind up at his place and look at his pseudo art collection.

"So let me get this straight," I say, returning to the conversation. "The guy who hated heights and didn't have artistic flair whatsoever went up in a helicopter for a photography project?"

"Yeah, and he flew to Vegas, too, for his bachelor party, no problem. Now, if you'll excuse me, I'm going to use the bathroom while we're in between innings still. Text me if you want anything from the concession stand."

While I'm alone for the moment, I try to digest all I've heard. I know it seems like a small thing, but the Decker I knew, the one I was married to, would not have gone up in a helicopter. Sure, I can maybe see him taking an easy art class for a graduation credit, but Decker couldn't stay on a hotel floor higher than the fourth, refused to zip-line when we were in Mexico, and made me pay extra for an aisle seat on our honeymoon flight to Paris just to make sure he wouldn't have to look out the window. He told me they drove to Vegas, too. Maybe Brian's memories of the bachelor party are a little foggy—Decker *did* say he was blackout drunk that whole weekend.

For as convinced as I am about Decker's aversion to heights, I also know Brian doesn't have a reason to lie about something as trivial as some dumb high school project. In fact, I believe Brian's anecdote wholeheartedly, which makes this pesky, gnawing feeling in my stomach that much more annoying. When you're married to someone, you know everything about them—it's part of the bargain. You're the one person who knows the other better than they know themselves. I'm embarrassed to think that maybe I had this whole heights thing wrong. Maybe it wasn't a crippling fear the way I had thought it to be, but rather just a discomfort or a preference. Did he refuse to go rock climbing that time we vacationed in Colorado, or did I just not give him the option because I *thought* I knew what he'd say about it? I hate to spiral out, but it begs the question: What else did I not know or could have gotten wrong about the man that I was married to?

Brian comes back from the restroom and wastes no time asking me for a favor.

"How about a quick selfie?"

"Excuse me?"

"Yeah, I just got the new iPhone. The camera is supposed to be bomb. Give portrait mode a try with me?"

I crinkle my forehead yet again as I contemplate the ask. Before I can protest, he pulls me into the crook of his arm and I give in. What's the harm in helping him test his camera? I tilt my head toward his. He softly places his hand around my shoulders and says "Smile" before snapping a few shots in quick succession.

Chapter 13

The Dodgers lose four to two, which is exactly the ratio of beers I've had compared to Brian.

For the last few hours, the biggest problem on my mind has been how I'm going to get the nacho cheese stain out of my ripped denim shorts, not what I was going to do with my husband's ashes. Even though I barely paid attention to the game, I still call that mini break a "win for the home team."

While we wait at the valet stand for the Tesla to loop around, a gaggle of drunken college bros passes us singing the lyrics to "Closing Time," a security guard ushering them to stop loitering and leave the stadium.

"You don't have to go hoooome," they chant. "Sing it!" They point to us to finish the line.

"But you can't stay heeeere," we sing, laughing as the bros turn around and fist-bump us.

"I had a good time with you at the game," Brian says, looking at me with his cocoa-brown eyes. They get bigger by the millisecond, like flowers blooming on time lapse. "It was fun to hang out. I'm glad we're...good."

"I agree," I say, content enough with "good." It's neutral, it's friendly, it's exactly where we should be.

"We should hang out like this more. You know, not just wait for years to go by before we run into each other at Whole Foods again."

I think he wants me to say "I agree" again, but "I don't know" is probably a more appropriate response.

Just then, I hear my phone ding four times in a row and my Apple Watch lights up erratically. I take out my phone, if only to silence it, but the SOS texts from one of the TIF interns are poking through one after the next like the creatures in a game of Whac-A-Mole.

Back flat on my feet, I read the texts and learn that an invitation list for a museum event that I prepped before my forced PTO has apparently been swapped with that of a liquor tasting event, and so now the demographic of tonight's Calder expose is skewing on the younger, more thirsty side, while the folks at the bar are wondering where all the expensive art is.

"Oh, shit," I say. "Shit, shit, shit."

"What's wrong?" Brian asks.

I ignore him as I go on to read more of the damning messages.

I know you're on PTO, but can you call me? It's 911!

Hello??? Charlotte, U there?

Actually, hold on. Maybe this will be OK. These 20 y.o.s are REALLY into the art!

And I'm told the people at the bar are having fun, too!

Yup. Ignore. Clients are happy. Crisis averted.

HUSBAND MATERIAL • 151

Do U think reporting will still be OK?

The last message sends a shiver down my spine. On the one hand, it's great that the clients don't seem to notice anything is wrong at their respective events, but on the other hand, this little list mix-up is likely going to mess up the reporting for both events. I need to get to my computer and adjust the metrics, otherwise when Marigold runs the recap report on Monday, it'll look like we totally missed the mark on who their target demo is—at least from the numbers side of things. And that's not a fuckup for which I'm willing to admit any fault. This would never have happened if I was still in the office.

"Char? The car's here," Brian says, trying to get my attention. "Is everything okay?"

I finally tune him back in. "No, it's not. My team screwed up something really major with two important clients and now all the reporting is going to be fucked come Monday."

"Hey, it's okay. Come here," he says, attempting to pull me in for a hug. I bob and weave and call the intern back instead.

"Hello?" she says, shouting into the line. It sounds like she's at a New Year's Eve party.

"What's going on with Calder?"

"Everything is fine! I can't talk… I'm schmoozing!" she screams before killing the line altogether.

"Wow, that girl was a loud talker. But I guess the good news is that everything seems okay," Brian says.

"Yeah, but it's not—trust me. Because of some stupid intern who couldn't read a file name correctly, not one, but *two* outcomes that were supposed to happen tonight, won't."

"So?"

"So my reporting is going to look like a third grader put it together. This is seriously so messed up, you have no idea. Can you just drive me to my office? I need access to our work

server so both these clients don't end up canceling our con-
tracts when their event recaps make no sense whatsoever."

"You want me to drive you to your office right now?"

"Yes, right now. I know traffic is bad, but it's not that far.
We can take side streets."

"I don't care how *far* it is. It's late. You're on PTO. I don't
think your boss expects you to be the one to fix this right
now. Can't this wait?"

Is he kidding?

"No. It can't. I need to put together an alternative group in
case the client wants to redo the event, and it wouldn't hurt
to run some preliminary reports to see just how screwed up
this embarrassing mistake looks on paper."

"The event is going well, Charlotte. Whoever you just
talked to said she had it under control and the client is happy.
Did you not catch that? Does that not count for anything?"

Brian's suggestion that I should just let fate play out at these
two client events screams DEFCON-1-level disaster to me.
Maybe it's not a big deal to him, but to me, it's data in, data
out. That's how it has to be.

"This isn't about whether or not the client is happy," I snap.
"This is about the numbers adding up like they are supposed
to. Someone dropped the ball. But if I can take control back,
then why not do it? Why not give these people the outcomes
they were expecting, the outcomes they paid for?"

Still standing outside the car, Brian is silent and shaking his
head with a bit of a smirk.

"What?" I ask.

"What if you just table the math of it all for just a second,
Char? What if you let people be pleasantly surprised by how
good things went tonight?"

"Yeah, and then what?"

"Then, when you're back in the office, you explain there

was a glitch and everything *still* turned out fine. This isn't open-heart surgery. An art party and some boozy event seem like situations with a little room for error."

"Do not belittle what I do, Brian. Just because I don't save lives for a living doesn't mean—"

"That's not what I meant. At all. You know that." He turns serious.

"You're right, no one is dying on a table right now, but this stuff matters—to me, at least. And I'm pissed. Can't I be pissed? Can't you just let me be pissed?"

"Then so be it," he says, throwing up his hands. "Be pissed."

"I will. And screw giving me a ride—I just ordered an Uber," I announce as I briskly walk away to flag down my driver.

The Uber from Dodger Stadium to The Influencer Firm took thirty-two minutes in bumper-to-bumper traffic and cost fifty-six dollars because of surge rideshare pricing. And when I got there, I was greeted with a disabled fob and locked entry. I tried texting a "911" message to Zareen explaining why I needed in, stat. But all I got back was a short and not-so-sweet: Client = happy. Reports = Marigold.

The next Uber drove me from my work to my apartment in Studio City. It took eighteen minutes, a decent amount of traffic, and cost seventeen dollars.

By the time I unlock the door to my apartment, I've wasted nearly an hour and the same amount of money as a bag of Leno's high-end dog food. And for what? I can barely answer that myself, as the only thing I have to show for it is an alert on my phone reminding me to tip and rate my drivers as well as an oversized shirt that smells like a combination of cheap beer and nervous sweat.

As I help myself to another one of Casey's LaCroixes in the fridge, I spot the two tickets to the singles cruise and remember not only that it's this Sunday, but that I agreed to go with Casey. Here's to hoping I can somehow get out of these plans, or that there's a onetime pop-up mummy exhibit she'd rather go to instead.

My Apple Watch lights up with a new text. It's from Brian.

Did you make it to wherever you were going?

Ya, I say, clearly still pissed—not necessarily at him.

Good. BTW you left your purse in my car...

His text is a subtle reminder of just how high I flew my freak flag earlier. I was so worked up that I left my bag with Decker's urn in Brian's car. I assured Debbie that her son was not rolling around in the back of my trunk, but I guaranteed nothing about him floating around in the back of Brian's Tesla. Am I unfit to take care of this myself after all? Was she right that I had no business handling his remains?

I call Brian immediately but it goes straight to voice mail. I dial back and the same thing happens. So I move on to a frantic text instead.

U have D, right?

Thirty seconds rolls by with no reply.

Right?

A minute.

Hello?!

Two.

My mind spirals as I begin to think the worst. Brian is pissed at me for acting like an ungrateful diva tonight. I don't blame him. I look down at my phone. Still no reply.

I can picture Brian ignoring my texts as he drives to Debbie's house to hand off the urn because *that's* how far I've pushed him. I don't listen to anyone. I'm a control freak. And above all, I've been a widow longer than I've been a wife and I can't play the sorry-I-was-drowning-in-grief card anymore.

Why, Charlotte? Why did you have to run to work right then and there like an absolute lunatic?

I'm usually a girl full of answers, but I can't even begin to tackle that one. The one thing I've kept an eye on so intently that it almost cost me my job (and frankly, still could) is the same thing I just happen to leave behind in someone else's car like it's spare change in the cup holder—all because I was so preoccupied with things at a company that isn't even acknowledging my employment right now. Did I really think the interns wouldn't be able to handle the event?

Just as I get up to grab my keys and drive over to Brian's uninvited, I get a ping back.

Sorry, took a shower. Yes, I have D. We are drinking brews, watching football. I can bring him back tmrw.

I think about offering to come get Decker (read: I absolutely want to go get Decker and bring him back to my place right this very minute), but realize Brian is probably a little "Charlotte'd-Out" for the night, especially when it comes to the urn. And who knows, maybe Brian actually is enjoying the throwback to SportsCenter and simpler times with his best friend by his side. Either way, now that I at least have confirmation of Decker's whereabouts, I can breathe a little easier.

Thx. Sry I kind of freaked out.

Speaking of...in med school, they teach you to pick up on the non-verbal signs of your patients.

What's that supposed to mean? I ask back.

I saw you get a little weird when I mentioned hanging out again. You clammed up then abruptly left.

I type and delete. Type and delete. I'm caught between wanting to apologize, deny, and explain myself all at the same time. Meanwhile, he fires off another text.

I want you to know I wasn't trying to be forward. We can hang, I'd like that. Or we don't have to if you don't want to. But we SHOULD clear the freakin' air.

A few seconds go by. Am I supposed to say something? Thankfully, he picks the text convo back up. Unfortunately, it's by stating the obvious...or rather the obvious*ly* swept under the rug: We kissed, Charlotte.

I inhale deeply and tuck my hair behind my ears as I wait to see where this conversation is going.

It was a long time ago, we were young, we were grieving, and I'm sure the Jack and Cokes had something to do with it. Bottom line: it happened, it was a mistake, and it meant nothing. Can we agree on that and move on?

Yes, that's right. I kissed Brian. Or he kissed me. You be the judge.

I wanted to be alone that night—that's the ironic part. But I knew it was physically impossible to get what I needed done on my own. That's where Brian—or more like, Brian's Jeep—comes into the picture.

His Wrangler was parked in my driveway, ready to be loaded with moving boxes to be shuttled from my nearly empty house in Highland Park to my rental apartment in Studio City. Brian was helping me bubble wrap dishes while we nursed our ~~second~~ third Jack and Cokes of the night. The next thing I know, Brian's hands were cradling my neck and we were kissing. And not just a quick peck on the lips à la Dodger Stadium, but a passionate, albeit sloppy, kiss with tongue and hands where they shouldn't have been, my shirt off and bra unhooked. I'm still not sure if it was the grief or the booze or the combo of both, but I don't how else to explain.

As quickly as it happened, I stopped it. I clutched my shirt and bra to my chest and ran off to the bathroom. From behind a locked door and a stream of tears, I told him to go. He begged me to come out—said he was sorry and that I couldn't finish the move on my own. I refused his help, shouting louder for him to leave.

I reread his text. I'm not sure how I feel about him boiling that night down to one convenient little thesis statement, but it's nice to know that *this* can be it on the conversation about *that* if I just let it be. We can drop it, which sounds and feels a lot better than just completely ignoring it, if I'm being honest.

OK. Deal, I send back.

I agree that it was a mistake. I'm not sure, though, if it meant nothing.

Chapter 14

There's a knock at my door that jolts Leno into a barking fit. Even though I'm already awake on this Saturday morning, I'm definitely still in pajamas, and the dilapidated topknot that's lobbed to the right side of my head suggests just how annoyed I am that Casey has let her phone die and forgotten her keys once again. But when I look through the peephole and see that it's Monica double-fisting two pints of Salt & Straw ice cream, I welcomingly open up the door.

"Surprise!" she squeals.

"What the hell are you doing here? I thought you went back to Turks and Caicos?" I throw my arms around her and give her a hug. I've missed my closest coworker/beauty consultant, to be honest, and that has nothing to do with the ice cream in her hands.

"No, Danny ended up flying back here for some big player trade and we just decided we'll pick up where we left off sometime around the holidays. That's life for you, eh?"

"Wait—so were *you* at the Calder event last night? I was

under the assumption it was just a complete and total intern fuck-show."

"Yes, and, Charlotte, it was the most *amazing* event ever, which is why I'm here. With these!" She holds up the ice cream like she's flashing her boobs to me. "You're the only other person who would be *as* relieved as I am that it miraculously all worked out, so I decided we should celebrate with ice cream for breakfast."

I cringe at the word *miraculously* but she has my favorite ice cream in hand, so I try to look past it—and the fact it isn't even 9:00 a.m. There has got to be a logical explanation for how both of the events managed to go off without a hitch—an explanation I will dedicate serious time to figuring out just as soon as Zareen reactivates my office key fob.

"Plus," she continues, "the event organizer at the museum overordered the ice cream for the sundae bar, so we all got to take home a bunch of free pints. Sorry, it's kind of early but figured you'd want a scoop or two before I leave to go catch Danny's Galaxy game?"

A scoop or two or six.

"Come in, put your stuff down. You and I both know it's never too early for mint chocolate chip," I say, already reaching in the cabinet for a couple of chipped cereal bowls.

"Screw the bowls. Where are the spoons?" she asks.

A moment later, Monica and I clink our heaping scoops together at my kitchen counter. I forgot how good and simple it is to eat ice cream straight from the container.

"So...where is he?" Monica's eyes get wide as she scans my apartment from wall to wall without moving her neck.

"Where's *who*?"

"Your husband."

I almost choke on a chocolate chip.

"Excuse me?"

"Did you really think Zareen wasn't going to tell me what fell out of your bag at the Voyager dinner? I want to meet your man! I want to see the urn!"

Clearly this conversation is sponsored by Monica's sugar rush. She's a direct person by nature, but I can't see her just casually bringing this up by the watercooler at work.

"Sorry...he's actually at a friend's house." Even though I'm trying to play it cool, I realize how weird that sounds, like I'm sharing custody of a child or something. But it's the truth—he's not under my roof right now and his absence is duly noted.

"Why didn't you ever tell me that you were married, Char?" Her tone shifts from high energy to slightly serious. "I tell you everything. You know I have irritable bowl syndrome. You were there for me when my dog died last year. I tell you about the petty fights I get in with Danny. I'm not saying we are total besties, but we're *work* besties. That counts for something, right? We spend a lot of time sitting across from each other, you know. At the very least, you could have told me you were struggling with something personal and we could have worked through it. Together, like we do with all of our projects."

I shrug my shoulders. I don't really have a good answer for her, just like I didn't have one for Casey. Truthfully, I do appreciate Monica's friendship and we are a great team. While *I'm* not an open book, I realize it takes a lot of strength to be one like she is. In fact, I'm envious of her ability to wholeheartedly confide in another. In me, at that.

"The whole thing is just weird," I summarize. "My husband dying is like an old wound I never want to break open again. So I just keep things separate, life before Decker and life after Decker. Professional life, personal life. Black, white. One, zero. It's just easier that way."

"Zareen told me the urn came back to you out of the blue?"

"It showed up on my doorstep last weekend. Thought it was a hard drive."

"Well, then, see? You can only do so much, girlfriend. Sometimes life has other plans. Or, as I've come to witness, no real plans at all. Hell, I'm supposed to be on my honeymoon right now, aren't I? Instead I've got a soccer jersey on and I'm triggering my IBS while hanging out at your apartment."

Touché.

"Also, there's no rule that you have to split your life into some weird, binary 'before' and 'after' he died," she goes on. "Those are two eras that *can* speak to each other, blend, blur and still be okay. Know what I mean?"

"I'm just trying to control what I can control. And to me, it makes sense that if I keep quiet about Decker, the pain stays silent, too."

"I'm not so sure that's healthy. Or scientifically proved, at that."

She sticks me with the data and I can appreciate that. "You're right," I acknowledge. "I'll try to be more open with you."

"Ugh, I can't eat anymore," Monica says, ditching her spoon in the sink. "I just got a massive brain freeze."

"Want to sit down for a few?"

I put the lids on the pints, store them in the freezer, and gesture toward my sofa in the living room. I have to admit I'm a little embarrassed at the disheveled state of my place, but oh well. She's the one who sprang a surprise visit on me this morning.

"So, what have you been up to with your time off?" she asks.

"Nothing really." I join her on the couch. "Last night, I went to a baseball game with an old friend. And this weekend I'm going on a singles cruise with my roommate. So as you can see, making excellent life decisions, really figuring out this whole urn thing, and definitely ready to be back at work with no distractions," I say facetiously.

"Go easy on yourself. You're not thirty yet. Prioritize your social life while you can still stay up later than 10:00 p.m. That said, I'm a little sad it doesn't sound like you're making any time for our friend Chad?"

"How do I say this? Chad's out of the picture," I regret to inform her.

"Nooooo," she says with eyes as big as the scoop of ice cream she just inhaled. "Just this once I wanted my match-making skills to pan out. What happened?"

"He wanted his future wife to sign a *sex contract*, that's what happened."

I get up and walk away from the conversation with Monica to open up my sliding glass door. I think it's time we got some fresh air circulating through this tiny apartment.

There's not much of a view on the fifth floor, but I can see the cars zooming up and down the 405. The white noise from the freeway puts me into a bit of a trance.

"Tell me about Deck," Monica says from behind me as she joins me on the balcony. "Did you call him that for short ever? *Deck?*"

I'm not sure I want to go there, but I'm also not sure I can avoid it. Shoving Decker under the rug hasn't really worked well for me in any situation thus far. So I take a pause to stare down the traffic once more before I gather my thoughts.

"No, not really. I called him *Babe*. And he called me that, too."

Monica smiles and her eyes light up a bit. "Babe. I like that," she says. "What else about him?"

"He was a really good guy. And I've been scared for a long time that I'd never find anyone better than him; that they just didn't make them like that. That's not me being a dramatic, emotional mess either. Tell me how many guys you know who are content and sweet, genuine and smart, charming and calming? I could go on and on and on about all the ways he was a better person than me. I miss him, Monica. I really do. But for as much as I miss him, and loved him, I've finally come to a place where I know he's not coming back and my only real choice is a new life. Which makes an already-complicated situation that much more difficult."

"What do you mean?"

"Since the urn came back, it's like I have one foot rooted in the past right now, which feels nice. I miss Decker. The water is warm when I think about him. But the other foot is ready, like ready to just spring forward. But I have absolutely no idea how to push myself in that direction."

"It's got to be tough with the urn—just a constant, physical reminder. It's like, I don't know, a shackle or something."

I pause and contemplate her comparison.

"But the thing is," I explain, "I'm the only one who can make him leave and I want to make sure I do that right—with a lot of love and respect. And that's a lot harder than it sounds, trust me. You know me, Mon. I crank out new business pitches in a half hour. I run reports on the fly. I solve things on the spot. But with this, I don't know. It's different. It's like moving in slow motion. I've only gotten as far as a stupid Google search or two. I thought I would be further along with figuring out where to put him and what makes sense in this situation, and instead I'm just stuck here wondering why the hell I can't seem to get myself into gear."

Talking it out like this makes me sweat so much, I have to wipe my upper lip with the back of my right hand.

"You will figure this out. Remember what I told you? Life has no plans. You didn't ask for this. You're doing the best you can. It'll all be okay. Give yourself some time. Those warm fuzzy feelings will come. Things will be clearer. I promise."

Monica puts a comforting hand on my shoulder and we stand on my balcony in silence, looking up to the sky.

"Hey, sweetie," she says after a while. "You okay? I've got to get going to the game. I didn't mean to derail your morning or anything."

"Oh yeah, I'm good. Don't worry about me. Thanks for the ice cream. Tell Danny I said hi."

"I will. And, hey, way to leave out the fact you went to the Dodgers game with *this* sexy guy."

She holds her phone toward me and I squint to see what the big deal is.

Brian has apparently uploaded our selfie from last night's game to social media and checked us in together at the stadium. Between his smile and the glow in my eyes after a few beers, we look "Facebook official."

"'Behind home plate. Ain't a bad way to watch the Dodgers game,'" Monica narrates Brian's caption. "Hey, wasn't this guy in *Luxe LA* with me a while back? He looks familiar. Anyway, will there be a second date? He's clearly into you, Char. Behind home plate, eh?"

I roll my eyes and dismiss the thought that maybe she *and* Casey are on to something with their in-sync seating observations.

"Relax. He's just someone who knew Decker and was nice enough to invite me to a Dodgers game because he had a spare ticket he didn't want to waste."

"When my grandpa died, my grandma remarried his best friend six months later. She said my grandpa would have wanted her to be with him. Those two went on to have an amazing, long marriage. Just saying," a chatty Monica blazes on as she slings her Chanel bag over her shoulder.

I don't know Monica's grandmother from a fence post, nor do I condone following along in her footsteps per se—ask any widow; that's some sticky territory. But her anecdote does make me think how impressive it is that Brian and I have somehow managed to evolve from *estranged* to *friendly* given the circumstances. And it makes me wonder what other exceptions to what other rules he might turn out to be if we do end up hanging out more.

As soon as Monica clears the doorway, I pull the selfie up on my phone and see it in my feed for myself. We do look happy. We do look like friends. We do look like everything in our lives is completely normal and fine.

But a few seconds later, I think back to the last time he uploaded a selfie of us and a shiver travels down my spine.

It's funny how basic things cease to be important when you suffer a large, personal trauma. I mean, it's not like I had just blacked out when it came to brushing my teeth, combing my hair, or restocking the toilet paper—I knew that all of those things needed attention. It's just that they became a very low priority. Suffice to say, the thought of a Target run was comparable to running a marathon.

But eventually I did leave my house. It may have only been two doors down to a hair salon, but it still counted. I just wanted them to wash my hair for me. But the stylist talked me into something more: hacking it off and dying it blond. Six hours and three hundred dollars later, I had a platinum pixie cut. And even though my life was not like any normal twenty-five-year-old's, at that moment I couldn't resist feeling giddy after spinning around in the chair and catching a glimpse of myself in the mirror. I looked different, but I felt more myself than I had since Decker died.

Later that very same day is when Brian Jackson came over

to help me pack up my house in preparation for the closing. Brian must have sensed the bit of momentary confidence the transformation had given me, and in between topping off our Jack and Cokes and taping bubble wrap around coffee mugs, he snapped a photo of us. It was a selfie, just like at the ball game. He uploaded it and tagged me—because that's just what you do when you're a millennial with long arms and your recently widowed friend is actually having a good day.

It started with a text from Debbie. Be cognizant of your image, Ms. Rosen. Did she not like my hair? Or did Brian tell her we kissed?

I didn't have time to process that before one of Brian's friends commented on the photo: Wow. New bae? That was fast! When three people "liked" that person's comment, I just about lost it. When I thought about how I just *kissed* the person who posted this photo, I *actually* lost it. I uploaded a vague, emotional, messy monologue to my Facebook page warning people to mind their own business and back off from mine. Post: public. Comments: disabled. Spell-check: forgotten.

It felt good at first. But then thirty minutes later, I just felt crazy and broken. I realized the only way to combat the rumors was to stop showing my cards altogether and distancing myself from the source of them. So I deleted my post, untagged myself from the selfie, and unfollowed Brian, tightening my privacy settings like a belt.

The unofficial life lesson from "Picture-Gate" was to keep things to myself. Which makes me question, even five years later, if I should really be this okay with casually hanging out with the guy who unearthed all of that?

Chapter 15

After Monica leaves, I determine now is the time to clue my mother in about *both* of last week's deliveries: the matzo and the man. She has Facebook, and if Monica has already seen the newest Brian post, then so has The Jeaner. I'd love to get ahead of what I know will turn out to be twenty questions.

It's a day earlier than our standing Sunday morning appointment, but my mom wastes no time picking up for me, her favorite (only) child.

"Hi, honey. Howareya?" she says, nasally as ever.

"Hi, Mom. I'm good. The matzo came. Thanks so much for sending it. I've already had half a box."

"Save some for the soup. I tell ya, I thought for sure those *dummkopfs* at the post service would lose it in the mail." When Jean Rosen throws out the German word for *idiot*, she means business.

"Well, no worries because it arrived and it's just as good as I remember it. But, hey, listen. I've got to tell you something. Your matzo wasn't the only thing to get delivered to me this week. Remember that J.Crew box I sent you a photo of with Leno sniffing it?"

"I sure do. Anything good I should order in my size? You know I love those colorful high-waisted chinos they sell."

That fact that I'm about to rip a huge hole in her madras print dreams weighs heavy on me, but I need to drop this bomb once and for all.

"It wasn't actually a package from J.Crew. It was…Decker's ashes. His urn got shipped back to me from the mausoleum and now it's in my apartment."

I wince as if I'm bracing for a slap to the face.

"What do you mean *it's* in your apartment? Decker's in your apartment?!" she shrills in reply. I have no choice but to hold the receiver four inches from my head until it sounds like she's calmed down.

"The mausoleum in Pala was in the path of a wildfire."

"I had no idea the fires were that bad," she responds.

There's not a day that the news doesn't pick up a story about the spread of this one, the lack of containment on that one, and so on and so forth. Personally, I had determined that when the fires start to rip across Ventura Boulevard and encroach on my morning commute to the office, that'd be the point I'd start paying attention. But clearly it's too late for that.

"Yeah, and so they returned all the ashes they had there to the next of kin."

"Are you sure they can even do that?"

"I don't know. I never saw a contract or anything. But it's a privately owned 'boutique mausoleum.' Do any rules really even pertain to them?"

"I can't believe it. They were right in the path of the fires and didn't have a backup plan? What's the matter with those people?"

"Dummkopfs," I say.

"So, what are you supposed to do now?"

That's the million-dollar question. In the background, I hear the ice maker on my mom's fridge grinding, as well as cubes bouncing off the bottom of an empty glass. My guess is that she's making herself a midday martini. This woman wastes no time imbibing under stress. I flash back to night one with Decker's urn, chugging a bottle of wine in the kitchen, and realize I am my mother's daughter in that sense.

"Well, did you tell Debbie?" she continues after a hard swallow of her fresh drink.

"Yes, of course." Although that meeting was stressful, it feels remarkably freeing to be able to say that I did it.

"And what happened? Did she force you to hand over his ashes so she could turn them into a clay mask because some beauty blogger says that's the key to looking youthful?"

It's a sharp-tongued statement from my mom, but she, of all people, knows full well how skewed Mrs. Austin's worldview is and how it has proved to be more than a little frustrating to our family over the years.

"No clay mask, but you're right. She did demand possession of the urn. She even showed up back at my apartment while I wasn't home, trying to fetch it for herself."

"Of course she did."

"But I told her I'm hanging on to it."

"Of course you are."

"And I've been bringing him with me everywhere I go now so she can't try to steal him back."

"Oh. Okay. Well, then." She pumps the brakes. "Always good to protect yourself, right?"

I can tell she thinks I may be taking it one step too far, toting him around with me in my bag like he's a phone charger. But—

"I'm just trying to do the right thing by Decker while avoiding Power Struggle Part II with Debbie. That's all," I say.

"Honey, there is no need to explain yourself to me. You are doing the right thing. Take as much time as you need. And I know it's hard for you, but make sure you ask for help when you need it," my mom insists.

"I know. I have been. I even had a friend call the insurance broker handling the mausoleum's claim. That was huge for me."

I immediately regret the fact I'm free flowing my thoughts like I'm at some weird slam poetry storytelling session.

"Oh, really? That's good. What friend?"

I tell her his name and it doesn't ring a bell. When I describe him as the groomsman from our wedding who looked like a young Pierce Brosnan, suddenly it clicks.

"Oh. I *do* remember Brian, now that you mention it." I'm sure she does. "It's been a while since you've seen him, hasn't it? How's *he* doing?"

I'm not about to get into the semantics of early-thirties Brian Jackson, who literally seems like he's tailor-made for any role in a rom-com. So I go with a short and sweet answer instead.

"He's good. We went to a Dodgers game last night," I say, purposefully failing to mention that he kissed me on the cheek in front of a crowd at said Dodgers game. "And he's very willing to help me with the urn *if* I need it."

"Hmm."

"What?" I ask.

"Nothing."

I know a Jean Rosen *hmm* when I hear one. "What is it, Mom?" I probe some more.

"Does a part of you feel like he came back into the picture for a reason?"

Monica's visit made me think about this, too. Brian is a good guy who went aggressively after his dreams. He's charismatic, handsome, and empathetic. He's great with kids and has a quirky sense of humor. Maybe I'm not crazy for thinking if this guy showed up on Tinder, I'd swipe right in a heartbeat. But Brian isn't just a Tinder profile. He's my late husband's friend. Widow Code would say it's a lane I should never swim in—even though I kind of cannonballed it once before. But what about now? What about five years later?

"I mean, it's possible," I finally say. "Although we have a bit of a past that I wouldn't mind rewriting." I leave it at that. My mom doesn't need to know we made out after Decker died.

"Oh, honey. We've been through this with the therapist before. You can't *rewrite* what happened to Decker. You didn't cause it. It wasn't your fault. It was an accident, remember?"

Dear lord. My mom was talking about Decker—not Brian. Maybe I need to pour a drink of my own here soon.

"Yes, I remember," I say, quelling any concern she may have that I'm doubting the facts. I'm not statistically culpable for his death, end of story.

"I just mean that you can make his final resting place final this time. That's what I meant by him coming back for a reason. And, you know what they say, two brains are better than one, so let Brian help," she says with the confidence of a stage mom. "Do you need me and your father to fly in for anything? Four brains are better than two!"

I definitely do not need my parents taking a red-eye to Los Angeles to help me sort out my complicated life, but I appreciate her unwavering support. For now, I think I can handle things.

Brian texts me and asks if I'm home so that he can drop Decker off. When I tell him that I am, he follows up by asking if I've got time for a surprise car ride. He says the air vents have been programmed to smell like chicken nuggets and he's got a cold brew with my name on it in a thermos. Clearly, he's not hanging on to any baggage from the way I acted last night and I owe him letting go and doing the same. I agree to be ready in the next twenty minutes.

Once he's downstairs in his familiar pickup spot, I hop in the Tesla that smells better than a bag of In-N-Out when hungover and press the button that fastens my seat belt. While adjusting it, I can't help but notice there's a basket with a baguette sticking out of it in the back seat. Wait. Is Brian taking me on a picnic? Is that what this little surprise is all about?

I face forward again in the passenger's seat. Even though I'm wearing white leggings, I could go for a Saturday lunch picnic with Brian, grass stains and all. A smirk purses my lips that I can't seem to help or deny.

"What are you cheesing about?" Brian asks.

"Nothing," I say. "Just smiling."

It's undeniable how comfortable things are with Brian. I can't think of another person who wouldn't have brought up my antics from last night by now. I mean this in the best possible way, but he's like a piece of low-hanging fruit. Brian represents someone I don't need to go on five awkward dates with before we start to get anywhere the least bit emotionally interesting. He represents someone I don't have to explain the complexities of my first marriage to. He isn't someone I have to convince that I don't carry around any heavy "widow baggage." He's someone who believes me that I'm truly fine and ready to get back into the dating pool. And Brian would never make me choose between hiding my past and having a future.

Next thing I know, Brian pulls off on the exit for Gower Street and makes a quick right turn. The car parks itself alongside what appears to be a construction site. I see nothing but chain-link fence, bulldozers, and piles of dirt and gravel.

"We're here," he says, sounding like a giddy dad on a road trip arriving at a Wisconsin cheese castle. He presses a button and our seat belts automatically retract themselves.

Out of the Tesla, Brian marches to the fence—sans picnic basket—and puts his fingers through one of the open holes as he stares out at the vast land. I position myself next to him and look out as well. Although I'm not sure at what specifically.

"So…what do you think?" he asks, as if I'm supposed to have an opinion about a mound of dirt.

"I think I forgot my sunglasses," I say, putting my hand above my eyes to shield against the bright rays. "And also a blanket." Forget grass stains, my pants are going to get destroyed by this mud.

"Blanket? Anyhow, this, my friend, is the future site of that five-story mausoleum you were googling at Alfred's. After you told me about it, I looked it up and saw that the Los Angeles City Council approved plans to add thirty thousand crypts. Which sounds like a lot, I know, but then I read on and saw that 75 percent of them were already accounted for. People are buying up the plots like Elvis is going to be moved here. Anyhow, at nearly ninety thousand square feet, this is going to be the most iconic resting place in the entire county. Not to mention, completely bombproof. Wildfires? What wildfires?"

"Well, thanks for the tour of a future grave site," I say. "Any other fun facts you'd like to share?"

Brian releases his fingers from the fencing and grabs my palms instead.

"I bought a plot," he says with a smile that's expanding at the speed of light.

"Come again? You…what?" I shake my head. Clearly I'm having trouble following all of this.

"Okay, well, I didn't buy it yet, per se. But it's on hold for me if I want it. I mean, you definitely don't have to put him here, Char. But I know you were interested in it, and I wanted to act fast."

"Interested? It was just a Google search result that I hadn't even clicked on yet," I say.

He steamrolls on. I don't think he's even heard me.

"And if this is going to be *the spot*, I didn't want you to get ripped off. People are going to end up reselling the crypts on the black market for much more than asking. I just need to let the guy know by Monday. Think you can decide by then?"

I look over my shoulder once again to confirm what I'm seeing: piles of dirt, a wide-open field, and no one working.

"When...when is this thing even going to be done?"

"Uhh, I think the website said a year? I bet it'll be closer to ten months if they've got their shit together."

I don't need a program to run the math on this completion date. I'm caught between showing my appreciation for someone who has, in theory, solved my greatest problem, and running for the hills—perhaps the dirt ones behind me—because I didn't ask for this and I'm afraid showing any hint of ungratefulness is going to create even more of a mess.

What I think is the sound of a bulldozer backing up is actually the beeping of a pager Brian has clipped onto his pants. I didn't realize doctors carried pagers anymore, the noise is so foreign.

"Shit, sorry," he says, unhooking it from his mint-green scrubs. "Oh, damn."

"What?" I ask.

"They moved our staff lunch up by an hour. It was supposed to be at one. Now it's at noon. We're doing some summer pot-luck thing in the courtyard at Cedars with the folks from Internal Medicine. I just brought a loaf of bread, though. Who has the time to make deviled eggs? Anyway, do you mind if we cut this short? I promise we will talk more about it later, but I've got to get you back to Studio City and me to Cedars all in the next half hour."

Those travel times are impossible and he knows it.

"Don't worry about me, Brian. I can Uber back to my place. I want to spend some time here checking out the grounds."

That's a lie. In fact, there's no place I want to be less than here, except contained in a car with a man who basically bought a plot of land for my dead husband. And here I was thinking his surprise was a picnic for two.

"You sure I can't drive you? I feel really bad. Didn't mean to stick you with an Uber bill. Actually, I think I might have a promo code for Lyft in my email. That's usually cheaper. Here, I'll send it to you?"

He fumbles for his phone.

"No, Brian, it's totally fine. Casey's work is somewhere over here, too. I'd love to pop in and say hi to her. I feel like I haven't seen her in a couple days."

Again, I'm lying. I have no idea where Casey's work is and connecting with her right now is not a priority at all, but I'm in need of a clean break, not lingering conversation on the semantics of rideshare providers.

"Okay, well, thanks for being spontaneous today. Text you later, okay?"

He steps toward me for a hug and plants a kiss on my cheek before hopping back into his car and pulling away from the construction site with two quick honks of his horn and a wave. I wave back.

Does he really think this place is a solution? *Is* it a solution? After all, it is—or *will be*, rather—a fireproof place that's centrally located to all who loved Decker. Short of having to hang on to the urn until construction is over, doesn't that check a lot of the boxes? Could rehoming the urn really be this easy?

I pull out my phone to open my Uber app. But when I press the home screen button, it's on the last thing I had open, which was Facebook. I admit that earlier this morning, before Brian picked me up, I was sitting in bed, petting Leno, looking—no, staring—at the photo he posted of us. There's just something that draws me to him. There's something that draws *everyone* to him, though. Just ask *Alexis* from the farmers' market. Or *Bella* from Internal Medicine. Which reminds me, he's off to the hospital right now, where he's going to mix and mingle with some cute nurse he has, or had—who knows—feelings for and sees every day at work. Then after the potluck, a drove of hot soccer moms will bring their bruised-up kids through his doors, fake like they actually think it's a hairline fracture, just to see Brian's megawatt smile.

The girls he's into, he buys them baseball tickets, not crypts. I'm a charity case, not a crush. *It meant nothing.*

My Facebook feed auto-refreshes and at the top is a post from TIF's newest client, WeHot. It's a picture quote that says: You're never more than 30 minutes away from a good mood. The caption goes on to explain that science shows a half hour of moderate exercise releases enough endorphins to change your mood dramatically, and invites their social media fans to drop in for a micro-spin class. I'm immediately attracted to the fact that they've backed their claim up with proved data, but more than that, I consider it a dare. Exercise-averse as I am, I wouldn't mind the mood change. Seeing that I'm still rocking my signature fun-employment looks—leggings, T-shirt, and sports bra—I call an Uber and enter the address for the boutique gym in West Hollywood.

Chapter 16

Who knew that when exercise classes aren't an hour long and themed to 2000s pop music, I'd actually be somewhat down for the sweat session? Read: That. Was. Fun. And the bonus? My client wasn't working today, so she wasn't looming over me, pressing for details on Gaga Glow—*and* I actually knew how to get my spin cleats off this time.

Like most things this week, WeHot kicked my ass, which was to be expected considering my aerobic capability caps at power walking to my Ubers before I get charged the late fee. But I stuck with it the whole time, and for that, I'm proud of myself—even if the motivation was just to test the theory that my mood would change after pedaling as fast as I could for thirty minutes. Did it work? Am I shitting out butterflies now? It's too soon to tell. But either way, I'm hopping off that bike with two things: a much calmer mind and an email from Zareen.

All the rest of the girls from the class have sprung out the door to catch the mobile rolled ice cream truck that posts up across the street before they drive and park at an intersection closer to The Grove. Jennifer Lopez shops there a lot and it would be a great Instagram moment if they could get her to take a pic with a bowl of shaved watermelon ice.

I'm the last one in the locker room, sitting on a bamboo bench and dabbing my brow with one of WeHot's signature iced-lavender rags. I open the email from Zareen, the first communication from her since being put on leave.

Good morning,
I hope you're finding your time off restful and insightful! I'm writing to let you know that a gentleman named Warren Holm-gren called the agency twice trying to reach you. I informed him you were on personal leave, hoping he'd relent until your return. Clearly, he isn't one to take social cues and pressed on for a personal email address. I countered by offering to give you his details instead. I'm unsure what could be so urgent. Perhaps it is concerning your husband? Either way, Mr. Holm-gren's information is in the attached contact card.
See you soon. Take care.
-Z

It only takes a simple Google search to realize that a) Zareen would be completely lost without me and b) Mr. Holmgren most likely does *not* want to talk about the urn. I click into his LinkedIn profile and see that he's a venture capitalist from Sili-con Valley. A "tech enthusiast" with a "knack for start-ups." His rap sheet includes being an initial investor in Groupon, Slack, and Instagram. Holy shit, this guy's got an eye for ROI.

I extract his email from the contact card Zareen sent and shoot him a message. Moments later, he zips me back a reply that says he's in LA for the weekend and wants to meet up. He goes on to say that he read about The Influencer Firm in *Forbes* and wanted to connect "one-on-one" with the developer behind the company's success to see what else I may have in my programming repertoire. I sit back and think this is my chance to give a bona fide tech guru a tour of my app. I double-check the projects he's been a part of and confirm he missed the boat on investing in Tinder. With all his tech bases covered *except* for modern dating, my guess is that if he saw what my app could do, I'd be able to sell him on it in a flash.

Sure. When and where? By keeping it short and sweet, I remove the hint of desperate excitement I secretly feel. Though impromptu in nature, this is a meeting I've been coveting since Suitor Zero—the first guy through my app.

Tomorrow is my only free day. The wife and I are going to see Hamilton tonight.

The cool thing about not technically having a job right now, or a boyfriend, or family that lives within three thousand miles, is that my schedule is as free as I want it to be. Except then I realize that tomorrow is Sunday. And Sunday is the singles cruise I promised to go to with Casey. I know it's in the evening, but there's no way I'm missing a one-on-one with Warren Holmgren.

It's not necessarily his deep pockets I want, so much as his deep roots in the tech hub of America. If I can get someone like Warren to back me, well, then I see no reason I can't add the clout-worthy salutation *Founder of...* to my LinkedIn profile in the next three to five years, ample time to give this thing a proper name. After all, I can't just call it "my app" forever. I always said TIF was just a stepping-stone and now I'm finally getting closer to taking that leap. As soon as I figure out how to schedule all of this.

I came here for the clear mind, right? So let's think this through, I say to myself. Warren said tomorrow. And while he may have discussing this over a forty-five-dollar martini in mind, I'm going to counter with breakfast instead so we can meet sometime in the morning. I'll sit down with him for an hour, two at the most, come back to my place, start getting ready by two, and I'll leave with Casey for the cruise by four. That all seems doable, right?

Let's meet at the bakery at Bouchon in Beverly Hills tomorrow at 10, I fire off.

Here's to hoping he's in the mood for a chocolate croissant.

I'm prepping for my meeting with Warren by creating a test version of the app for him to try out. It doesn't require much from the custom-coding standpoint, but it does require a second iPad. Without access to our extra stock at TIF like I had for the Voyager dinner, I need to go fishing through Decker's stuff for his iPad, assuming it'll still work once connected to a charging cord for a bit. So, for the second time this week, I climb up and reach for the box of Decker's belongings. I pop off the no-longer-dusty lid and can't help but notice the bright red folder from the bank where Decker's life insurance benefit policy is. I probably should have done a better job of putting things back in order after I pulled out his Dodgers jersey, i.e., I should have shoved this folder to the way bottom of the box and piled everything else that's left of his on top of it. It's a lot easier to have a run-in with a Dodgers jersey he loved to wear than with the gateway to his life insurance policy—one of the coldest reminders he's gone.

When I pick it up, I realize—not for the first time—that no one my age should come into a sum of money like this. A surge of cash you didn't have the day before. It's like the lotto—except surrounded by a lot less lucky circumstances.

I have never taken from the life insurance fund before. I've never really needed to. I paid off Decker's medical bills from

the profit on our house sale, and everything else—his schooling, his car, etc.—were gifts from his parents. With no debts
to worry about, there certainly was a degree of temptation to
spend frivolously when I suddenly came into the money after
he died. When you're dealing with an impossible kind of pain,
you just never know if a new car, another dog, or a full-back
tattoo will be the things needed to take the edge off. But to
be honest, my only plan was always to save the money for a
down payment on a house with a yard for Leno whenever I
was ready to do that whole thing again. I haven't been ready.

I take a quick inventory of where I am at nearly the five-
year anniversary of Decker's passing. I know his urn coming back threw a lot of stuff off track, but Brian Jackson may
have solved the mystery of where to place him. I return to
work in a week, and once I start writing code and running
reports again, things will go back to normal. It'd feel good to
do something philanthropic in the meantime, which reminds
me that Debbie urged me to make a donation to Decker's old
fraternity. I know she can be pushy about what people should
and shouldn't do, but I don't mind the idea of pledging something in his honor for their fund-raiser. In fact, it puts a nice
bow on the crazy week I'm about to wrap up. My only question is: Is a thousand dollars appropriate?

I open the folder, expecting there to be a withdrawal ini-
tiation form. I've never done one before, but I remember that
being Step One of the process as explained by my assigned be-
reavement banker. There are no helpful papers in the folder, so
I log on to the bank's website to initiate a digital check instead.
I've never done this before either, but I'm in the business of
user experience and can figure out how their website works.

When I look at the sum of the account, it seems to be off
by about ten thousand dollars. I think back to when I got all
the policy stuff from the bank and try to remember if I ever

made a withdrawal one drunken night when I was grieving like crazy, but I understand myself well enough to know that's impossible. It's time to call the 24/7 800 number.

After taking several minutes to verify who I am and what I want through a series of Social Security numbers, pin numbers, maiden names, and so on and so forth, I'm finally on the line with a real-life representative.

"Okay, ma'am. I see it here. The withdrawal form was made out to *Cash* in the sum of ten thousand dollars."

I almost laugh at the absurdity. "That just can't be right."

"It's been the only account activity thus far."

"When was it?"

"Let's see here… In the September after your husband passed. I can certainly transfer you to Loss Prevention if you think it's an error, but I'm almost certain the claim would fall outside of the statute of limitations by this point since it's been almost five years and you haven't reported any suspicious activity on the account. Have you been checking your statements regularly?"

Whenever I get mail from the life insurance bank, I toss it in the garbage. I know that sounds irresponsible of me, but I also know I haven't made any changes to the account since it was opened. So what's the point of engaging with monthly reminders of my husband's death if these documents aren't telling me something I don't already know?

"Is it possible for me to download a copy of the withdrawal form you're talking about?" I ask the account rep.

She walks me through where on the website I can download the form and I thank her for her time. My computer dings, indicating that the download has completed. When the PDF finally opens on my monitor, I see the form made out to Cash, clear as day, signed with my name just as the rep said.

Except the handwriting is most certainly *not* mine.

My head is spinning as fast as my heart is racing. It's time to call my go-to guy for shit hitting the fan: Brian. His phone rings twice then cuts to voice mail, which tells me it's not dead—he's just not answering. He's probably just—

With a patient. Everything OK? he texts.

My fingers start to dance over my keyboard as I type and delete all the different ways to tell him that someone stole a cool ten grand from me because I wasn't emotionally equipped to open my mail, let alone dispose of it properly.

Not rly. Can U come over after work? I fire off without rereading. Inviting Brian to my house to deal with some Decker drama is both familiar territory and risky business. But we're adults now. We've moved on from what happened the last time we were in this boat. We've declared it a mistake we'll never make again.

Crazy shift followed by 7am tee time tmrw morning. Don't think I can come over tonight, sry.

I don't know why, but as I reread his text my heart sinks a little bit. Maybe he's not in the mood for *this*? Maybe spending his lunch hour with Bella cleared up the hesitations he had about her and now they're back on track? Maybe I just got used to Brian being available for anything and everything Charlotte-Decker-related this past week? Or maybe…he's just busy, like he says he is.

The screen lights up again seconds later: I can come over after golf tho. Maybe around 2 or 3?

I toss my phone to the side without a response. His reply makes me sound like a consolation prize, a charity case. I don't want to talk semantics right now. I've got an iPad to charge, a presentation to load, and a five-year-old financial disaster on my hands.

Chapter 17

"So as you can see, I've pretty much perfected its mate matching functionality," I say to Warren after completing a thorough demo of my algorithm from my iPad to the screen of his (Decker's). All of the Apple tech is fitting, considering Warren looks eerily like Steve Jobs.

"It's impressive. Truly. What are you calling this thing?"

"I don't have a name for it yet. But I'm open to ideas," I say.

"Well, from my vantage point, whatever you end up calling it, it certainly seems to have the potential to be a full-blown, industry-changing dating app. You should get on that." He sets the iPad back down on the table. "I want to ask you: Where do *you* see this going, Charlotte?"

"Call me crazy," I say. "But I'm thinking of selling my project to some big online dating firm in the next five years and then I'll work on it for a bit, and then move on to solving the next big tech dilemma."

He breaks off a piece of his seventy-two-layer, fifteen-dollar buttery croissant and tosses it to the back of his molars for a lengthy chew. He tilts his head back and forth as if he's contemplating just how lofty a goal that might be.

"If that's what you want to do, I'd say you're well on your way to doing just that. But I can do you one better. Don't sell it to one of the big guys. *Be* the big guy. Trust me, I know plenty of people in the tech world who would be all over investing in something like this."

Butterflies dive-bomb in my stomach. Hearing something so promising from a person like Warren Holmgren is a big deal. It's like LeBron James saying your free-throw form is good, but would look even better in a Cavs jersey.

"That's totally my goal...to take over the online dating world!" I exclaim, sounding like I'm delivering a Sunday sermon. I decide to tone it down a tad when I ask the next question: "So what's a good next step for me? For the algorithm?"

"At this stage of the game, you need two main things: capital and beta testers. I wouldn't worry so much about capital; the idea is solid. Plenty of people I know, including myself, would be willing to back it. So what about your beta testers? What are they saying needs to be tweaked before you go to market?"

"Um..."

"You *do* have beta testers, right?"

"Um..."

"Let's try this. You do *know* what beta testers are, right? People using the app to confirm its functionality and success ratios?"

I mean, yes, I know what beta testers are, but no, I don't have anyone dabbling with the program right now. While I'm confident that my algorithm is as good as it gets, something in me just isn't ready to release it into the hands of the wild. But, hell. *I've* used it enough to know all of its ins and outs. Do I really need a focus group?

"Essentially I have been my own test subject for the last three years," I say, hoping that's good enough.

"I see. And are you happily married now?" he asks, taking a sip of chai latte. There's a crumb stuck to his lip and I'm trying hard not to get distracted by it as I dig for an answer that won't make me sound as flakey as his croissant.

"Me? No, I'm not married. I used to be, but that was before I invented this algorithm."

"So, then, are you engaged now? To someone new?"

"No. But with every date, I verify through this very program, I can feel myself getting closer to that goal."

"Interesting. And how many dates have you gone on recently?"

"One last week," I say, referring to Chad at Monica's wedding. Warren takes his circular glasses off and rests them on the table. He rubs his eyes and I can feel his mood shift into something I can only describe as lukewarm. I'm not sure who should speak next.

"So, what do you think? Are there any other questions I can help answer?" I inquire.

"Well, I have to be honest. I'm starting to get a little confused here, Charlotte. Let's unpack this a bit. You aren't married, aren't engaged, and aren't seriously dating any one particular person. Then last week, you only fashioned yourself *one* date. But all the while, you're telling me that this... this piece of programming, which hasn't been tested by anyone but you, might I add, is the key to a happily-ever-after for everybody else?"

There's no professional way to rebut a guy like Warren Holmgren, so I stay quiet and let him continue poking holes in what I thought was a perfect piece of tech.

"Also, didn't you mention that you were married before *without* the help of this software?"

"Yes, but without going into hoards of detail, I was young and that marriage was simply not meant to be."

"And why is that?" Warren asks.

There is not enough caffeine in my double-shot vanilla latte to help navigate a viable answer to *that* question. I could, in theory, pull out the urn, set it on the table, and put the whole thing to bed. But instead, I figure that trying another angle—one that does not involve human remains—might be a better approach to stopping this line from going limp.

"I'm looking for a *lasting* love. One that yields me a husband and partner with whom I can truly grow old. You have to understand, Mr. Holmgren, that *that* is what every little girl dreams of when she is young. It's not about the wedding day, so much as it's about a special forever love. Someone who can be there with you through it all—ups, downs, lefts, rights. In today's society, it's impossible to know someone's intentions. There are so many distractions and social media platforms. You know, the kinds of things that make finding love super messy. My app will cut through the clutter and help figure out *who's* real, *what's* real, and what are the chances that this person is *the one*, because my future users are the type of people who don't have time to waste."

I put a figurative period on the end of that sentence and it feels like I just aced my interview. It's a mic-drop moment for sure, and now I wait for whatever the tech-master has to say in return.

"It's certainly compelling, Charlotte, don't get me wrong." He puts his glasses back on. "But, frankly, the more we talk, the more shortcomings I'm starting to see in your product as it stands right now."

I take a hard swallow as I linger on the word *shortcomings*.

"What do you mean?" I ask.

"For example, does it work for men? You spoke earlier about

this software helping *women* achieve their dreams of Disney-princess-style love. But what about if a *man* were to use the app? What if he wanted to plug in big tits and a round ass because that's all he's really looking for at the end of the day? Could he get that?"

Tits is not a word I expected to come out of Warren's mouth during this meet-up. And a round ass? What the hell is he talking about? My app isn't Instacart—you can't just go shopping through a virtual aisle and put a pear-shaped Brazilian booty in your basket. Even though this plot twist has the possibility to derail me big-time, I take a deep breath and regain focus. I've been thrown bigger curveballs in my life.

"Yes, I can certainly rejigger things so that it can work for a man looking for a woman, or a man looking for a man, or a woman for a woman. However, the functionality isn't so literal. You don't necessarily order specific traits. Rather, it aims to vet a person's online tendencies and use them to determine how this person might act as a partner in real life, so you know if going on a date with them would be worth your time. Make sense?"

He takes a sip of his latte and nods his head while looking out the window. Is that a smile I see? I feel like the line just might be tightening back up again.

"Sure, but I still think being able to specify physical traits is the single most important thing this app should offer given where we're at in today's society. Let me know if you can add that as a feature and we can pick the conversation back up next time I'm in town."

"But—"

"It's been a pleasure, Charlotte. Keep in touch. And do yourself a favor: get some beta testers. And decide on a name for it, too. *Algorithm* isn't a sexy word. Okay?"

Warren knocks the knuckle of his middle finger twice on the

top of the bistro table before slipping out the front door and into the back seat of a matte black Bentley. Either he has a personal driver, or that's the fanciest Uber I've ever seen. Moments later, his driver peels away and I'm left sitting alone at Bouchon, no closer to securing an investor to take my app to the next level.

"I don't like the look of this," Casey states. Her face is slathered in a seaweed mask. "Why aren't you getting ready?"

"Yeah, I don't think I can go tonight," I respond with minimal eye contact from the couch. "Do you know how to switch from Netflix to cable on this thing?"

Casey grabs the remote out of my hands and turns the television to black.

"You're going, Rosen. Not in those sweatpants or that chocolate-milk-stained shirt you're wearing, but you're going," she orders. She plops down next to me on the couch and presses on. "I don't get it. What's the matter? What happened?"

I never wanted things to get deep with Casey. Telling one another when we were low on toilet paper was where our relationship excelled. But I reckon that if I'm really leaving her high and dry on the day of the singles cruise, I owe her an explanation. Albeit an abridged one.

"I had a meeting with an app investor today."

"Yay!" she squeals, putting her palm up for a high five. I spare her the celebration and lower it for her.

"It didn't go well."

"Oh." She slumps.

"And last night, I was digging around in a box of Decker's things and found his life insurance policy folder. Long story short, it looks like some asshole went through my garbage, found Decker's life insurance policy papers, and hacked my account for ten grand. And because it was almost five years ago and I have no real proof, there's really nothing I can do about it. So, yeah. Not a good day in Charlotte's world."

"How do you know it was someone random who did it?"

"The bank sent me a copy of the transfer form."

"So?"

"So... I didn't do it. It's not filled out in my handwriting."

"Right, but you said you have the policy folder here. Maybe someone didn't go through your trash for access to the account. Who else knows you have that box with his stuff in it? Better yet, who packed it?"

I give Casey, a true crime aficionado, credit for thinking of something I did not. But rest assured, I'm the only one who packed that box. Sure, Brian helped with the china and the mugs, but the second the house sold, I myself packed everything daunting of Decker's (policy stuff included), then made four more piles: "Mine," "Theirs," "Donation," and "Trash."

There were some things that went straight to the trash, like a half-open box of Nut Thins and an electric razor that was on its last leg. "Donation" consisted of mostly clothes and some PS4 games. "Theirs" was a pile for Kurt and Debbie, which was just a pared-down and less meaningful version of "Mine," which had everything else of Decker's I never thought I'd get rid of. No one else was invited to that sorting party, and no one else touched the boxes of "Mine" with policy stuff in it.

But it does hit me that just because Debbie didn't pack it doesn't mean she wasn't ever near it. Even though our relationship had been strained, Debbie did stop by my apartment on what would have been our first wedding anniversary all those Septembers ago to bring me flowers. Even though I knew she resented me for the decision I made to pull Decker off life support, hand-delivering a bouquet of flowers fresh from her cherished gardens made me wonder if deep down, she knew she would have done the same thing. I wondered if she was secretly grateful that the onus didn't actually have to fall on her in the end.

I can still picture them: hand-wrapped bulbous sunflowers from her garden. They were so gorgeous, they looked fake.

"Do you have a vase for them?" she'd asked.

"Yeah, somewhere in here."

She and I rifled through my moving boxes until I ultimately found a glass vase, too small for the bouquet, but it was all I had access to at the moment. By then, she apparently already had access to the something else: a policy transfer form.

"How could she do this?" I say to Casey.

"Who?"

"Debbie," I mutter, still trying to make sense of this in my head. Granted, I was knee-deep in sadness and completely distracted, but the woman doesn't strike me as someone slick enough to pull off a heist like this.

"Well, that makes perfect sense, Charlotte. The woman already tried breaking and entering earlier this week. I'm pretty sure she has it in her to steal from you."

"But why, though? What could Debbie Austin possibly need that money for? I feel like she carries that amount in cash with her at all times."

"Perhaps her financial status is just like everything else of hers: a facade. Probably needed the cash for a face-lift. Speaking of, I need to wash this face mask off before it sticks to my skin for good. You back in for the cruise, or what? Personally, I think it'll be a great distraction for you, and I promise I'll help you hack her financials, or whatever, as soon as we get home."

I pull Debbie's name up on my phone for the second time this week, but before I commit to pressing Call, I remind myself to breathe. It's not my style to confront someone without all the facts. So while I can confidently accuse her of stealing from me, it'd be nice to have time to research what she used that money for and have the full story.

"Fine," I concede to Casey, determining I owe that much to the person who just helped me figure out Debbie has wronged me for the last time.

The apartment looks like a pseudo sorority house as Casey and I take turns sharing the mirror in the bathroom. As of five seconds ago, I've affixed the last hot curler in my hair with a bobby pin. It's funny—I haven't put curlers in my hair in nearly five years. Granted, I chopped ten inches off right after Decker died, but still I never found myself back in the routine even once my hair grew out.

Because these things have to set for at least twenty-five minutes to create the soft but polished waves I am looking for, I'm using the time my hair is tied up to do something useful with my hands. Right now, that means googling the Austins' lawyer. I'm not sure if they'll have it posted, but if I can find out their retainer fee, perhaps I can link it to the missing withdrawal amount.

After Decker's accident, his family filed a bullish wrongful death civil lawsuit against the organizers of the race. Attorneys warned them from day one the judge was likely to throw the case out since Decker had PFO, a birth defect. Assuming Casey is on to something with the Austin family financials not being all they're cracked up to be, they could have tapped into the policy money instead of having to use their own so there'd be nothing to lose if the case went cold, which is exactly what it did.

"So if I send you the link to his Facebook profile, can you run him through the wringer?" Casey is standing in the hall-way wrapped in a towel with wet hair. She is staring at me, more like through me. In one hand, she's armed with a piece of peanut-butter-covered matzo, and in the other, she's holding her cell phone.

"The what?" I say, looking up from my phone screen.

"Your app thingy. The one you funnel all your guys through."

"Yeah, I know what you're talking about, but that…that's an incredible name for it. Drop the *w* and call it The Ringer."

Suddenly, the smoke clears from the bullshit research I was just doing, and I repeat the name at least three more times in my head. *The Ringer. The Ringer. The Ringer.* According to Warren, I still need to figure out how a user can filter by breast size *and* land on a name. Sounds like I can check one of those off the list.

Finally having a name for my app takes the branding of it to the next level and gets me one step closer to actually merchandising this thing. I set my phone down and stare into space. I go on to imagine all the fonts and color schemes that will go best with my future company's newly appointed moniker. Truly, there could be no better name for a product that is designed to drill down into the people who use it and spit them back out with a ring on their finger—The Ringer. I freaking love it.

"So will you run him through it or not?"

"In exchange for complete ownership of the naming rights, sure. I'll do it." I zone back in and wait for her to agree.

"In exchange for the naming rights? God, you're so fucking weird, Rosen. But fine. I just sent it, FYI."

"Who is this guy anyway?" I ask, going back to lining my lips like it's a paint-by-numbers project. My phone dings, confirming receipt of Casey's hella on-it cyber stalking.

"His name is Justin. I met him last night at a Web-Toes Anonymous meet-up deep in The Valley. Supercute librarian during the day, drummer in a band by night, looks like Pete Wentz, and… I just so happened to spend the night at his house. So, can you just run him already and tell me how many babies we'll be having?"

I've never run my app for anyone but myself. But I suppose if I plan to make The Ringer a universal product, Warren was right—I need beta testers. And there's no reason that Casey and Justin can't be my first guinea pigs. I will just need to swap her info in for mine and then plug in his profile attributes. All in all, this should take me far less time than it takes for curlers to set my hair.

"Yes, I'll do it right after I finish getting ready," I concede. "You know better than I do—these lips won't line themselves."

"Pro-tip," Casey says, grabbing the pencil away from me. "Line just above your natural lip line for that Kylie Jenner look. There. All set."

As Casey trots off to her room to change for the cruise, I get an incoming text from Brian. He's at my place. I remember now that I hadn't really responded to him yesterday when he'd offered to come over, but I guess he assumed it was fine. I call down to the doorman and tell him to let him up.

Moments later, I can hear Leno's toenails clicking against the hard surfaces as he goes to greet his favorite long-lost friend.

"Knock, knock?" his voice says from around the hall.

"I'm in here!" I shout from the bathroom.

"Well, aren't you just a vision," Brian says from the doorway.

"Thanks. You'll have to excuse the whole Medusa thing I've got going on right now," I say in regards to the curlers.

For the record, he looks good, too. In his golf polo and plaid shorts, he looks like he's just finished walking the Topman runway at Fashion Week.

I scurry my way out of the bathroom, still in my robe and fuzzy bunny rabbit slippers. I spring onto my tippy toes to fetch a water glass down from a cabinet above the sink. Brian's six-foot-something frame towers over me, offering me the assist. We both exchange a silent smile at each other.

"Want some matzo?" I ask as I rehydrate. "My mom sent me a bunch of boxes."

"No, thanks. I'm not hungry." Brian takes a seat at one of the bar stools by the kitchen counter.

"You seem kind of quiet." I break off a piece of matzo. "I thought for sure by now you'd be telling me about the kid you saw yesterday who was throwing up Windex."

"Sorry. I'm just exhausted. Last night was…brutal."

"Lots of runny noses, eh?"

"No. I wish. A four-year-old choked on an apple slice in day care. The workers weren't certified—botched the Heimlich. We worked on her for a while, but couldn't save her."

Is he just trying to trump the time he told me his patient had the bubonic plague?

"I'm serious. It really sucks." There's a somberness to his voice and I know he's not kidding around. I know Brian came over to lend a delayed ear to my urgent texts yesterday, but I want to be respectful of the fact he's exhausted, he's sad, and now is not the time to start bringing any life insurance policy fraud evidence. So I table my own drama. For now.

"I'm really sorry to hear that, Brian," I say.

"Who's ready for a singles cruuuuiiise," Casey sings as she comes into frame. "Don't mind me, just making a little pineapple-rum mixer. Anyone want one? Char, you, of all people, may want to pregame before this. Loosen you up a little before we head out to Catalina."

Suddenly, three's a crowd in our tiny kitchen, especially after Casey spills the beans that I'm sailing out to Catalina Island with a bunch of singles for the evening. Not exactly the most appropriate follow-up for just learning he had a rough night at the hospital.

"You're going on a *singles cruise*?" he asks with a hint of judgment in his voice.

"No. Well, yeah. But I didn't sign up for it on my own or anything. Casey won the tickets in a raffle. She asked me to go with her," I say, trying to sound as neutral as possible. Instead, I sound like a car engine sputtering out its last bits of gasoline.

"Got it," he says, without any further commentary.

I need to shift gears. I don't like where this conversation is going, so I make a move and head toward more familiar territory.

"Hey, can you help me with something??"

"Sure. What is it?"

"I wrote a check for a donation to the frat fund-raiser. Here. Could you give it to the treasurer? I'm sure you're still in touch with all them. It'll save me the trip to USC. I don't trust mailing it."

As he looks it over, there's enough of an awkward silence for me to wonder: Is he mad at me? Suddenly, I feel compelled to go back into how the cruise wasn't my choice, I don't even really want to go, I only agreed to it because I'm about five years behind on hanging out with my roommate, and so on and so forth. But instead, I just keep quiet. I know myself, and when I don't have time to process the data and I'm put on the spot, I'll just end up spewing things off that I don't really mean. I remind myself: this is a harmless outing with my roommate, and he and I are just friends.

"Got it," he says, folding up the check and putting it in the front pocket of his polo shirt. "Sorry again about not being able to come over last night. What did you want to talk about?"

Well, since he asked.

"I was trying to make a transfer from Decker's life insurance policy to the fraternity's PayPal for the donation. Long story short, turns out that ten grand went missing from that account and it really jarred me."

"Did you find it?" he asks.

"No. At first I thought it was someone random who went through my trash and stole my identity, but then Casey suggested it could actually have been Debbie, and now I kind of agree with her. I mean, there was this one time she came over, and—"

"Never a dull moment, Charlotte," he announces, hopping off the stool in my kitchen as his pager goes off. "I've got to get home and ready for work. Do you want me to take the urn? I figure you're probably not going to want to lug it on the ship, and if you're both gone, then who's playing security guard?"

We both look at Leno, who is ripping the stuffing out of a toy I just bought him.

"That's actually not a bad idea," I say. "You don't mind? Can you bring it back—"

"First thing in the morning. Yes."

I put the urn in a Trader Joe's reusable grocery tote and hand it over to Brian.

"You two have fun tonight," he says before he goes to let himself out.

"Brian, wait," I say. "Is everything good?"

"With?"

I go out on a limb: "Us?"

"Yo, Rosen. Our Uber is five minutes away. You need to get dressed," Casey says, coming around the corner wearing red patent leather platform shoes, fishnet stockings, and a T-shirt as a dress as if she's off to Coachella. She's holding up a preselected outfit for me—a revealing minidress I forgot I even own.

At that, Brian flashes a soulless smile and makes a satirical saluting motion with his hand at his head before letting himself out.

Chapter 18

onfession: I didn't wear the minidress. Assuming I would have been able to get it over my left thigh, it's a dress that reveals a little more skin than I'm comfortable exposing to the type of people who voluntarily go on a singles cruise to Catalina Island. It was, however, a good reminder that one of these days I should focus less on paring down Decker's things and more on making a donation pile of my own.

Instead I went again with a comfortable fave, "summer wedding chic," which manifested itself tonight in the form of a halter dress with green palms printed all over it. With the Sea-Band and Apple Watch on my wrist and a dark-berry overly lined lipstick, I look like a cross between a pinup model and Casey's angelic alter ego. This is what happens when your dramatic life leaves you with five minutes to get dressed.

We get out of the Uber and immediately it's a sensory overload for me. Hundreds of people looking like they are going to some sort of adult prom are darting their way over toward a midsized yacht that's rocking ever so slightly in the water behind us. Cue my vertigo.

"Everyone must check in before boarding the boat! Come get your name tags and your wristbands over here! Remember: no bracelet, no booze!" a woman shouts from the registration desk on the dock. She looks about my age, yet also like she's somehow made a career out of being a professional sorority sister. Kudos to her.

"Come on, Char. Let's check in and start drinking," Casey squeals, dragging me by the arm toward the registration table. Her matte black, pointy fingernails are digging into my skin, which I can feel is starting to crawl with every step we take closer to the ship.

"That guy is cute," whispers Casey about a man standing in front of us in a line of about ten other singles waiting for their turn at the registration desk. He is, I agree. But right now, all I can think about is the sinking look on Brian's face tonight when he heard I'd be spending my night aboard a boat full of drunk single people. Even though I'm not interested in hooking up with anyone here, *at all*, maybe for him this is what it was like for me when I found out he was having a work picnic with Bella.

"Last name please?" the grown-up sorority girl fires off. Upon closer inspection, I'm jealous of her hair, body, and face-framing bangs.

"Rosen," I say.

The woman proceeds to scan a row of preprinted name tags that are laid out on a table behind a sign that reads: "Last Names N–Z."

"Ahh, Rosen," she repeats as she picks up a name tag. "Are you…Charlotte?"

"That's me," I say with the enthusiasm of being called in for root canal surgery.

"Okay. Here you go," she says, handing me the name tag and a wristband. I'm awaiting further questioning, such as blonde or brunette? College educated or entrepreneur? But I guess they don't take dating data as seriously as I do.

I stick the name tag to my chest and attempt to apply the wristband on my own using a combination of my left hand and my teeth. I guess I don't go to enough outdoor music festivals to have perfected the art of putting on one of these things.

"Need a hand?" says the cute guy from the line.

"Sure," I say. "Thanks."

The man, who's named Jake according to *his* name tag, applies my wristband in about two seconds flat, smiles, and says, "Let's talk more inside" before sealing the quick interaction with a wink. I forgot that every philanthropic action tonight isn't about being nice; it's about potentially getting laid. It's like night one of *The Bachelorette* here and that was this guy's staged limo exit. In which case, I wish I just gave my molars a chance to help adhere the damn thing to my wrist instead of letting the a-little-too-smiley "Jake" think I actually care to talk to him more inside.

Once appropriately tagged and banded, I look up and realize that Casey has already beelined it onto the ship without me. Although she's probably at the bar, I don't want to risk waltzing into the lion's den solo, so I take out my phone to shoot her a text—there's too much noise for my Apple Watch to pick up my voice. In doing so, I see that I have one sitting in my inbox from Brian. I must have been too busy fidgeting with my wristband to have noticed it come in.

Did you decide about the plot? it says.

Crap. The truth is, I—

Haven't even thought about it? his next text says.

Sry, I say back before further questioning.

It's fine.

I imagine the sinking look on his face once he realized I hadn't thought about the plot on Gower Street yet. I know he has to get back to the crypt broker (god, that sounds so weird) tomorrow, but I just can't tell my mind to process this any faster.

Casey grabs my shoulder with one hand and holds a piña colada with the other. "Thought I lost you," she says as I cut my phone to black. "Let's get inside before I get yelled at for taking my drink off the ship."

She escorts me onto the boat and I soak it all in. The inside of it is like a casino meets hotel lobby meets man cave.

"So I signed us up for the first round of all-inclusive speed dating," Casey says. "It starts in ten minutes."

"No, thanks. I'm good," I say. She gives me a look like my answer isn't the hall pass I think it is.

"What part of 'I signed us up' didn't you understand? We're doing it," she dictates.

"I don't even know what *it* is. All-inclusive speed dating? Does that mean my nausea comes with an actual vomit bag? Because it would be great if that was the case."

Just then, I feel the boat jerk forward. We have officially set sail on the open water. I flag a circling cocktail waitress who looks like she's been plucked straight out of The Flamingo in Las Vegas to work the event tonight and order a bourbon and ginger. If anything, the ginger ale will quell my stomach nerves while the bourbon numbs the mounting fact that I don't want to be here. Why couldn't our first hang sesh as roommates have been a 3-D movie or one of those BYOB wine painting classes?

"It means it's guys *and* girls," says Casey.

"Isn't that how all speed dating works?" I question.

"Yes, but with this round, you may be paired with a guy

for one conversation, and a girl with the next one. Either way, you have sixty seconds with each person."

"With all due respect, Casey, I think you know by now that I'm purely into men."

"So then you'll make a few friends while on the hunt for your next lover. I said don't freak out. Just roll with it, okay? I'm going to freshen up my makeup in the ladies' room. I feel like I'm very shiny."

"You're not," I assure her.

"Yeah, but I *feel* like I am. Don't go anywhere, homey."

With Casey out of sight tending to her phantom sweaty forehead issues, I neurotically tap my Apple Watch and check it for messages again. There are no new ones.

I proceed to speak into my watch and fire off a good old-fashioned Is everything OK? text, but when I do, the message to Brian gets kicked back as undeliverable. Assuming it's a glitch with the watch, I take out my phone and try again. No dice with that either.

Dear god, I think to myself. It has started—the lack of cell phone reception has officially kicked in as we have made it far enough away from the coastline to be unable to connect with the rest of the world. Here's to hoping there are no icebergs out here.

"Bourbon and ginger?" the cocktail waitress calls out as she hands me my order.

"Yes, thank you." I claim it and tip her a dollar. "Hey, can you tell me the code to the Wi-Fi as well?"

"Wi-Fi? There's no Wi-Fi, honey."

"There are stickers all over the ship that say Wi-Fi Enabled," I gently point out.

"Yes, but the event organizers had us disconnect it for the night. Said they want their participants focused on each other, not their phones. Sorry, sweetie. I feel your pain." She lets out a frustrated huff and walks away to deliver the rest of the drinks on her tray.

I'm calling bullshit. They didn't cut the internet so we could focus on each other; they cut it—along with deciding to serve bottom-shelf bourbon, flat ginger ale, and host this thing on a Sunday night—to save money. Cheap asses.

Regardless, no service and no Wi-Fi mean no way to deal with the ominous It's fine text Brian sent me. I dread the thought that he may assume I'm ignoring him when something is clearly on his mind. This is the worst possible situation right now.

"Alright, Char-Char. It's our turn to hit the speed dating tables," Casey says as she sneaks up behind me.

Wait, no. Maybe *that's* the worst possible situation right now.

"Do you know there's no internet on this ship?" I ask as she ushers me to a row of ten bistro-sized tables, each with two chairs at them.

"Who cares?"

"I do. It's like we're in some sort of a black hole!"

"Relax. Your Tinder account will still be there when this thing ends. Just sit down before there are no seats left."

The joke would be on Casey if only she realized that I haven't really checked Tinder since Decker came back. I guess your new-husband priorities just kind of fall by the wayside when your old husband returns. But regardless, I find the one open seat on the "stationary" side of the speed dating table, which means every sixty seconds when the whistle blows, I will not move but rather someone new will be sitting across from me. Casey is sitting on the rotating side, her face looking like it has more white powder on it than a frosted beignet. Somehow, it works for her. A guy who looks like a young Tom Hanks is the first to sit down across from me.

"Hi, I'm Liam," he says, shaking my hand. His palm is cold and sweaty. "I guess you're my first 'date' of the evening?"

"Charlotte," I say with a forced smile as I return the shake like my hand is a dead fish.

"Sixty seconds are on the clock... GO!" shouts the moderator for this event.

"So, what do you do for a living?" I robotically ask as I take a sip of my now watered-down bourbon and ginger.

"I'm a hedge fund manager. And I also collect classic cars. I have about eight in my garage right now."

"Wow, very cool," I say, noting that hedge funds and classic cars might not actually be such a bad combo.

"Are you more of a Mustang girl or are you into Corvettes?"

"Corvettes," I say, as if I really have an opinion on the matter. "How old are you?"

"I'm thirty-six. You?"

"Twenty-nine."

"Right on. My little sister..."

Liam trails off about something related to his younger sibling while I maintain eye contact but feel around as discreetly as I can in my bag for a pen. Sixty seconds isn't much time to work with, but the fact that he is a hedge fund manager and car collector is worth some extra exploration for the sake of the app. Even though there is no cell service on this godforsaken boat and I can't plug these data points into my app right now, I just need ten seconds to jot down Liam's info on the back of a cocktail napkin before the next round starts. It's not ideal, but it'll have to do.

"So, what kind of a guy are you looking for?" he asks just as the whistle to the next round blows. "Dang, that went by fast. Here's my card. Get in touch if you'd like."

I note that he says the word *dang* when frustrated—as opposed to *damn*—as my next date settles in across from me. It's a woman. And not just any woman. It happens to be Gemma from WeHot. It's a little foreign seeing my client here at a dating event. It's like spotting your teacher out shopping for groceries. But that's the risk I ran going to an event like this. You never know who's spending their free time and disposable income on a *singles cruise*. For all I know, maybe her roommate dragged her here as well. That said, the fact that I somewhat know her will make telling her I'm not romantically interested in women slightly less awkward than having to break that news to a total stranger.

"Well, hello, hello," I say to Gemma.

"Charlotte. So funny seeing you here."

"Same to you. Well, I'm not sure how to put this, but I'm here for the boys," I spew out.

"Me too. But happy to play along and go through the *getting-to-know-you* motions. So…what's your last name, Charlotte?"

I smile at this more relaxed version of my uptight client before telling her, "It's Rosen. You?"

"Sutherland. I'm born and raised in LA. How about yourself?"

"New York City. Brooklyn."

"Really? I didn't know that. And you're not in show business obviously, so how'd you find yourself all the way in sunny SoCal?"

She's right. Hollywood is what brings most everyone here and I'm not an exception, even though she thinks I am. I could skip over that part of my life, or I can try dabbling in something new: being honest about my past.

"Actually, I started my career in casting and craft services. That's where I met my husband. I was married, but I'm a widow now. My husband was born and raised in LA like you. Went to USC, did the whole lacrosse thing. Anyway, after he died, I just ended up getting a job here that I really loved and decided to stick around ever since. I don't think I could handle an East Coast winter again, to be honest," I joke.

Yes, that whole exchange was clunky. But it felt amazing and empowering to just rattle the awkward truth off to a person I hardly know and who's about to shift seats in three, two...

"And rotate!" says the moderator.

"What was your married name?" she asks. I know we need to change partners, but I like this follow-up question over the other possibilities, such as...how did he die? When did he die? etc.

"Austin." I indulge her before she moves.

"Go around me," Gemma says to the suitor who was supposed to take the seat in front of me next.

"Are you for real right now?" he says. "This isn't how speed dating works, lady. You get one minute. It's my turn with her now."

She flicks her hand at him like she's shooing away a fly. Clearly, she's not budging, so he shakes his head and skips over a seat, leaving me forever wondering if the guy, a young Denzel Washington look-alike, could have been my soul mate.

"And begin!" shouts the stopwatch-wielding moderator from a distance.

"What are you doing, Gemma? You have to rotate." I can't believe I'm voluntarily policing this event.

"You look so different," she says. "Your hair. It was blond back then."

"Excuse me?"

"And short. Wasn't it? It was a pixie cut, in that picture of you I saw five years ago."

"Okay, you're actually freaking me out right now. What are you even talking about?"

"Are you sure the name *Gemma Sutherland* doesn't mean *anything* to you?"

"You're a client of The Influencer Firm," I announce matter-of-factly.

"That's it?"

"You're a *valued* client of The Influencer Firm? I don't know what you want me to say right now, Gemma. But I really don't want to get in trouble by the lady with the whistle, so could you please—"

"Christ. I fucking knew it," she huffs to no one in particular and looks to the sky as she bites the tips of her French manicure. If she were a man, these nervous tics would be key body language data points for me. But for now, she just looks like she can't follow the rules of a simple round of speed dating. She leans in like she's about to tell me my underwear is showing and whispers, "Look, I'm not sure who all I'm going to piss off by telling you this, but I really don't care anymore. Enough time has gone by and I was *promised* that they told you; that you knew." Just then the whistle blows on this round of speed dating.

Gemma doesn't break eye contact with me. Instead she just puts her hand out to block the next guy from trying to take the turn that is rightfully his. He rolls his eyes and obliges. Another potential soul mate, down.

Gemma mumbles to herself then says: "Decker—"

"Whoa, whoa, whoa. Wait a sec. How do you know who Decker is?"

"—has a son," she blurts out.

"Gemma, I don't know what is going on here, but clearly we are blurring some sort of client relationship boundaries here. I'm going."

I get up from the stationary side of the table and she reaches across, putting her hand on my arm and directing me back into the chair.

"He has a son with me."

My concern for this woman's stability and sobriety is rapidly growing. It's my turn to lean in and whisper.

"I don't know who you are or what you're talking about," I say, stirring the melting ice in my otherwise-empty cocktail glass on the table. "But this is not appropriate, and I am leaving."

"I know you don't know what I'm talking about, which is precisely the problem. I was told that you knew about our son and that you wanted to be involved in his life, but you just needed some temporary distance since it was so soon after Decker had passed. And I understood that—I…I accepted that. But then years went by and you never contacted me, nobody brought you up, and I couldn't figure out why you wouldn't want to be part of Decker's son's life. So, clearly someone lied and I'm not going to play into that anymore. I'm done."

"What are you talking about? Who lied?"

She just shakes her head as if I was asking her a yes or no question.

"*Who* lied, Gemma? You better start naming some names if you want me to keep taking you seriously."

The truth is I haven't *started* to take her seriously, but she doesn't need to know that.

"I know it looks like I have my life together. And I do now, somewhat. But even after the money, the secrets are still choking me and have been for the last five years. I just don't think I can be the one who pieces this whole thing together for you," she says as she gets up to leave the speed dating table. I drive my fingernails into her forearm the way Casey did when she dragged me onto this cursed boat.

"Sit down," I demand. "We're not done here. Not even close."

"Is there a problem over here?" The woman with the stop-watch approaches the two of us. "The flow seems to be getting clogged up over here, and it's very important all our patrons get to experience the entire speed dating panel. That is what they paid for."

"Screw the speed dating panel," I say, loud enough for Casey at the other end of the table to dart her eye contact away from her turn with young Denzel and over toward me instead. She furrows her brow like a mom telling her child to knock it off from across the room. I lower my voice. "Gemma, come with me, please."

As I escort Gemma away from the speed dating area, there is a look of panic that washes over the moderator's face. I know that look well. It's the look related to what happens when your data gets screwed up. When the outcome you expected and worked toward has suddenly been thrown to the dogs. And for that, I deeply apologize to her because I understand that gut-wrenching feeling. I make a mental note to grab her business card before I deboard the ship and send her an email with notes on how to adjust her metrics in the event she's ex-pected to do a report-out of this dumb event.

We find a quiet nook adjacent to one of the mobile bars and I attempt to interrogate her without scaring her off.

"You brought my dead husband into this. Now's your turn to prove that you aren't just blowing smoke up my ass. So I'm going to ask you one more time: Who's lying to me and about what?"

She says nothing, just stares at me blankly.

I shake my head and look to the sky. This bitch opens a can of worms but won't pour them out? What's her deal?

"Okay, then. Let's try this. What *can* you tell me? Besides the fact that you apparently slept with my husband and got pregnant with his child?"

"No, no, no. That's not *at all* what happened. This was long before you were ever in the picture, I swear. My son is twelve years old. This...this happened in college."

"What exactly happened?" I probe.

"It was an accident. A stupid one-night stand and I got pregnant. We both agreed that we weren't ready to be parents and we weren't going to be together, so the plan was a closed adoption. He said his mother would never let that happen, especially if she knew it was a boy. Her only son having a son? Yeah, no way was she going to let the Austin name slip away that easily."

For what it's worth, that does sound like Debbie. But I'm still not buying this bombshell.

"So I told him not to say anything to anyone and I would just handle the adoption on my own. This was my fault. I was his TA, and even though I was only two years older, I should have known better. I didn't want to ruin anyone's life over some drunken night," she goes on to explain. "I thought I could go through with the whole adoption thing, but as my pregnancy ticked on, I just couldn't do it. I'd gotten used to the idea of being a mother. I couldn't imagine just handing over this sweet thing, this piece of me, to a perfect stranger and agreeing to stay out of its life forever. What if I never got pregnant again? So I backed out last minute and didn't tell anyone. In my head, I rationalized that it wouldn't change anything. I was just trading one secret for a different one. I still wasn't going to be with Decker, so he'd never know. But then things ended up getting kind of out of hand."

Gemma begins to cry and blot the tears with the soft spot of her ring finger. She angles herself toward the wall.

I position my body to the side of hers and put my hand on the small of her back. "Why? What happened?"

"I gave up my job as a TA and dropped out of school as soon as I started to show and stayed as far away from USC as I could. I moved out of my neighborhood. I went off the grid completely. Then, once my baby arrived, it was like complete chaos mixed with no sleep mixed with a dark cloud of regret. I messed with the fate we had already decided, and the guilt I felt from that was super intense. It's never gone away, actually."

"So nobody ever knew you were pregnant except for Decker? Nobody knew you had a baby?" It sounds far-fetched, but I need to get her facts straight.

"My parents knew. But I'm not close with them. They live in Florida."

"Well, who did you tell them the father was?" I ask.

"I said I didn't know." She cries harder into her hands. "And that didn't exactly motivate them to help me out at all. In fact, the only thing it motivated them to do was swear I'd tell anyone who asked that I got a sperm donor as part of some feminist movement I believed in. I'm still really pissed about that."

"Okay, so if your mom and dad weren't part of this, then someone else has to know about your son. I mean, you said *they* lied. Is it his parents? Do Debbie and Kurt know about this? Is that who the 'they' are?"

"Charlotte, I'm sorry. I've already said too much. Just know, I didn't plan for this. Any of this. I wasn't prepared for this, I shouldn't have opened my mouth, and I'm sorry to leave you hanging. I have to go."

"Where are you going, Gemma? Huh? We're on a boat in the middle of the ocean right now. Just stay here. Talk to me, will you? Talk to me woman to woman. What's his son like?" It's my last-ditch attempt to data mine.

"Loved," she says, turning away from me and marching

over to where the ship has set up something called "Privacy Pods." They are little makeshift cabanas people can go in to get away from the crowd and continue forming their connections. She finds an open one and locks herself inside, which couldn't be further from the point of those things. How convenient it is for her to end the conversation on her own terms, barricading herself like a coward so she doesn't have to deal with me. Little does she realize, I don't need her to come out to get my answers. I'll compute this on my own. She's dealing with a Numbers Queen.

Chapter 19

Follow-up questions start flowing through my head like white-water rapids surging down a rocky river. My skin is hot to the touch. I blink twice to clear the dark spots, but I just feel dizzy. I want to refuse what I've heard tonight in every single way, and I believe that I can. But only if I can discredit the authenticity of what Gemma has told me. I cannot do that without my app, my algorithms, and at the very least, some goddamn internet access.

When Brian came to my door with *the news* about Decker, I froze up, I broke down, and even though I couldn't believe it, I believed it. With no data or facts at all.

This time, it's different. This isn't news; this is garbage. I don't believe. And so, I'm remaining in control. There, I said it. I just don't believe her.

Do I believe Gemma knows Decker? Yes. That's obvious from her ability to piece together elements of the past on the spot. Did they sleep together? I mean, it's possible. Decker was entitled to a history with other women before me just like I had hookups and exes myself. Did Gemma have a kid? So she says. But did she have *his* kid? No. There's no way.

Perhaps there's more truth than she cares to admit behind what she told her parents. She told them she didn't know who the father was. How convenient, to pin paternity on a dead guy who can't be DNA-tested, who can't defend himself, and whose family is a complete and total cash cow. All it would take on Gemma's part to pull this off is what it takes me to go on a date with any guy. A computer, social media, and ample time to research. It's really not that hard to have targeted Decker.

But despite the holes I'm already poking in Gemma's story, it doesn't change the fact that she's put this out there. So one way or another, even if just for this moment, the thought that my own husband, the man *I* was supposed to have children with, already had one, independently of me and without my knowledge, is weighing on my mind. I think now about the fact that there could be a piece of him still alive.

I pause for a moment knowing full well I must regain my composure. The only way I can do this is to bathe myself in the cold, hard facts. *What do you know for sure, Charlotte?* I grab on to the low-hanging fruit: I know Decker. I know him better than anyone else and there is no way he had a child, accident or not, adoption or not, and didn't tell me.

I spot my favorite cocktail waitress and order another drink. This time, a gin and tonic, as well as a few sheets of paper from the back office. I pace back and forth, cracking my knuckles. She comes back a minute later with a stiff cocktail and stack of bright pink Post-its. Those will do. I give her a ten-dollar tip before retreating to a bathroom stall. I'm not trying to take a page out of Gemma's book and isolate myself, but until this boat gets back to shore, I need a home base. I need a place where I can be alone and think. In my day, I've had many makeshift offices. This one—a plumbing-challenged women's restroom on a boat—is a new low. But this one is also far more necessary than all of the others.

I'm off-line until we dock—I've accepted that. So for now, I'm taking advantage of what limited resources I have and writing down everything I can remember about Gemma and our conversation that may come in handy with linking her to what is bound to be a big, fat lie. Decker wasn't the kind of guy who would have a drunken one-night stand with his TA. Even if he did make that mistake, he also wasn't the kind of guy who would just accept that some chick he knocked up was going to put their unwanted child up for adoption and never follow up to see how that went, or how she was doing. He had morals. And a conscience, too.

I start making a list of things to look up later, writing each on a separate Post-it and sticking it to the back of the stall door.

Are blondes more likely to lie than brunettes?
Boob job…pre or post Decker?
Mutual friends?
Double-check the timeline…

Nearly two hours later, I feel the boat jerk to a halt in the middle of scribbling another rapid-fire note on a Post-it. I've never been so happy to be back on land and immediately peel them all off, keeping them in order, and place them inside my bag.

I locate Casey by the sight of her red patent leather shoes and head straight toward her. She is conversing, laughing, and drinking with one of the guys from the speed dating table.

"Hi, excuse me, sorry," I interrupt the two of them. "We need to leave, Casey. Now."

"Why? Did you get your period or something? I have tampons…"

"What? No. We just need to go home. I can't explain it all right now, but someone on this ship claims to have known Decker, slept with him, got pregnant, and now I've written down all this data that I have to put through my system so I can prove there was no connection between the two." I fan the fluorescent Post-its her way to drive home the point.

"So…why do *we* have to leave?"

I can't believe how oblivious she is being. I'm telling her that a bomb has been dropped and she's showing no sense of urgency to move with me to get out of the way of it detonating.

"Umm, because I need to know if the two of them could have possibly ever hooked up and I don't have my algorithm set to run like that right now and I can't tweak the code unless we are off this boat."

Was that all one sentence?

"So you need to see if they were compatible?"

"Exactly." She's finally getting it.

"Isn't that the same thing I asked you to do with me and Justin before we left tonight?"

"Who the hell is Justin?" I ask.

"The librarian. The drummer. The guy I had the one-night stand with. I sent you his profile. You told me you'd run him through your app after you were finished getting ready. Did you do it?"

"Not yet, Casey. You know Brian came over right after you asked and then I had to hurry up and get dressed for this stupid thing. When would I have had time to do that?"

"I don't know. But you *said* you would do it."

"I'm sorry, but I think this is just a tad more important than seeing how things with your hot hookup might work out in the long run. My life has literally just been turned upside down. Again."

By now, the guy who was lingering around her has left and it's just she and I bickering in front of the bar.

"You want to know what's so funny, Charlotte?" she says, a little too cool for my liking.

What could possibly be funny right now?

"Nothing about me is ever important enough for you, except for the whole facet of my being," she spouts off.

"I have literally no idea what that even means," I say of her philosophical-sounding statement. "I'm just going to order myself an Uber."

I pull out my phone and she pushes my arm down.

"No, take a second and think about it. You've never once been to any of my oddity exhibits. You never ask me anything about my life unless it somehow makes yours easier—if I can walk your dog, if you can have some of my wine, drink one of my LaCroixes. And you don't do what you say you'll do... even the little things. I mean, I bring your freakin' mail up for you. I pay our tab at the bar with my hard-earned cash. I ask you to come with me to things like this for free. And you can't even take five minutes to tell me if Justin was husband material? But at the same time as you not giving a shit about me, you need me. For everything. You needed me to keep you from being alone when your husband died. You needed my furniture to replace the stuff you bought with him so you wouldn't have to sit on a sad memory every time you watched TV. You needed me because I'm a homebody, but also not the type to ask you to go to barre class, or talk about what happened on *Grey's Anatomy* last night. I'm all that you need, and nothing that you don't so that you don't have to be inconvenienced by your past. Go ahead. Tell me I'm wrong."

"You're a random Craigslist roommate who I happen to not have been killed by yet," I say as if delivering the final line of a rap battle. "Now, if you want to stay here with these losers, so be it. I'm heading home."

"Bullshit. There's nothing random about me. You picked me on purpose, and you know it. I'm an escape route for you and I'm not going to be that anymore. So I guess you better call that Uber and leave me here with 'these losers.'"

I stare at Casey, the queen of questionable decisions. How could she completely tune out everything I just said about Decker having a child? It took a lot for me to open up to her about him, and now the story has just taken a turn for the worse and she couldn't care less. If anyone is being selfish here, it's her.

"Suit yourself," I say. "And also, I don't need to run that Justin guy through the algorithm. Librarians tend to like people who actually think before they speak."

As soon as I get home, I pop open my laptop, fire up my spare double monitor, and begin going down the almighty Gemma rabbit hole. Tonight, I'm in the market to prove something.

As I get settled in, I determine that there is no information too insignificant to feed into my algorithm. So I begin sticking all the Post-its to the wall behind me. I need to see exactly what I'm working with, like a detective working a beat.

As of right now, my algorithm is coded to do two separate things. During the day, it tracks influencers. At night, my potential relationships. What I need for this particular situation is essentially a combination of both. So I hunker down and tweak the code to act more like an online yearbook. Something that can distill Gemma's pictures, give me a rundown of her favorite activities, the scope of her friend network—things like that.

But in order to feed it, I've got to give my program a head start. I punch her name, Gemma Sutherland, into my search bar and find her easily enough on social media. I want to drill down on the accounts, but her Instagram profile, the most visual of them all, is locked. All I can see is her bio: WeHot. Amateur Blogger. Pro coffee drinker. Mother.

I quickly create a fake Instagram profile for myself under the pseudo name @SoCalSweatSesh. To do so, I pull twenty user-generated photos posted from the event at WeHot the other day, which helps me pose as a superfan of the boutique gym. I click the "request to follow" button on @GemmaSutherland's profile and hope she's off the boat and interested in connecting with another "like-minded" wellness guru...or whatever the hell I'm pretending to be right now.

Meanwhile, I plug in the URL to her blog and hit Go. It hasn't been updated in two years and the formatting is absolutely atrocious. I can barely follow the layout and none of the photos are aligned in any sort of methodical way. It's a coder's nightmare, but I try to look past the programming issues and search for more nuggets of truth.

The blog does not turn out to be the gold mine I thought it would be. She only has five posts and two of them are recipes for cooking brussels sprouts and the other three include her training regimen for a 5K, a manifesto on what is happening to the health insurance system these days, and finally, an ode to Pinterest. It's no surprise that she's as basic as they come, but I know there has to be more. There always has to be more to a girl who has the balls to sidebar a girl she hardly knows on a captive ship and tell her she had a baby with her late husband.

That's when my phone pings with a notification from Instagram: @GemmaSutherland has accepted your follow request. And I'm in.

Where the blog was lacking in information, the social media stream more than makes up for it. It's a treasure trove of pictures, mostly of her—mirror selfies of her six-pack and perfect hair. I'm tempted to save a couple to my collection, but then I quickly remind myself that this woman slept with my husband.

Scrolling down, there are a couple of images with who I imagine may be her son, but they are all strategically positioned to retain his privacy. For instance, there is one where he is hanging upside down on monkey bars, but his back is to the camera. The caption reads, "When did my monkey become a middle schooler?!"

Even though I can't see his face in the pic, I get lost in the thought that this might be a little version of Decker. I pinch my fingers on the screen to zoom in on the image. The boy is wearing a camouflage T-shirt and his jeans are dirty from playing. He has longish blond hair that's hanging down like strings of spaghetti. I can only assume he has a smile on his face in this moment. Maybe he has Decker's overbite.

I think back to how old I was in middle school. I do the math and realize that Decker was probably a sophomore at the time this kid was conceived—not even old enough to legally have a drink at the bar or to rent a car.

Between our first date and our five hundredth date, he never casually—or formally, for that matter—mentioned a child out of wedlock. While I could understand how someone would choose not to lead with that kind of information upon first getting to know someone, I can't figure out, if this Gemma thing is true, why he would keep the fact he got a girl pregnant from me, his partner. His wife. There's a time and place for all kinds of honesty once you make that commitment to someone. Decker was a guy who understood that.

I go back to looking through Gemma's photos. Eventually in the stream, I spot an image of two Christmas stockings hanging from a mantel. The embroidery on the smaller one says: Aiden. *He has a name*, I think to myself. A trendy one, at that.

As I go on to recount more of our conversation, I think back to Gemma alluding to Debbie and Kurt being in the know about this. So I run what I've gathered so far about Gemma into my algorithm and have it spew out stats regarding a possible link to Debbie or Kurt Austin. My search comes up dry. They aren't friends on Facebook. They don't follow each other on Instagram. They aren't connected on LinkedIn. And they live worlds apart, according to their respective zip codes. There is virtually zero connection between them and I find that to be impossible given how Gemma *says* they are related.

I drill into Debbie's profile on my second monitor and comb through all of her online photos. If she knew she had a grandson, rogue or not, she would post it. Maybe she wouldn't tag him or drive extra attention to it, but I'm determined to find some visual wherein this kid is accidentally pictured in the background of a family dinner.

I dig and I dig and I dig, but I find nothing. As frustrating as that seems, it's actually a breath of fresh air. It's entirely possible, and extremely likely, there is no relationship between the Austins and Gemma Sutherland, despite what she claims. Without so much as 1 percent of a link anywhere online, it serves as further evidence that there is no proof this kid was fathered by Decker.

So my next step is to go down the rabbit hole one step further and attempt to link Gemma to at least one other guy during the same time frame who's a plausible match to be Aiden's real dad. For me, it is not enough to just prove Decker isn't the father. I need to show there's sufficient evidence for the father being someone else. I need to search for someone who is like Decker, but didn't just suddenly pass away and become an instant pond for this girl to go life-insurance-money fishing in.

I use what I know and recall how Decker was an education major and a star athlete at USC. There's *no way* he'd dabble in hooking up with faculty from some other department and then risk getting kicked off the lacrosse team—or worse, out of USC completely, which also happens to be his father's alma mater. It just wouldn't be something that fell in his moral scope at all, I don't care how many Bud Lights were involved that night at the party.

In fact, I reckon it takes a specific type of person—an immature thrill-seeker; maybe a guy like douchebag Chad—to have the balls to hook up with his teacher and not use protection. That's when I get the idea to create a ranking system, similar to a March Madness basketball bracket, to narrow in on the real person who fathered this kid.

I go through every photo I can get my eyes on from Gemma's past feed—from the one where she's doing a beer bong at a frat house, to the selfie with her favorite barista, to Thanksgiving dinner eight years ago—and throw it into my algorithm. No photographed man is off-limits for my data mining—if he has testicles and was in a photo with her around the time this child was conceived, he's the potential father. I even go so far as to download a facial recognition program so even if she didn't tag them in the post, my algorithm will find out who they are based on similar-looking images on other social platforms.

An hour later, I've found a bottle of wine to keep me company and my bedroom wall is slathered in fluorescent-colored Post-its. But despite its chaotic nature, I've narrowed it down to a "Final Four" of sorts and guess what? Decker is not on there. In no way, shape, or form have my statistics shown any viable link between her and him—other than the fact he took a class she once TA'd called "Intro to Socialism." But so what? There must have been a hundred people in that class and not all of them wound up being accused of fathering a kid. So that link doesn't worry me; it's a dead end.

Like Debbie, Decker and Gemma have no social footprints to each other. I breeze through his birthday Facebook messages—the ones I swore I'd never revisit—and see no well wishes from her. You'd have thought the mother of his child would have hit his wall with at least an "HBD."

And frankly, the more I look at her, the more I can't even really see him being all that into her, looks-wise. She's attractive, sure. But she's way too LA and also the complete opposite of me. I like to think that I'm my own husband's type, for fuck's sake.

As I bring my dirty wineglass back to the kitchen, I check the clock on the microwave and see that it's nearly two o'clock in the morning and there's been no sign of Casey. I can bet that after tonight's blowout, she won't be making an appearance at apartment 518. In fact, I'd say there's a good chance she found her way back to that guy from speed dating and is banging him at his dingy apartment right now. Or who knows, maybe she's at *Justin's* place just trying to stick one to me.

I wish I could pull an all-nighter and drive my investigation home, but I'm exhausted and Leno needs to be popped out for a pee before we go to bed for the night. So I take one last look at my wall before heading outside. Absorbing what I have done, I can't help but feel proud. This is me, thriving under adversity. This is what I wish I could have done in the hospital.

Chapter 20

"Charlotte. It's 7:00 a.m. I promise you I was going to bring the urn back before noon," a groggy-eyed Brian says as he answers the door in gray sweatpants and no shirt.

"Sorry, I know it's early," I acknowledge. "Can I come in?"

Before he has a chance to answer, I roll past him through the foyer and straight into his living room. I set my bag on his Chesterton sofa like it's some sort of old habit. In my hand is the stack of sticky notes from my wall. I begin placing them, in order, on a blank wall below his flat screen. I've even stapled the profile pages of a few key people to the correlating Post-it. Sure, it may look like a police lineup as I press them onto the wall, but I figure in different light, with fresh eyes, there is a better chance I will see the truth.

"What are you doing?" he asks. By now he's fetched a T-shirt and a pair of glasses.

"You said you wanted to help me with things, right?" I don't make eye contact. I just continue re-creating the bracket.

"Yeah, but—"

"So then help me figure out why my client told me she slept with Decker and had his baby in college."

He takes a few steps forward and looks up at the wall. "What *is* all this, Charlotte?" Brian asks with the same shock and horror of stumbling upon a gruesome murder scene. "Why are these names on my wall?"

"It's a relationship map. A ranking of everyone who that girl most likely had sex with according to her social media interactions since the start of her various online profiles."

Brian moves closer, taking better note of my display. He's now gazing at it like it's a piece of art hanging in the Louvre—squinting, tilting his head, contemplating. He peels off the Post-it with the name "Marcus Linton" on it and puts it back.

"Sorry for all the stickies. I found out on the boat last night and I didn't have any Wi-Fi, so I started scribbling—"

"Why am I not on here?" he asks, pointing to the wall behind him.

"Excuse me?"

"If this is about all of the people who Gemma Sutherland might have slept with, then why am I not here?"

"Wait. How do *you* know who Gemma Sutherland is?"

"Her name is right here, Charlotte. Right in the middle of your...web?" He peels off the bright pink Post-it with her name and hands it to me as a reminder. "I mean, I know half these people from USC. Curious why Marcus Linton made the cut and I didn't?"

"Are you really asking me this?" It feels like bad timing on his part, but I can't help but explain my rationale. "I mean, besides her TA-ing at the same school you went to, there are zero links between the two of you. Same for Decker. Hence how I know she's lying about getting pregnant with his child. Their connection starts and ends with him being a student in her socialism class. Your connection? Is nonexistent."

"That's interesting, because I did know her."

I'm sure he means he knew *of* her and I feel bad that he seems devastated that a cute blonde with big boobs wanted nothing to do with him back in the college days. It's times like this when I especially hate being the bearer of bad news, but you can't argue with what the facts show. You can't argue with what's on the wall.

"Come on, Brian. Are you seriously annoyed this chick wasn't into you? I know you can get anyone you want, but you wouldn't want this one. Seriously. She seems certifiably insane. If anything, you should be glad I ruled you out."

"Ruled me out?"

"Yeah, congrats. You're not in the running to have had a rogue kid with this crazy, gold-digging woman. I mean, using her ex-student's death to prey on his wealthy surviving family? Please. I'm not falling for it."

"I don't think this is healthy, Charlotte. Why don't we take five on the couch? I'll get some cold brew going. We can work on a crossword puzzle together."

A puzzle? I just told Brian someone confronted me about having a secret baby with my dead husband. Now is not the time to be derailing me with coffee and crosswords.

"Yeah, sure. After we look these people up. Gemma was in love with someone, but it wasn't Decker. I need to figure this out."

"She was in love with *me*," he says, seemingly out of nowhere, gripping the handles of two coffee mugs. "Not Decker or—" he looks at my wall chart "—whoever the hell *Mitchell Heath* is."

"Very funny. Can I have a little cream, please?"

"Look, I clearly wasn't planning on having this conversation with you this morning, but you seem adamant," he says. "So here's the truth: I'm the one who backed off on things with Gemma. I liked her, but not as much as she liked me. So I sidelined her. Like I did with every girl when I was nineteen years old."

"Did you go out late last night after work? If so, I think you still might be drunk," I playfully accuse him.

"Stone sober, actually." Clearly not in a joking mood. "I don't like to drink so soon after losing a patient. It's a dark habit a lot of doctors fall into."

"Where's the urn? I should go," I say, not feeling like going tit for tat on whose loss is worse.

"You don't need to go, Charlotte. I was just trying to—"

"I'm sorry about your patient, Brian. I really am. I, of all people, know that death isn't easy. I know all about the *dark habits* people—not just doctors, mind you— fall into when you lose someone. But the reality is, tomorrow you get to go back to work, and chances are, there will be new problems for you to solve. Problems you get to check off the list and move on from. I wake up tomorrow and that urn is *still* my problem and *still* not going anywhere."

"I've offered a solution for rehoming the urn," he reminds me. "You've ignored it."

"Buying a crypt at some fancy place doesn't just make my problems go away. You can't just solve them on the spot for me."

"Hey, I didn't buy it. And I said you didn't have to go with that, remember?"

"Then why did you even put a hold on it in the first place?"

"Because for some reason, you seem stalled with this whole urn thing. You're a strong person. The strongest I know. And it pains me to see you this way—stuck. I was just trying to do something—anything, really—to show you moving forward is actually a possibility here. And I'm not just talking about helping you with things with the urn either. What about your meeting with Warren? How'd that go?"

"My meeting with Warren? Holmgren? How do *you* know about that?"

"Warren's kid was a patient of mine before he moved their entire family up to San Fran. I knew he was in tech and saw on Facebook he was in town for the weekend for *Hamilton*, so I called in a last-minute favor and he did me a solid by calling your work and pretending to have just happened upon you in a magazine. I thought he could help you with your app thing."

"My goodness, why are you trying to do *everything* for me? I didn't grow up like you and Decker, okay? I'm not used to things just getting handed to me and I don't want to start that now. If you talk to your buddy again, do us both a favor and tell him he doesn't have to take on this charity case, will you? And also, I'm calling bullshit. I *don't* think you think I'm strong at all. In fact, you clearly think the exact opposite. That I'm just a weak little girl who had a bad thing happen to her and now she needs things delivered to her on a silver platter. I mean, really, what are you compensating for?"

Brian walks away into his bedroom and a minute later returns with the urn. He sets it down on the coffee table.

"You know, I finally figured you out, Charlotte Rosen. You just want to look at a computer screen—or a wall with a bunch of sticky notes on it—and go with whatever it spits out, even if that means rewriting history. Even if that means ignoring actual reality."

"I'm quite in touch with reality, thankyouverymuch." I put the urn in my Birkin. "How else would I have been able to take my own husband off life support if I didn't understand *reality*?"

"You've got to stop routing back to that day. Not everything is about that decision you made five years ago. *This* sure as hell isn't." He gestures to my Post-it bracket.

"This is about preserving Decker's memory."

"*This* is about manipulating information to fit the narrative you want to hear. What *if* Gemma was in love with me? What *if* Decker had a kid and chose not to tell you about it? Life is messy. Life is complicated. I want you to be free of these numerical, mathematical shackles you put on everything. Real relationships and real-life situations have an actual arc to them and sometimes chips fall where they may."

I assess the web of sticky notes I've slathered on his wall like an oil spill. I hate to admit it, but I think Brian was right to get real with me just now. Sure, this relationship map looks like it's about Gemma, but it's really about me. It's about the way that I've set up rules—so many of them for so long. I've put stakes in the ground and roped off restricted areas every which way regarding how to move on, with whom, when, where, and why. And I've done an excellent job—especially this last week—convincing myself it was never Brian and could *never be* Brian.

I start to peel off the stickers one by one and Brian steps softly into my peripheral.

"Hey, don't worry about those right now. Let's sit down," he says.

We make our way over to his signature comfy couch. If every therapist I have ever seen had a couch like this, I probably would have kept a weekly appointment.

"You're right," I say. "This is dumb."

"It's not, Charlotte. You're passionate about the truth and that's a good thing. More people should be like you. So don't apologize. In fact, I should be the one apologizing. I didn't mean to infer that you didn't care about my patient. I know you do," he says. "And I'm sorry for the soapbox about the way life is just now. It's not the same for everyone and I shouldn't have freeballed like that. I guess that's the problem with going with your gut sometimes, you know?"

I'm looking into his brown eyes, a little sleep crust in the corner of them. All I can think in this moment is how good it feels to sit next to someone so comfortable with taking accountability and apologizing.

That and how he is my 95 percent match.

Last night, in the midst of all my research, I ran him through my algorithm. Not to trace him back to Gemma, but to see where the two of us would land. That's when I saw we would make a near perfect couple. I don't know if I can—or should—ever do anything about that. Why? For starters, it feels like we just got into a fight and we're in that tiptoe peacemaking phase. Secondly, he may not have yet stated his direct opinion on the Decker-Gemma bombshell, but Brian sure made it clear that *he* and Gemma had some type of a thing. And finally, Brian said it himself and I happen to agree: maybe I'd be better off divorcing myself from numbers and percentages for a while. Clearly, it's gotten to me.

I look at him for a moment more, and before he can look away or say another word, I kiss him—this time on the lips, this time on purpose.

A second or two passes and he springs back, blinking his eyes hard like he's waking up from a dream. A second or two passes and he's still speechless. The guy who has always known what to say to me and when.

I grab the urn while he's still sitting shocked on the sofa and let myself out. For as quickly as I made the decision, I flood my own mind with doubt. That's the problem with going with your gut sometimes.

Back home, I lie in bed with Leno curled between my legs. Casey isn't home but she was. At least that's what the note on the fridge that says "Sups annoyed with you. Need to talk" tells me.

It's the start of my second week off from The Influencer Firm and I feel no closer, no more at peace with things since Decker's urn came back. In moments like this, I dig for therapy advice and beg for it to come to the surface. Right now, the mantra that rises is "Let it crumble."

I've caused a defect in every relationship that could possibly offer me support or solutions in this situation. With Casey, I kept her at arm's length on purpose. With my parents, I refused to move home or even visit semifrequently. With Monica and Zareen, I was all business. And with Brian, I sent him mixed messages followed by bolting the one time the two of us needed to talk most. If relationships were binary things—1 or 0—I have always picked 0.

Like branches on a tree, I've snapped them all off one by one. And now what's left is a naked stump. I didn't set out to do this, and it is no one's fault except my own.

I go to pull up the schedule for a grief group, but I get stalled seeing that the internet browser on my phone is still on the page I left off in my research from last night: the picture on Facebook of Brian dressed up as Superman for Halloween with the adorable Clark Kent kid standing by his side. I've seen this photo before. But right now, recognition hits me like a crack of lightning. Brian isn't the only person in this picture that I've seen before.

I enlarge the photo, expanding it to full-size on my screen, and zoom in on the caption, which I've actually never read. It says, Trick or treating with my best little buddy, Aiden.

This isn't just some patient. This is Aiden. This is Gemma's son. And it's also the same kid from Debbie's pool party last week. The one who charged into the house, like he knew his way around the place, and requested a pool noodle.

The revelation that Brian knows hits like a dodgeball hurled straight to the stomach. He claimed he knew Gemma, but I didn't think he *still* knew her. It takes away any appetite I may have had and replaces it with a sickening emptiness instead. I look again at the photo. Now I know what Brian was compensating for—and who he was covering for.

I screenshot the photo and get ready to fire the smoking gun off to Brian. How could he not mention this? He saw me struggling to piece this all together and this whole time he knew? All this time and I was never worth the truth?

Let it crumble rises once again to the forefront of my thoughts and I set the phone down on my nightstand, taking a few deep breaths in through my nose and out through my mouth. I've finally figured out who the "they" were that Gemma referred to. I thought it was just two people. Debbie and Kurt. But it was *Brian*, too.

I'm so mad, I begin to cry. Hysterically. I cry the way I've wanted to cry since the urn came back, but was too afraid to be heard. I don't care anymore, though. I'm so mad, and even more so because I'm not entirely sure at whom. The picture confirms what I didn't want to believe: people who I thought were in my corner this whole time were working together to keep a huge secret from me for years.

All because of Decker. Decker who had a kid and kept it from me. This is *his* secret mess that others have been cleaning up and hiding from his wife. But are you even allowed to be mad at someone who isn't alive anymore?

I wipe my nose on my forearm and head over to my laptop. The home page of my algorithm is pulled up. The cursor is blinking at me, taunting me. I'm only a few keystrokes away from exporting the results of a "Decker-and-Charlotte-stats.xls" report. A part of me is curious to know what percent match we truly were.

The thought of running a script I'm so familiar with against a person who I was already in a relationship with has never crossed my mind. Not until everything I knew about him imploded before my very eyes. Of course, I've worked with the algorithm enough times that I can sit here and make a fairly educated guess where the two of us would shake out, but frankly, I could see it going both ways. We married each other, therefore we could—and probably should—be a 100 percent match. Then again, Decker was a guy who got a girl pregnant and never told anyone. But does it matter now anyway? He's already dead—it's not like divorce is an option.

I look over at the urn just sitting across from me on my nightstand. I thought I'd feel lighter having cracked the case, but instead I feel like I'm in the throes of some sort of weird emotional hangover. My husband's ashes needing to be re-homed was complicated enough. But now, the urn's return has managed to unearth things I think a lot of people thought were done and dusted. And at this point, Brian and Debbie have no idea that I. Know. Everything.

Perhaps I should circle back to confronting Brian, the author of the twenty-two—make that twenty-three—frantic text messages sitting in my inbox, but after letting things crumble, I've decided I've got nothing to say to him right now.

So instead, I lean into the emotional wave I'm on and let it take me somewhere I haven't been in ages.

Chapter 21

"Hi. I'm Lucy," says a Martha-Stewart-looking middle-aged blonde woman who stands up from her chair.

"Hi, Lucy," the room responds in unison.

I treat going to grief group like a visit to the gynecologist: an uncomfortable hour wherein you know you are doing something good for your health, so you just suck it up and make a personal agreement to reward yourself with a giant ice cream after—and not the fat-free frozen yogurt kind but a double scoop of malted cookie dough from Salt & Straw. In a chocolate-dipped waffle cone.

The first available drop-in grief group being held this morning is in a meeting room in a Los Angeles Public Library branch off Laurel Canyon Drive. I've never been to this exact meeting; it's women-only. Most of the attendees here appear to be a bit older than me, but I'm used to that being the case. I sit quietly, respectfully, and listen to Lucy's story in preparation for any words of comfort to grab on to. The kind I so desperately need right now.

"I lost my husband of twenty-three years when he was killed in a workplace explosion," announces Lucy.

The room lets out a series of gasps and a few members start to tear. They must be newbies. Sure, it's gnarly to picture, but a workplace explosion doesn't shock me. It just tells me there's another person in the room to whom I can tell what happened to my husband and she won't be horrified either.

"I saw a therapist this week for my grief. My husband's death anniversary is next month and so summers are always really tough for me. His death anniversary is even harder than our wedding anniversary. Does anyone else tend to ride the *death anniversary* train like I do?"

Several people raise their hands. I raise mine, too. The sound of the air-conditioning kicks on. The room needed a little white noise.

"Anyhow, my therapist explained something about grief last week in a way that really resonated with me. It's amazing how you can read every book on the subject, scroll through every on-line forum, and keep coming to these groups, yet still be able to learn something new about how to process our favorite emotion."

A whir of low-volume laughs breaks up her somber intro-duction.

"So I thought I'd share it with you all in case anyone else might find what I learned helpful."

Lucy pulls out a sheet of yellow paper from a legal pad with the stages of grief written in a circle: anger, hurt, confusion, etc. It looks as if each of these words is a number on a clock.

"You're probably all very familiar with each of these. For years, I tried to work through them one at a time and con-quer each individually." Lucy taps her pen from one emotion to the next, like it's the ticking second hand.

"But that's not how it works. It starts right here in the middle of it all, in what the therapist called No-Man's-Land,

where you don't really feel any of these. You just feel numb."
She makes a dot in the middle of all the words and begins to
draw a circle that fans out like a spiral, bigger and bigger with
each loop of her pen. "Then it starts to get real."

Her pen strikes through the middle of every word. She explains that grief is about bouncing around from emotion to
emotion with no real rhyme or reason. Some days, you'll be
overcome with anger, others it will be more about the denial.
There's no method to the madness.

"Grief isn't like a storm you can track. You never know what
will trigger it or how severe it will be. For me, when I'm driving
in my car and I'm all alone and in the quiet, BOOM. It hits me
there. And also, much like a tornado touching down, I never feel
like I have any time to prepare and head to safety when it does."

Many women in the room nod their heads in agreement.
The car thing gets me, too. Most days, my grief is pretty mel-
low and it is what it is: just a trip to Trader Joe's. But in the past
especially, it would be a destinationless drive with a singular
focus: making sure my legs were touching the same piece of
fabric that touched his so that I could still feel his presence, so
we could still be connected. Because I wouldn't know how
to function if that didn't happen.

"Anyway, my therapist said the best thing to do is learn how
to treat each specific stage of grief so that whichever one your
brain settles on in a given day, you'll at least be equipped to
function. Today, for me, it's sadness. So I'm working through
that. *Sadness.* Thanks again for listening."

"Thank you, Lucy," the room says in concert.

About twenty minutes later, the session wraps. I didn't say anything during the group chat. That's not unusual for me. I come
here less to talk and more to be reminded that I'm not alone.
That all of our stories are essentially the same. I come here for
proof that life goes on, because sometimes, you just need that.

The women in the group, including myself, get up to mingle. Lucy is behind me in line waiting to refill her white Styrofoam cup with the cheap stuff supplied by the library.

"Thank you for sharing today," I say as I turn around and free up the coffeepot. "Your diagram was very helpful. I always like to learn new ways to process old feelings. I'm Charlotte, by the way." I put out a hand for her to shake, and she accepts. Her fingers are cold, her nails are painted red. I don't see that very much anymore on anyone: bright red nails. She reminds me of a receptionist at a dentist's office.

"Oh, you're most certainly welcome, Charlotte. Again, I'm Lucy. When did you lose your spouse, hon?" she asks as I pump a little expired pumpkin-spiced creamer into my barely drinkable java.

"Um, almost five years ago, actually. He died in an accident at a big race."

I add that last detail because I've been to enough of these to know that the question of "how" is always what comes next.

"Like a marathon?"

"Yeah, kind of like that."

"Oh, god. That is so hard," Lucy says, validating me.

You may not notice, but there's a widow code of ethics going on between us right now. I've ended my last sentence in a way that Lucy could hear the period I put on it. I'm not open to sharing more about how he died with her right now. So she won't ask for more details.

"Anything in particular you're struggling with today, Charlotte?"

Where do I begin?

"I'm worried about my memory of him," I say.

"Ahh. Well, Charlotte, as someone who's been widowed just a tad longer than you, I can assure you that the memories never go away. Sure, they fade a bit, but you'll see something, or you'll smell something, or a friend will mention something, and trust me, you'll wind up right back on track."

"Not like that," I explain. "I'm worried that the perfect way I remember him, that everyone remembers him, might not be how he *actually* was. Don't get me wrong—he wasn't a bad guy or anything. It's just, he had a past that not many people knew about, and ironically, it's coming into frame now after he's gone."

Lucy smiles and nods. "I see. What happened to your husband's cell phone after he died?"

"It was in the zip pocket of his shorts when he ran the race. It was smashed. I never got it."

"Okay. I ask because my husband couldn't have his phone on the floor at the plant, so he kept it in a storage locker. After he died, his company unlocked it for me and put all his belongings in a gallon-sized Ziplock baggie. His phone didn't have a lock on it or anything. And I admit, I went through his phone. At first, just to look at old pictures. But then I listened to his voice mails and I read his texts. Gary never cheated on me, thank god. But, he had a horrible gambling problem that I had no idea about. He texted his bookie more than me. He withheld half his paycheck from me; I had no idea his salary was double what he was bringing home. It all went to betting. As disappointing as that was, I had hoped it would have led to a treasure trove of excess funds, but all it led to was a crippling bookie debt. I didn't tell anyone about it. I've just been slowly inching toward squaring up with his bookie, taking weekly withdrawals from his life insurance policy. See any creamer around here?"

I gesture to the carafe hiding behind the decaf coffeepot to the left.

"Thanks. So does that help you any?" Lucy asks.

"It does. But my husband's secret," I tell her, "can't be zeroed out like a debt."

239 of my field

She sets the creamer back down on the table and stirs the contents of her Styrofoam cup.

"Gary was in his job for thirty years. He sliced every single one of his weekly paychecks in half to gamble. I'll be paying off Gary's debt for the next twenty years, Charlotte," she says, topping off her coffee. "I turned sixty in April. Do the math." Lucy laughs at the absurdity.

"Look, I don't know why he never told me about the gambling. I guess it's because he knew it would hurt me. But at the end of the day, nothing about his problem changes the experience *I* had with him. It was sunbeams and rainbows, as far as I knew—respectful, reliable, always there for me. But I get that's hard to explain to other people—they'll push me to focus on the negative—so I just don't bring it up at all. I take care of it privately myself. In fact, you're the first person I've told this to, actually."

"Really? Why me? I won't tell anyone, I promise," I quickly reassure her.

"Charlotte, dear. I didn't tell you because I thought you were good at keeping secrets. I told you because sometimes you just know who you can trust. Now, if you'll excuse me, I need to make the rounds before the library kicks us out of the meeting room. I hope to see you back here again, Charlotte. It was nice talking to ya."

With my mom so far away, I can't tell you how badly my heart needed to hear a *ya* right now.

The thought of Decker choosing not to tell me something feels like it goes against all that is holy in a marriage. But something in Lucy's anecdote triggers a new thought. Would Decker withhold something significant from me if it meant not hurting me? What if he thought about this—really thought about this—and came to the conclusion that it was better I did not know he got a girl pregnant? If I did know, I'd worry about it. I'd stew about it. I'd be confused about starting our own family and if our first child would really be ours or just mine. I'd struggle if we never had a boy and the Austin name never had a proper chance to live on. I know myself. And Decker knew me. I trusted him a thousand percent. I trusted him with our relationship—with our future. He wouldn't do something to hurt me. He would, however, choose to protect me at all costs. Are those the same things?

As I buckle my seat belt, I spill a little of my grief group to-go coffee on my lap. So I pop open the glove box and reach for a spare fast-food napkin. That's when I notice something else in there: my engagement ring.

There comes a moment for every widow when they decide to stop wearing their wedding ring. That moment happened for me over the kitchen sink the first day I moved into the apartment with Casey. I was always in the habit of removing it and setting it on the counter when I washed my hands. The soap made it extra slippery and susceptible to falling down the drain. As I was toweling off, Casey asked about the ring and I told her it was an heirloom I'd been meaning to take to the vault. After that, I never put it back on. Nor did I take it anywhere but to a box in my closet for safekeeping, which is where I thought it was—safe and out of sight—this whole time.

But then I remember. On one of my last trips to Goodwill to drop off the remaining Decker stuff, I decided to bring the ring along with me, stop by a secondhand store, and donate whatever they'd give me for it to an inner-city youth lacrosse team. But at the last minute, I got cold feet. I tried convincing myself it was a noble thing to do, but then I thought about the journey that ring took to be in my life and I couldn't accept it culminating with some lowball offer from a skeezy pawnshop in Sherman Oaks. So I separated it from the errands pile, tossed it in the glove compartment, and figured it was safe enough in there tucked between the owner's manual and paper napkins until I could actually find time to look up renting vault space at the bank. I guess I never found the time.

I slip the ring on for the first time in years, but it gets stuck around my knuckle. I'm up about ten (okay, fifteen) pounds since we were married. That's what years of stress eating combined with sitting in a chair for hours on end writing code will do to a person's body. But regardless of its placement on my finger now, I twist my wrist to the left and right and let the sun ricochet off the center stone. Little blips of reflections from the diamond dance on the car's ceiling like a twinkling constellation in the night sky.

I think back to the day Decker gave it to me. We had made it to the top of Runyon Canyon, pausing to take in the scenery and catch our breath. I redid my sweaty, Sunday morning ponytail as I spotted and pointed out the Hollywood sign. "Look!" I said with excitement taking over every feature of my face.

"Yes, babe. I know. The sign. Can we head back down?"

I knew—well, thought I knew—the heights were bothering him. But maybe his rush to start our descent was actually just the preproposal "let's get this show on the road" nerves.

I breathed in from the top and reflected on the fact that Los Angeles is such a smoggy, beautiful beast. It was hard to believe that in a city so big, the two of us from drastically different roots, coasts, and backgrounds somehow gravitated toward each other, became boyfriend and girlfriend, and managed to have a loving, loyal, *real* relationship in a city full of fake. Yes, Decker was attractive, but on the inside, he was a prize—a total gem of a person. Soft-spoken, thoughtful, gentle, kind, and with a quirky sense of humor I'm fairly certain was only meant for a handful of people to understand. Myself included.

When I looked at Decker, I always came away with the thought that he was my best friend. We had fallen for each other like bags of bricks—quick and hard. In LA, settling down with a girl who "works in entertainment" before the age of thirty-five is a foreign concept. "There are just so many distractions, so many options." That's what everyone told me about the dating scene here, and I not only believed it, I had accepted it like some tax you have to pay to live here. Yet here we were: me, twenty-four years old, him, twenty-six; fingers interlocked at the top of the mountain, and most certainly doing the damn thing.

"Ready for brunch, babe?" Decker asked.

"Yup. Starving."

He kissed my lips and down the hill we went.

Halfway back, a blonde lady with too much plastic surgery (a dime a dozen) passed us walking the cutest dog I'd ever seen.

"Oh my god, Decker. Look at that pupppppyyyy!" I squealed, giving his arm a squeeze and dragging him over for a closer look at the insane cuteness.

"Excuse me, can we pet your dog?" I unapologetically asked on behalf of both of us.

Before she even responded, I was bent down and giving this little French bulldog all the attention in the world. Everything in me wanted to snatch the puppy, run, and deal with the repercussions of doing so later.

"How old is he?" I asked, submitting to all the licks and kisses.

"About six weeks," his owner said.

"Awww, you're just a baby, aren't youuuu?" I said in that high-pitched, crazy-dog-lady voice people can't help but use when canoodling the cutest-ever six-week-old Frenchie.

"You can pick him up if you want to," the lady said.

"Isn't he adorable?" I said to Decker as I rocked the puppy like a newborn baby in my arms.

"He's very cute, yes. What's his name?" Decker asked.

I grabbed hold of the little bone-shaped tag around his neck and turned it toward me. It said LENO.

"Oh my god."

"What?" Decker asked.

"This dog is named *Leno*. Stole your 'firstborn's' name!" I turned the tag toward him as proof and couldn't resist smiling.

"Turn it over," Decker said. "What does the other side say?"

I flipped the tag over, unsure of why it mattered *what the other side said*. The coincidence of the year had already taken place—a dog named Leno, just like Decker had always planned for himself. But, as it had turned out, the romantic gesture of the year had not.

"MARRY ME, CHARLOTTE?-D" was engraved on the other side of the dog tag.

I looked up at Decker, who was smiling ear to ear, then back to the blonde dog owner. By now, she had removed her giant sunglasses and was asking if it was "okay to leave now."

Decker gave her a twenty-dollar bill before she scampered away down the mountain. He then crouched down on one knee. The whole thing was still a blur, but what I knew for sure was that I was clutching a puppy and he was holding a ring.

"What is going on here?" I said.

"Charlotte Eliza Rosen, will you make me the happiest man on earth and please, *please* marry me?"

I shifted Leno into my right arm and gave Decker my left. He placed the two-carat perfect emerald-cut diamond on my left finger, then stood up to kiss me on the lips. I nuzzled my face into the crook of his neck and started to stream tears of joy.

Back in my car, as I twirl the ring on my finger, I put my hands to my face and feel those same tears make an appearance. They are tears of relief. Relief that the good memories are not all gone.

Chapter 22

She's clipping the stems of a dozen white roses over the farm-house sink in her kitchen. And for the record, it looks like Alexa let her down with changing the security code on her front door because entering the Austin house in the middle of Debbie's Monday afternoon neighborhood pool party was as easy as cutting through room-temperature butter.

"That's him on the diving board, isn't it? That's Aiden? Decker's son?" My question is fired at point-blank range and cancels out the sweetness in the summer aromatics that previously occupied Debbie's kitchen: SPF 30, freshly squeezed lemonade, and the beginnings of a robust floral arrangement. I've never spoken to Debbie like this. My interactions with her have only ever toggled between wanting to be in the good graces with my husband's mom, and wanting to be in the good graces with my *late* husband's mom. In either situation, there hasn't been much wiggle room for me to suddenly sport a confrontational personality. But by now, I'm ready to get to the point. It's not like I have any allegiance to Gemma, but I agree with her on one thing: *no more lies.*

She turns to face me, finally. The touch of rosiness normally seen in her cheeks is void. She's gone pale and her lips are separated as we both wait for words to fill them. For the first time since I've met her, Debbie is speechless—lost and confused. I know those emotions well and we won't get anywhere if she stays stuck like that. I decide to tone down my incorrigibility.

"Let me back up." I prep for an explanation. "I talked with Gemma. For quite a while, actually. Was no one going to tell me that Decker had a son?"

Debbie lets out a defeated sigh, positioning her hands on the kitchen island for stability.

"It's not what you think, Charlotte," she says softly, refusing legitimate eye contact while leaning over her gigantic marble kitchen island.

"What's it, then? Because I've really been trying to figure this out."

"Well, no one told you to go play detective. And now look. This is not how we wanted you to find out," Debbie says, standing up tall in an attempt to reclaim her signature status.

"Please don't do that," I say. "The urn coming back to me has nothing to do with you being exposed as a liar. And a thief, too."

"A thief?" She goes back to slumping over the counter. "In what regard am I a *thief*, might I ask?"

"The time you brought sunflowers to my new apartment after Decker died."

"Yeah, and? I remember that bouquet well. Arranged it with pops of white ranunculus."

Is she really making me spell this out for her right now?

"You stole transfer paperwork from Decker's policy box

and forged my signature on a ten-thousand-dollar withdrawal. Ring a bell?"

"You've damn near lost your mind, Charlotte. Do you think Kurt and I would ever need a loan from our son's life insurance policy? Do you realize how ridiculous that sounds? Look around this place, will you? We're doing quite alright for ourselves."

"You gave it to Gemma."

"Gave *what* to Gemma?"

"Hush money you didn't want traced back to your own bank account. She mentioned it."

"Well, if she mentioned it, I guess that hush money isn't working so well, huh? I don't mean to be rude, but if Gemma needed *fifty* thousand dollars, we could—and would—give it to her. But there was no *hush money*. Gemma is not like that. She has never been about money."

The way Debbie talks about Gemma, it's like she must know her—well. Better than me, I wonder? Are the two of them closer than I ever was to my own mother-in-law? I can feel my facial expressions lose elasticity and she must be able to tell that I am sinking, too.

She puts her hand on my shoulder and says, "Why don't we continue this chat in the living room. Okay?"

Continue this chat? I want to leave. I want to surrender to a massive panic attack. I want to give up on everything. But alas, I can't go just yet because if Debbie is inviting me to take a seat in the living room, there's more to this story.

Debbie flips her blond hair over her shoulder and sits down next to me on the sofa in the living room. Normally she opts to put some distance between us and takes the seat across from me. I wonder what this closeness is all about.

"Now, I have no idea what happened to your money, but I can call Kurt's personal finance attorney right now if you think that'll help," she says, what I determine to be one of the first and only times she's actually been genuine to me. "Would that help you, Charlotte?"

"What would really help me right now...is if you just say it. I want to hear someone just say it out loud. Say it loud and clear. 'Decker has a son.' I mean, doesn't he?"

I look to Debbie and she nods.

"So then just say it, please."

She lets out another big breath. "Decker has a son. Aiden Michael Sutherland is his biological child," she says, finally corroborating the story like I requested. "That's him on the diving board with the long hair."

Debbie is a cold woman, but after she points him out, she puts her arm around me. I'm not sure if it's a sign of affection or an attempt to stabilize me after she drops the truth bomb. But like a rock hitting a windshield, I begin to crack and split. I begin to cry.

"Sandra!" she shouts. "Can you bring the picture album from my bedroom down here, please? And a box of Kleenex, too."

Debbie looks to the ground as she rubs my back softly. This close to her, I can see she's not wearing any makeup. This is essentially an unheard-of state for Mrs. Austin. Even when we were in the hospital with Decker on life support, I caught glimpses of her touching up her lip liner with the mirror of a pressed powder compact. Of course, she is vain, but in that moment, I want to believe it was just a nervous habit of hers—like she didn't actually care if her lips weren't the perfect shade of red when her son lay dying just a few feet away. But today, she's gone au naturel.

"Here you go, Mrs. Austin," Sandra says, plopping down a large photobook not unlike a wedding album.

"Thank you. Here, Charlotte. Why don't you have a look

at some of these photos and help yourself to a tissue or two? I'm going to get some tea started."

Somehow my trembling fingers are able to open the book. I see photos of Aiden over the years. As I turn the pages, some include Debbie and Kurt pictured with him. A few pages later, even Gemma makes an appearance, back before her hair was as bleached as it is now. I eventually get to another angle of the Superman/Clark Kent photo with Brian that actually appears to have been taken in the front foyer of this very house. I've been here a hundred times. How the hell did I miss that detail?

As I go through more photos, I finally land on one with an uncanny, indisputable resemblance to Decker.

"Hi," I catch myself whispering as I brush my fingertips over the protective plastic.

The photo is of Aiden hanging upside down from a set of monkey bars. The same one on Gemma's Instagram, but this version is taken from the front. His sandy-blond hair looks like a lion's mane and he's smiling with the brightest, biggest blue eyes. Suddenly, I feel myself smiling, too. Decker still exists in this world, just in a different form, a different body. This is...crazy.

"He's a cutie, right?" Debbie says with a smile as she brings two cups of tea into frame. "Do you want me to call him in here?"

I know she's not trying to spring a full-on meet and greet right here, right now. Instead, she's offering me a plain view, something greater than any of the photos in this book. From where I sit, I can see him. Frolicking, laughing, splashing. From where I sit, I get it. This is Decker's son. He's every bit as beautiful as I thought he would be. But right now, I don't need more of Aiden. I thought maybe I wanted that when I got here, but I don't. I know he's not going anywhere. This family won't let that happen. So when the time is right—if the time is ever right—I'll know what to do.

"Can I just ask a question?" I say, not allowing Debbie to answer. "Why did Gemma wait until *after* he died to tell anyone about Decker having a son? Doesn't that seem a little too convenient? Like, how easy to poach a grieving family that also happens to be super well-off? I'm just struggling with the authenticity and the timing of all of this."

She waits for me to finish blowing my nose, then responds.

"I mean, don't think for one minute that we didn't consider that. But like I said, we've never given her a penny and she's never asked. The girl keeps to herself. She hardly accepts the gifts we give Aiden and even scheduling these weekly summer pool dates is like pulling teeth. She feels like she is inconveniencing us. She never sticks around. She feels like she's intruding. I have to remind her constantly, 'That's my blood. That's my grandbaby. It's fine!' But then Kurt reassures me. Gemma's not our daughter-in-law and she knows that. She doesn't have to invite us over. She doesn't have to stay for dinner. She doesn't have to tell us what she's up to these days, where she's working, things like that. She's sweet enough to us, but there's no intimacy. It's probably pretty confusing for A, don't you think?"

I listen to her put it like that and feel for the moment she realized she had been a grandmother for years and never even knew it. Her son was alive, in a way, this whole time and she never knew it. Then when she finally found out, she didn't automatically just get Super-Grandma powers. After all that, Debbie doesn't even get to be a *normal* grandmother. The situation is laced with muddiness and complexity and, honestly, I don't envy the fact she has to navigate this.

"Are you not angry about any of this?" I question.

"At whom should I be angry? Decker for having a child out

of wedlock and never telling us? He was an adult at the time. He made a mistake that he *thought* he had corrected. How can I fault him? Or should I be mad at Gemma for not going through with the adoption? I can't change that. I never knew about it to intervene in the first place. So that leaves being upset at her for not telling us sooner? Gemma thought she could handle being a mother on her own. And maybe she could have gotten through her hard times without any help if she just grinned and bore it, but the fact is…for whatever reason…she spoke up and now we know. Now it's real. Think of the alternative. I could have gone my whole life never knowing that a part of Decker was still out there. So, no, I'm not mad. I'm grateful and I have been since these results came in."

She flips to the back of the photo album. Tucked into one of the plastic page protectors, there's a piece of paper that she slides out and hands to me. It's doesn't take more than a three-second look to see that it's a positive paternity test. It's the kind of information that makes things final, but it doesn't make them any simpler. I fold it back up and hand it to her.

"How did you get this?"

She inhales and looks out onto her glistening pool deck, slowly exhaling. She yanks a tissue from the Kleenex box and blots her eyes.

"A shaving razor of his. Or maybe it was an old toothbrush. I don't know. Kurt handled all the stuff with the lab people."

"I would have loved to have seen this sooner," I say.

"If I turned around and gave you this, if I told you that your late husband has a child with another woman and I have proof, then what? How do *you* move on from that, Charlotte? I know the connection you and Decker had. He was infatuated with you. He put you first. I never thought a son could love a woman more than his own mother. He proved me wrong. You had a beautiful connection, you two, truly meant for one another." She grabs my hands, wrapping both of her palms around them. "I want that again for you, Charlotte, but I'm not ignorant of how hard that will be. Decker was so special and I'm not just saying that because I'm his mother, I promise. Aiden would only ground you to a memory of something that is over and not ever coming back. And what if you couldn't see Decker the same way after knowing about this? *I'm* forever bound to him. Let these messy imperfections, let the heaviness, the sadness, the grief be *my* cross to carry. That's the whole reason we agreed to keep this between us, put distance between you, and protect you so that you could just...move on."

I believe Debbie. I believe the tears falling down her no-makeup face. I believe that the hardened exterior, the choice to put him in a mausoleum one hundred miles away, the visits that stopped, the communication that was curt, that all of it was just a cover-up for a master plan—not concealing a secret for the sake of withholding information from the girl who was no longer part of the family, but rather a combined effort to campaign for Charlotte to be okay—for once and finally, all at the same time.

My eyes connect with a framed photo sitting on an end table. It's of Debbie, Kurt, and Decker from Christmas nearly twenty years ago. From their matching sweaters, to their bright white smiles, to the kitschy North-Pole-themed backdrop that's hanging behind them, it all screams "perfection." But I notice something else. Evidence that secrets—especially the ones not meant to hurt anyone—are everywhere we look, even when we don't see them. This isn't a signature of the Austin family, this is real life, and not acknowledging that means I'm living in a dream world of sorts.

That is when I feel him.

I feel Decker around me in the most undeniable way.

My life flashes before me like pages in a flipbook.

A job that I'm good at and that I love, whether it loves me back right now or not.

A decent apartment with a roommate who splits the rent, even if she's a little pissed at me right now.

A dog that loves life and loves me, even when I rush him around the block.

A husband who wasn't a monster.

A life after a death that isn't so bad.

I'm doing okay, all things considered. No dream world needed.

The warm energy courses through my veins for a few seconds longer. I think he's proud of me for pushing through everything I've endured, everything I've learned, and the unfathomable decisions I've had to make because he had to die. And I feel he's pushing me to make one more.

I've brought the urn with me on a variety of occasions since its return—sometimes planned, sometimes not. I have it with me now. The intentions behind putting it in my bag today were unknown when I left for Debbie's. It was a reflex. But I can say with confidence that whatever gut feeling I started with has morphed into decided action.

"Here," I say, taking the urn out and putting it in front of her. "You should have this."

"Really? You're leaving it with me? Are you sure, Charlotte? Because I feel like I can finally be at a place where I am okay with you having it."

Under ordinary circumstances, I would take a pause to insert something snarky. *Gee, Debbie, I'm glad YOU are finally okay with HIS WIFE having it*, but I know how she feels. Because I have arrived at the same place.

"Yeah, but I'm okay with *you* having it," I volley back. "Like, really, really okay. Like the most *okay* I've felt about anything with the urn since it came back to me. And I feel like I should just run with that. So please, Debbie. Take it. Put it where you want. Just let me know where he ends up so that I can try to visit whenever I can."

Debbie tilts her head and offers me a warm, sincere smile. I bathe in that peace for just a moment and she does, too. The thing that binds us may be gone, but we've actually never been closer. And while I don't expect this to be the beginning of any sort of newfound relationship, it's a box we can check off. A moment we can both be proud of.

Debbie picks the urn up and carries it ten feet over to her fireplace mantel. There are large candles and some picture frames adorning it already, but she shoves those to the side and makes room for the ceramic pot. I'm sure she'll need to futz with it later to get the decorative balance just right, but she seems pleased with it for the moment.

"I'm putting it right here. And it's going to stay here. And just so you know, you are welcome to visit whenever you want. Let's be frank, I have no idea how to change that security code anyway, so just let yourself in. That would be fine."

We both let out a laugh that feels like an air pressure valve has been released. We've gone through an unfair amount of heavy shit, Debbie and I, and to be able to make a simple choice that feels right for both of us is an amazing accomplishment. I'm impressed by her levelheadedness and ability to prevail in a way that allows me to forgive her for the way she's treated me in the past. I don't think you can judge anyone for how they act in those moments or how they choose to live their life after. I turned into a crazy numbers guru. She turned into a heartless control freak. Clearly we were all just doing the best we could and this kind of clarity takes time.

Just then Sandra appears. "Excuse me, Mrs. Austin, your blue rose bushes have arrived."

"Oh my goodness, my babies are here? How I've been waiting to plant these beauties!" Debbie proclaims with the excitement of finding out she won the lottery.

"Go on," I say, giving her permission to clock out of this conversation. "Get to it."

"How do you feel now? Any better?"

"I mean, it's a lot to process. And I'm still not sold on Gemma's motives, but I'll get there."

"I know. And I agree. You *will* get there. Just remember, if it's any consolation, Gemma never came straight to *us* with this. She went to Brian. Right in the middle of med school, too. Now, I know the Jackson family very well. They paid for Brian's education, even after he switched majors. But his mother was adamant over lunch at Villa Blanca one day that there were no more handouts to be given. So you've got to think: this couldn't have ever been about money. She wouldn't have gone to Brian if all she wanted was a payday. One look at his Facebook page and you could see he was little more than a broke med-school student. It would have been a dead end for her."

My heart nearly stops. Brian knew first. That hurts.

But what's even more painful is that Brian wasn't actually the dead end for money Debbie thinks he was. He just needed to be in the right place at the right time to score: my house in Highland Park on the night he was helping me pack up.

Chapter 23

Last night I kept to myself. And I truly mean *myself*. See, it was the first urn-free night I've had with the knowledge it wasn't coming back to my apartment—ever. I was worried I'd feel a void or some sort of seller's regret after leaving him with Debbie, but I'm all good. I feel confident that Decker's final resting place is final this time because, frankly, Debbie isn't moving now that she's planted those blue roses, right?

"All good," unfortunately, is not how I feel about any of the other relationships in my life right now. Casey didn't come home again last night and Brian was speed-dialing me so much I had to shut my phone off. I had nothing to say, text or otherwise, to a person who's made a five-year hobby out of deceiving me.

I'm standing in the lobby of my building after a walk with Leno, scrolling through Instagram as I wait for the elevator. One ill-timed movement of my thumb, and I accidentally pick up Brian's first incoming call since powering my phone back on.

"Charlotte, hi. I've been trying to reach you," he says. He sounds exhausted and frazzled.

"I know."

"Then why didn't you answer any of my messages?"

"No. I mean, *I know*. As in…everything. Gemma, Aiden, you, Debbie, the money."

"Look, we *need* to talk," he pleads. "This isn't a phone conversation, okay? Can I just come over tonight?"

There's a beat of silence. I know the ball is in my court to take him up on the offer, which will no doubt color in some of these more fuzzy details. As a data person, that should be what I want. Right now, in fact. But, honestly, I'm not ready for all that. I'm still just…processing.

"No, you can't," I say. "I…I've got somewhere I need to go tonight."

I hang up the call. Lucy said after grief group that sometimes you just know who you can trust. Right now, that's not Brian. It's Casey. Five years of unwavering friendship and I owe five minutes back to her. So I take a photo of the poster that's pinned to the bulletin board by the elevators—the one that says "CURIOSITY EXPO—TONIGHT!"—return Leno to the apartment, and refer back to the image as I punch the address into my Uber app.

I pay the five-dollar cash entry fee at the door and enter a dingy, yellow-wallpapered boardroom at a run-down hotel not far from our place. In exchange they offer me a wristband that I'm told is redeemable for as much as I can drink. I decline. I've had enough experience with wristbands lately.

There are about twenty attendees moving slowly across the room like ghosts from table to table. The event is set up like a flea market: each vendor has a card table and on it whatever they decided to bring in from their rusty conversion van that I'm sure doubles as an illegal dwelling space.

Casey's pale legs stick out against the ornate gold-and-maroon hotel carpet. I spot her with a Pabst Blue Ribbon in one hand and a rabbit's foot in the other, talking to a mini crowd. To see her in her element, holding the foot of an animal, makes me proud.

She spots me and I wave like a stage mom. Casey rolls her eyes, admittedly not the reaction I was going for. "And that's the story of how a rabbit's foot became a symbol of luck," she says as the people disperse.

"Wow, would you look at this turnout." I gesture to my right and left. "Pretty good for a Tuesday, yeah?"

"What are you doing here, Charlotte?"

"I saw your flyer in the lobby of our building when I went down to walk Leno and I wanted to come check out your expo."

"Okay. Let me ask it another way: *Why* are you here?"

"I wanted to make sure my roommate was alive. You haven't been home at all. Sue me, I was worried."

"I left you a note. I said I was mad. Why would I want to be in the apartment and deal with your diva ass?" Casey turns her back to me and puts the rabbit's foot on the table. She busies herself positioning it, changing its direction three different times in five seconds.

"I know I've been an asshole," I announce. "Sure, a lot of shit hit the fan for me over the last week or so, but that doesn't excuse anything. I'm a grown woman. I need to be able to handle my business and still be a good friend, roommate, wing-woman, you name it. I shouldn't have tried to get you to leave the cruise early. I should have run the script on James."

"Justin," she interjects.

"Justin," I quickly correct myself. "I should have come to

your shows before tonight. I should replace the food I eat of yours. And most of all, I should have told you that you were right. You were not an accident. You were not a Craigslist rando. I did pick you for a reason. I picked you because you were the easiest person to play keep-away with, yet still be forced to keep me company, if only during the hours we were both asleep a room apart. I never got a chance to be afraid of losing my husband because he was gone too quickly. But after Decker died, my biggest fear was being alone. Not winding up alone, just *being* alone. I didn't know who I was without him. I didn't know who I was as a *widow*. And I didn't want to find out. But I knew I would have to face that if I was left alone for too long. So I scoured the internet and I settled on you. Someone I knew I wouldn't allow myself to have a breakdown in front of. Someone who I could feel safe with knowing you were just feet away every night when I turned the light off and realized it was just me under those covers. You were the perfect person for all of that and I picked you because of it."

Everything I'm telling Casey is true. But I've actually never articulated—*admitted*—that's what was going on when I signed my name next to hers as a cosigner on the lease for our place. Embarrassing and weak as it is, it feels good to tell the truth not just to her, but to myself.

"So you weren't just using me to get the lease because of my pristine credit?" she asks.

"No. I was using you for your never-ending supply of La-Croixes and spot-on fashion advice."

"Well, thank you. Thank you for saying all that. I know it wasn't easy and that nothing lately has been easy for you. So I appreciate it. And now, since we're forming a circle of trust here, I have something kind of major to tell you. I'm going to move out at the end of our lease. And before you go there, that's not some knee-jerk reaction to this little tiff we got into, okay? The Museum of Modern Art has offered me a curator position that starts in the fall. It's not as interesting as what I'm currently doing with the oddities and all, but the pay is better and it comes with actual health insurance. So, yeah. I'm taking the job and I'm going to rent a studio around the corner from the museum. I've never lived on my own and it's something I guess I just want to try."

"Wow. Congrats on the new gig. I had no idea you were job hunting."

"That's because you never ask me about my life, remember?" She winks at me. "So, yeah, thanks for being cool about that, but I figure telling you now gives us plenty of time to find you a new roommate. Or put in notice. Or—"

"Chill. I'll be okay and we'll figure that all out later," I assure her.

"Did *you* just tell *me* to chill? Because if so, that was fucking awesome. High five!"

I slap my hand against her and she smiles.

"I'm going to let you get back to doing your thing. Come home tonight, okay? The place just isn't the same without you."

"I will. I'm probably not going to be able to afford a Netflix subscription at my new place and I've got to finish this season of *Black Mirror* before moving day."

I roll my eyes at her snarky reply. It kills me that she won't meet me halfway in this tender moment, but I'll take her dry humor if it means we are all good.

"And, hey," she adds as I'm walking away. "Don't bother running Justin through your algorithm. I stalked him on Instagram last night and he totally has a girlfriend. What a jackass."

Back at my place, there's the most billowing bouquet of peonies I have ever seen just outside the door. I check the label and they are for me from Brian, complete with a card and all. The card, however, isn't just a slip of paper clipped to a stem. It's full-sized, sealed in an envelope.

I unlock my door, and Leno lights up at my return like usual. Before I pet him, I set the flowers and the case of rosé with Casey's name on it on the counter. I know she asked for me to replace just the one bottle I drank, but I owe this girl way more than that.

Sitting on the floor with Leno chewing his toy in my lap, I wish I had Casey's bra-knife handy to slice open the envelope from Brian. Instead, I use my finger. The paper cut from last week has since healed.

Straightaway, out of the card drops a check written out to *Charlotte Rosen*, signed by Brian Jackson, in the sum of ten thousand dollars.

Dear Charlotte,

I've been wanting to tell you something for years. But it was news that only someone who was close to you should share and I stopped being "close to you" after the night I helped you move out of Highland Park.

The irony is not lost upon me when I think about us and the fact that when I'm finally back in your life and things are really good with us, I have a greater obligation that will wreck it all. Again.

There has never been such a thing as "the right time" to say this. But in addition to being the strongest person I know, you're the smartest, too. At this point, you probably don't need me to say it, but for what it's worth: Decker had a son with a woman before you were ever in the picture.

After Decker died, Gemma reached out to me on Facebook. At first, just to say hi, to see how I was doing with losing D—she knew we were friends. Then she asked me to coffee. The first thing she said when she sat down was, "So I'm sure you know that Decker and I slept together once." It wasn't a question. It was a statement. And I knew right then there was more to the story. She told me about Aiden right after that.

Decker knew about the baby. He thought the child was adopted by a nice family in the suburbs. But that never happened. And when Gemma heard the news of Decker's passing, the reality hit her that she was a single mother of an eight-year-old boy whose story of conception was a complete and total lie. Every night she thought about how the father of her child was now dead, ruining the chance for her son to ever meet him or know him.

Clearly she was overwhelmed by her choice to do this entirely on her own and in secret. I had to help. The only way I knew how was with money. I couldn't ask my parents for it and didn't have the means to do something about it myself, so I took money from Decker's policy.

When you asked me what I had been up to for the last four and a half years, what I really wanted to say was: saving up to pay you back. That's what all those ridiculous side hustles were about. Ironically, I just donated my last batch of plasma a week before Debbie called me about the urn. And now here we are. I never wanted us to amount to this: just some payback and some paternity proof, but I don't really know how to tie up this loose end.

I'm so, so sorry.

-Brian

A small part of me had been wishing I wasn't so good at playing detective after all, but this letter confirms it. Brian took the money and gave it to Gemma and Aiden. Kudos to him. That's a lot of baggage to hide while just seamlessly sliding back into someone's life.

When I left Debbie's house, I left with more than just proof Decker fathered a kid before our time. I left with proof that relationships aren't about things like probability.

Take Brian, for instance. Brian is a 95 percent match with me, which leaves just a 5 percent chance he'd ever do something like lie or steal from me. But he still did both of those things.

So what am I supposed to do now? On paper, which is exactly what I'm looking at, this is a matter of blatant betrayal. But on the other hand, his letter is pure honesty laced with good intentions.

I've sifted through hundreds of guys since Decker died, holding them up against what I know a good relationship looks and feels like. Honesty and good intentions top that list for me even though they are hard qualities to come by. That's why I haven't dated anyone seriously. That's why I haven't *slept* with anyone since Decker.

That's right. Little Miss Tinder hasn't had sex with another man since Decker died. Mourning a spouse while simultaneously having desires for someone else is fraught territory, to say the least. But the confusion of it all isn't everything.

There's a horror to the universe when you lose someone you love. But there's also an awesomeness when someone new and amazing arrives. I know that, but I've never been ready for that, despite how all my outward efforts to find love would appear to differ.

I wanted to deny so badly that I was still struggling from my husband dying, that I thrust myself into a program that would help me find a future with someone else. A future I'd have complete control over, which included knowing before date one that that person would never have a chance with me.

"Daddy's home," shouts Casey from the doorway, waking Leno from the cutest puppy sleep in my lap and jogging me out of my untimely revelation. Immediately, our apartment smells like a deep fryer. She's stopped at In-N-Out on her way home.

I tuck Brian's card into the kitchen junk drawer and steal one of Casey's fries, which are covered in cheese and chili sauce.

"Okay, I will definitely *not* miss this when I move out," she says of me snatching her food.

"Can you throw me a bone, please?" I bargain with her. "I'm just coming to terms with the fact my husband has a son, giving my husband's ashes back to his mother, *and* reeling from seeing the skull of a double-headed flamingo at a curiosities expo. And one more thing. Remember my missing money? Turns out everyone's favorite children's doctor is the one who stole that ten grand from me. I'm very fragile right now, if you couldn't tell."

"Wow," she says with a mouth full of cheese fries. "Crack open a bottle of rosé and tell me more about it in the living room?"

I'm not so sure how rosé pairs with greasy fast food, but I'm game to take Casey up on the invitation for a fireside chat. I'm tempted to say that I owe that to her—to open up, have a little "girl talk" in the living room over a bottle of wine—but actually, I owe that to *us*. Parameters about how to move on, when, and with whom were put up around her, too. From the first day of living with Casey, I've always wanted to break those walls down. I've always wanted to be Casey's friend. Why? She's one badass chick. Not to mention, loyal to a fault.

An hour goes by and we both have a pore-minimizing mud mask on our faces. I have officially caught Casey up with all things Brian-Debbie-Gemma-Aiden. And unlike the way she acted on the boat, she actually seems to care this time—especially about the part Brian's played.

"Sneaky bastard, eh?" Casey says.

"I mean, I see why he *thought* it was a good idea. I just don't see how he didn't realize there'd be serious blowback doing what he did," I explain, two glasses of rosé in.

"Oh, I'm pretty sure he knew there'd be blowback. But I'm also pretty sure he knew for as fucked up as it may all have been, that every player in this game had the capability to cope with it in the end. You know? Like, this actually *isn't* the worst thing y'all have been through. So, let me ask you this. Now that the truth is out there, how do you feel about him?"

"Decker?"

"I was going to say Brian, but, sure, we can start there. How do you feel about your husband?"

Like the time Monica came over and asked me about Decker, I find myself staring out into the traffic on the 405. Every headlight zooming down the highway looks like a shooting star on land.

"I'm not sure I'll ever have an answer as to why he never told me about this. I know 'Hey, I knocked someone up once' isn't considered table conversation any more than 'Hey, make sure I'm cremated if I drop dead, okay?' so I kind of get it. But I'd like to think I was worth the whole truth. So that's hard. But he was a good guy. I'll always say that. I'll always believe that."

Casey clinks her wineglass against mine as I brush away the start of a single tear.

"And Brian?"

"I think he's an idiot."

"Oh, good," she says, relieved. "Then there's still a chance for Brilette to happen after all."

"Excuse me?"

"Charlotte, let me explain something to you. How do I put it? Brian has a thing for you and *you've* got a thing for Brian. And before you start denying that, let me tell you why. Because if you *didn't* have a thing for Brian, you'd want to kill him for what he did. You would have started this whole thing off guns blazing telling me how you never want to see or speak to him again before I could set my In-N-Out on the counter and unlace my Dr. Martens. But you didn't. You were sarcastic about the shit-day you had, him taking your money was the last thing on your laundry list of complaints for the day, and you just summarized how you feel about it all by calling him an idiot, which all of us are at some point or another. Am I wrong?" She holds up her arm, which still has the wristband from the boat party on it, then points at me. I think she's alluding to the way I acted when deboarding the ship.

"Kidding," she says. "But it *is* possible to forgive and look past things. You know?"

"I just have no idea how to look past this—or deal with it at all," I confess.

"Do what I do," Casey says. "Get a tattoo."

Chapter 24

Zareen gave me two weeks off to figure out what to do with the urn. Turns out, I made that decision in a split second. So as the days tick on, what I really think she was giving me was time to make some much-needed progress in other areas of my life. Progress that isn't as tangible as just turning his ashes over to someone else and checking this debacle off the to-do list.

The longer I am away from my desk, the more evident it becomes that I'm about five years into seeing the world through a lens of how things are supposed to be, not how they are, and that's not sustainable. At least that's what I was taught when the worst thing to have ever happened to me unexpectedly reappeared at my door a little over a week ago. No longer can I force-feed my future to fall into place a certain way. No longer can I strip out the difficult people, the hard conversations, the unplanned-for events. No longer can I pretend that mourning and new love cannot coexist.

Since Decker's return, it's been a crash course in how my

computer isn't always right. It can't just push out a magical solution to every single problem, no matter how many times I tweak the code. Despite how badly I want it to, it can't make every story perfect. I echo what Brian said back in my apartment: that the real world functions with an arc. That trials and tribulations aren't things we can program to be wiped out or ignored. Instead, we have to find ways to accept them, cope with them, and let them enrich the overall story. And mine, I'm beginning to understand, is one that's always being written.

It's the next day when I find myself pacing at the curb, waiting for Brian's Uber to drop him off at King Cobra. As I see the car pulling up the ramp a few minutes later, my stomach does a triple axel. I've lived my entire post-Decker life being scared of anything nonlinear. Now I'm intrigued by what it feels like to just go with your gut. And after talking to Casey last night, my gut said to text Brian this morning and tell him to meet me at a tattoo shop Casey recommended.

Brian shuts the door to the Uber and slogs his way over to me, emotionless. He doesn't seem particularly enthusiastic and I can't blame him. I didn't give him any details and shut down his opportunity to ask questions via text. But between shutting him down like a jackass, and the letter he wrote me that revealed *he* was the even bigger jackass, I figured two jackasses texting back and forth about the logistics of an impromptu tattoo appointment was not the best way to ensure we'd actually meet up here.

"Hi," I say. "How are you?"

"Tired. Haven't slept. What are we doing here?" he asks.

What *are* we doing here? It's a good question. And if I think about it too long, I'll change my mind. But for now, the answer I'm going with is a simple one: "I'm getting my tattoo covered."

My hand trembles as I hold out my arm and expose the *D* tattoo for what is bound to be one of the last times. I've never made the decision to permanently ink myself in five seconds flat based off a fleeting comment from my kooky roommate, but here we are.

"Right now? Are you sure?" Brian tips his black Wayfarer sunglasses up to see the *D* tattoo a little more clearly. He looks good for a serious lack of sleep, and his gray joggers coupled with a Clippers jersey, nothing underneath, is an excellent look on him. Debbie said it best when she was explaining med-school Brian: a poster child for disheveled living. But as I look at him now, I have to admit his whole post-turning-thirty look begs to be featured in a spread in *GQ*.

"Yes. Right now. You have your ID, right? They don't let anyone in without it."

"Yeah. I'm just… I have questions," he says timidly.

"And so do I. Let's talk about them in the chair."

Brian is staring up at the ceiling from the chair next to me. I'm also keeping my eyes gazed at the ceiling as I can feel my armpits sweating. A small *D* tattoo I got over five years ago pales in comparison to the pain I feel now with this cover-up job. It's like cats scratching at a sunburn but I have to stay still. There's no going back now. In this captive position while my tattoo artist is jamming to the Metallica in his headphones to stay focused, I decide it's time to hash some stuff out. I know I should be the one who breaks the silence, but I'm not yet sure what the first thing out of my mouth should be.

"So…you stole from me," I blurt out in some sort of weird, half-joking way.

Brian turns to me. His eyes wide like he got caught with a hand in the candy jar. I immediately regret this approach, but such is life when you go with your gut.

"Charlotte. I—"

"Let me guess," I forage on, trying to smooth over my clunky start. "You 'didn't want me to find out this way.' Debbie used that line on me and it didn't make anything better."

"Clearly, yes, you read my card. I took the money. And when I gave it to Gemma, I told her that you said you'd be open to meeting Aiden 'one day.' I regret it. I was just trying to handle a sensitive moment the best I could. She hasn't stopped asking if anything has changed on that front for years. I should have known that one day she'd take matters into her own hands and find out for herself what the deal was. I can't speak for Debbie, but that's why *I* didn't want you to find out this way. But now you have everything you need. I explained what happened and returned your money. What more do you want from me?"

Twenty-four hours ago, he's right—that's all I would have needed. Cold, hard facts and a check that would make Decker's policy go back to looking like I thought it was for the last five years: clean and balanced. But those things are doing nothing for me right now. I want...

"I want to know...did you take it when I locked myself in the bathroom so I could sob alone? Or was it when I was looking for my bra behind me on the floor?"

He cracks the bones in his neck.

"I'm not some douchebag who took advantage of a grieving widow. You know me better than that. I would never do that. But after that line was crossed, the idea just came to me. We talked earlier that night about what your plans were as we packed up your place, and I knew you weren't going to touch the funds for a while. I also knew you weren't coming out of the bathroom until you heard that door shut behind me. So I just took the transfer form and put it in my pocket, not sure if I'd ever actually make the withdrawal. And now here we are."

"Here we are," I repeat, defeated by his explanation. "Why didn't you just ask Debbie and Kurt to step in then? Everyone knows they're loaded."

"I did. I went to them immediately after. They refused to believe the kid was Decker's. They wouldn't even look at a photo of him unless paternity was established, which I was eventually able to prove," he says.

"Wait. *You* did the paternity test? Debbie said Kurt handled the labs."

"It took a while for me to find it, but I located his electric razor in some of my old college boxes and brought it to the lab at the hospital for testing. Debbie wanted no part of this until things were confirmed, so I dealt with Kurt, gave him the results from the lab when they were conclusive, and they both have been involved in Aiden's life since the results came back. But by then—"

"You had already taken my money and didn't need anything from them."

"I could have asked them for a loan, sure, and replaced your money right away. But I was trying to keep the spill contained. This was my mess, not theirs. If I roped them into it, I was afraid they'd already be off on a bad foot with Gemma, and she didn't deserve that. They didn't know Gemma like I knew Gemma."

"Does that mean that you and Gemma…?"

"No, never. But I am the one who invited her to the party at the frat house the night I'm pretty sure Aiden was conceived. She was a couple years older than us. I met her through an upperclassman. Thought she was cute. We talked a bit before the party, exchanged some flirty texts. I guess she thought we were 'hitting it off' or something, but I never wanted anything serious. So, I ended up ignoring her at the party. Typical Brian Jackson during the college years. Anyway, next thing I know, Decker tells me the following day he hooked up with 'that cool TA chick.' It kind of surprised me, to be honest, but I just fist-bumped him and that was that."

"That's enough," I say with frustration. I'm disappointed, but I can't tell in whom. It's a situation wherein everyone seems guilty, but everyone seems innocent, too. "You know, a whole lot of shit could have been avoided if people actually talked about things instead of just covered them up with money and lies. Why didn't you tell me? Why didn't you *ever* tell me anything? I can't even imagine keeping this kind of a secret."

"I didn't tell you because I didn't know how to tell you. I've never known how to tell you. Do you think I really believe a few paragraphs and a check and some flowers actually cut it? That that's what you deserve after all this? Hell no. But I don't know what I'm doing here. I've never really known what I was doing here. The only guide I've ever had was just trying to put myself in my buddy's shoes in a really tough situation. What would Decker have done if he were here? He would have helped Gemma."

"He would have told his wife."

"And I missed the mark on that."

"Conveniently."

"No. I missed the mark on that because I'm *not* Decker. I'm nowhere near as good as Decker. I'll never try to claim that I am. But I will claim that I tried to do the best that I could. I tried to minimize the damage. Maybe it didn't work, but I will never say that I didn't try."

I look at Brian, who at this point is wiping away tears. He doesn't need a tissue, though. He needs my mercy.

"All set, miss," my tattoo artist says.

I look down at the inside of my wrist. Where there was once a dime-sized, script letter *D*, there's now a quarter-sized blue rose.

"I love it," I say.

★ ★ ★

"Does it hurt?" Brian asks from a patio table at Alfred's.

"Nah, but in a day or two it'll be a bit itchy, if I remember the healing process correctly."

"I have an ointment for that if you need it. So, is it my turn now?" he asks.

"To get a tattoo?"

"To ask some questions."

I knew that's what he was getting at, but I was trying to pump the brakes a bit.

"Sure."

"Everything's out in the open now. All the numbers add up, you have your cash, you have the data, you have the explanation. You finally have it all. Even a solid reason to never talk to Debbie or me ever again. Isn't that what you wanted? Doesn't that make everything much simpler?"

"How do you figure?"

"Well, for starters, you don't owe Debbie anything anymore. You can do with the urn what you want."

"I've already given it to her. Permanently, actually. What else you got for me?"

"What has been going on between us? You kissed me in my apartment. You're not going to tell me that was a mistake, are you?"

There have only been a few times in my life that it felt like the air was being sucked out of the very space I was in and this is one of them.

Like I said before, it's been a while since someone considered: What does Charlotte need? What is Charlotte missing? But it's been even longer since the someone doing the considering was me. And right now, I'm zeroed in on what I need— moreover, *who* I need—right now in my life.

I thought my forced PTO would only be about finding a

spot for Decker after his death. Turns out, it was also about finding a spot for Brian in my life. As complicated and messy as that sounds, it's no more of an impossible feat than rehoming the urn, which I managed to do in an instant based off of a gut feeling. And if I just take a minute to ask myself what I need and what I am missing, the answer is pretty clear: Brian Jackson.

"No, it wasn't a mistake," I say. "I was just making sure I feel the way I do about you."

"And that is?"

"I like you, Brian. I just… I like you."

He leans over and kisses me softly on the lips. It doesn't last more than a second or two. But when his lips touch mine I can't help but think how good it feels to let go and live in the moment.

Epilogue

It's been a few weeks since a) I deleted Tinder, and all other dating apps, off my phone and computer. And b) I returned to The Influencer Firm. Things were weird at first, obviously. Other than Monica and Zareen and our freelance Human Resources lady, no one on the staff really knew what had happened to me or where I was that whole time. I'm sure my unexplained absence provided the interns with plenty of fodder for bathroom gossip, but so be it. I ended up really enjoying my time off.

We landed the Voyager account. Sure, the guys were impressed by the few slides I showed them, but that's not what sealed the deal. Marigold came up with a really cool idea to do a "mannequin challenge" video in our office of everyone wearing their shoes. It showed off our cool digs—and all the cute girls we employ—as well as our creativity. They signed the contract during my second week off.

As such, things have been pretty busy getting their account set up. So much so that I was moved off the less demanding

WeHot account to focus on getting Voyager live by September 1. Not only did that account shift free up my resources a bit, but it saved me an awkward conversation with Zareen. Plus, it removed future contact with Gemma over work servers. I can't give HR another run for their money like that.

We're on good terms, though—Gemma and I. And, well, Debbie and I, too. After things cooled down and the urn was officially rehomed, Debbie coordinated us getting together at the next pool party. Aiden got to see his dad's ashes and meet the woman he married—not to mention give her a hug.

I don't plan on making it a regular thing, seeing Aiden. But Debbie said they do something for his birthday each year, and this year's a big one—thirteen—so I'll be there. I'll need to first do a little research on what teenagers think is cool these days, but I'll definitely be there. Probably with Brian.

With all that going on, you'd think jumping back in the work pool would have been hard. Especially considering all the custom coding Voyager is requesting for their reporting. But it's been fine, despite my two-week break. If anything, it's just been a little more time-consuming than usual because I'm training Marigold on the keystrokes while I'm at it.

Yes, you heard that right: I am training Marigold, who is poised to help open the SoHo office in New York in the next couple of months. And, no, I'm not giving her faulty codes so she purposefully screws things up when she tries to repeat the same thing at her desk. This isn't about sabotage, shockingly. It's strategy. After convincing Zareen that account management and a junior coder are really the only faces who need to physically be in New York, she is letting me handle back-end Voyager stuff from my desk in LA. As such, I resolved it would behoove me to turn Marigold into my little rock-star sidekick. Loading her up with training now means that someone else gets to stay late at the office running reports. As for me? I'll go home early to walk Leno and cook dinner with Brian. Yeah, we're giving that whole dating thing a try now.

I've been a widow longer than I'd been a wife. And Brian's gotten the hang of Brian *without* Decker. He's a different person now. He's his own person now—not just Decker's friend and frat brother. As time goes on, things change. And real life has an arc to it, remember?

Alfred's? Brian asks in a midday text.

I grab my purse and slither out of the office without telling anyone. The post-urn me has put a priority on people over numbers, and right now, Brian wants to share a pastry—and a kiss, if I'm lucky—and so I'm there. I'm totally in.

In his signature scrubs, Brian sits in the same spot on the patio that we met at a month and a half ago, except his hair is a little longer now and I've seen him naked by this point. Both are a plus to me. He's sipping from a cup and there's another one set on the table, which I'm assuming is for me. He's always thoughtful.

"This seat taken?" I ask as I pull out the metal chair from under the table.

"Careful, the chair is—"

"Hot as hell!" I finish his sentence as I scorch my thighs, my favorite pastime.

"Sorry. Tried to warn you," he says with a smile flanked by two deep dimples.

"How's your day?" I ask, taking a sip of my crème brûlée latte. It's cooled to the perfect drinkable temperature, just the way I like it.

"Good, except I'm so damn giddy about us these days it's hard to concentrate."

"Really?" I blush at the thought that I don't need to verify the authenticity of the things he is saying. I just know them to be fact.

"I don't think I realized how long I've been mesmerized by you. I just came to a place of acceptance that the most we would ever be was Whole Foods hot bar acquaintances. Now, it's like, I've won the lottery. Just this morning I was testing this kid's knee-jerk reflexes. He kicks me square in the nose and I just start laughing. I didn't even care my nose started gushing blood, I was just…happy. Anyway, can I take you to dinner tonight?" Brian asks.

"Sure. What's the occasion?"

"Oh, nothing. Just that I want to date the hell out of you."

Brian leans across the table and kisses me on the lips for the second time since getting to Alfred's. His kisses feel so good that I lean his way and claim one more before both of us need to get back to work.

"Deal. And also… I really want to try Twisted Fork in Universal City, so I hope Italian sounds good to you."

When I get back to the office, my phone rings with a number from the San Francisco area. I answer.

"Charlotte? It's Warren Holmgren. Are you sitting down? I've got some great news for you."

I deleted Warren's number when I knew Brian had his hand in setting up our meeting. Although it was annoying to find out my interaction with Warren wasn't as organic as I would have hoped, I forgave Brian for puppeteering the thing. At the end of the day, it was a thoughtful and resourceful move on his part that showed he was actually paying attention to me when I was talking about my tech passion and hopes for the future. Regardless, I haven't followed up with Warren since, so the fact he's calling me out the blue and sounds as excited as he does right now is beyond me.

"Get this. I pitched your idea to my dev-team up here, and they are all-in on it. They are the target demo themselves…

tech guys in their upper thirties who just want to zero in on finding a wife before their whole lives pass them, so they are willing to take it on as a passion project."

"Wow," I say. "Are you serious? That's...amazing!"

He spouts off the terms of the deal, which, to no surprise, makes him a part owner. But the next thing he says is what catches me off guard.

"We need you here, Charlotte. We need you in Silicon Valley in the trenches with these guys if this thing is going to take off."

"You need me to move?"

"Yes. LA is for show business. Up here is for tech. You know that. So do you think fifteen days is enough time? I figured you'd put your notice in today with your current job, give your boss two weeks, then take a day to move up the coast?"

"I...I don't even really know what to say."

"Well, HR would tell me you need to officially say *yes* before we zip over the relocation paperwork. So, do you say *yes*, Charlotte?"

This is exactly what I've been working toward since day one on the job at The Influencer Firm. But as exciting as it is, I'd be lying if I said I wasn't conflicted. As of about, I don't know, an hour ago, I think I became Brian Jackson's girlfriend. And I don't expect a guy like Warren to understand how big of a deal that is, but it is. I'm not so sure long distance with him is what I had in mind for us right now. Plus, I like my life here. And I think I'll like it even more now that I stopped running every part of it through a computer script.

"Hmm, can I think about it?" I ask Warren.

"I'm sorry. What did you just say?"

"Can I think it over and let you know sometime tomorrow if I accept the offer?"

"With all due respect, Charlotte, you do realize that I'm

offering you an opportunity to become an entrepreneur with real Silicon Valley money and tech power backing your every move? What is there to possibly think about? We'll cover a hundred percent of your moving costs, if that's what this is about."

I can tell he's growing irritated that I'm not jumping all over the opportunity he's presenting.

"It's not about moving expenses. It's about moving in general. My gut is telling me to stay in Los Angeles," I free flow.

"That's career suicide. You *can't* do tech in Los Angeles," Warren firmly states. "If you want this app to get off the ground, then we need you in San Fran. And we also need your answer. Now."

But what does Charlotte need?

Charlotte needs to slow down.

Charlotte needs to step away from the numbers.

Charlotte needs to be close to her neighborhood Salt & Straw and her new favorite grief group.

Charlotte needs to start seeing her same world through a new lens.

Charlotte needs her own version of a do-over.

"If you need an answer now, then the answer is *no, thanks.*"

Even I'm shocked about how calm I am about turning down his offer. Maybe this will be my only opportunity to bring my brainchild in the world. Maybe it won't be. Maybe it's not even what I want to do with my life anymore. Either way, I feel fine about it. Whatever the outcome.

"Wow. This is a first. Good luck, Charlotte." He hangs up the line before I can say, "You, too."

As I set my phone back down on my desk, I don't feel the panic I should knowing I just walked away from the biggest opportunity of my professional life. But despite turning down the fancy business card, swanky Silicon Valley corner office,

and whatever else was included in that bright and shiny relocation package, I feel lighter and brighter than I ever have
staying right here.

Giddy as hell ;), reads the text from Brian that has just popped
up on my Apple Watch. I smile, knowing that my gut was
right about seeing where this goes. Because I can get used to
giddy. I *want* to get used to giddy.

"Okay. Where were we, Marigold?"

★ ★ ★ ★ ★

Acknowledgments

The idea for *Husband Material* came to me one day when I overheard a bizarre story on the news while washing the dishes. I never thought it would spawn a full-blown manuscript—but look what we have here! There are many people to thank for helping me bring this book into the world.

I want to begin with the widows I interviewed to ensure my writing had authenticity and nuance to it. I am not like Charlotte, but I was able to locate a few brave women, from all walks of life, who are. These ladies were willing to talk to me, a virtual stranger, about the most painful parts of their pasts—often on a whim, often for hours at a time. Their stories and strength inspired me; inspired Charlotte. My utmost, humble thanks to:

- Caroline Brogan—Rest in Peace, Joe,
- Wanda DeJesus Engracia—Rest in Peace, Pablo.
- Lindsey Kraft Lange—Rest in Peace, Ron.
- and Robyn Woodman

Now on to a big round of applause for my editor at Gray-don House, Melanie Fried. Her sharp, literary eye helped craft this unique idea into an edgy work of art. I am grateful for her spot-on creative direction, which allowed me to invent some of the scenes that I love most in the book. She also wins the fastest reader/responder award. Bravo to the entire Graydon House team!

Thank you to my agent Danielle Egan-Miller of Browne & Miller. She is the ultimate cheerleader and the definition of a fearless leader. I'm grateful for her representation, brutal honesty, and always on-it work ethic. Cheers to another great novel—and here's to many, many more.

To my family, especially my mother/momager: thank you for your ongoing support. Kris Jenner has nothing on you.

To you, the reader. You holding this book means more to me than I can possibly express. Thank you for coming back for more. I hope you enjoy the escape. Let's talk about it on social media (@emilybelden) or at your next book club.

And finally, a shout-out to Margo Lipschultz, who initially acquired *Husband Material* after hearing a short synopsis of the idea. Her faith in my storytelling allowed me to explore a world unlike my own for a few years, which to me, is the greatest perk of being a writer.

"Full of Fire."
—*Library Journal* (starred review)

"Exhilarating."
—*Booklist*

"Satisfying."
—*RT Book Reviews* (Top Pick)

"Provocative."
—Abby Stern, author of *According to a Source*

Turn the page for a sample of Emily Belden's delicious first novel, Hot Mess, a juicy look behind kitchen doors.

Available now wherever books are sold.

Chapter 1

"Are you going to be okay?"

His question gives me pause. Will I be okay? Was "okay" a hypothetical three exits ago?

All things considered, I'm hurtling through time and space with a guy whose recovery from a serious cocaine addiction matters as much as the rise of his chocolate soufflé tonight. So I answer honestly.

"I don't know." My voice sounds far away.

"Well, if you're not sure, change. You'll be walking at least five miles between ushering people to tables and the bathroom and running back and forth from the kitchen."

"Oh, shoes. You're asking if I'm going to be okay in these shoes." I glance down at my black platform wedges.

"Yeah, babe. What the hell else would I be talking about?"

He grabs the bottom of my chin and plants a quick kiss on my lips before he rinses a whisk in the sink.

The shells of seventy-five hard-boiled eggs are in the trunk of a car I rented to shuttle all the shit required for tonight's guests, I took an unpaid day off from work to be here to help and my parents are about an hour away from arriving to this special "comeback dinner," which will be the first time they've seen Benji somewhere other than the headlines in the last thirty days.

And he's worried about my shoes?

"I'll be fine," I say sweetly, knowing now is not the time for a true audit of my emotional well-being. Tonight is about Benji's big return and my confidence that all—including my shoe choice—will go as smoothly as the house-made butter at room temp that he's just whipped up.

I find my reflection in a nearby Cryovac machine and take out a tube of my go-to matte pale pink lipstick from my makeup bag. I sweep it across my bottom lip, then fill in just above my lip line on the top for the illusion of a slightly fuller mouth. After all, I know at least half the guest list is here to see what the woman behind the man looks like.

Speaking of lists, I can see Benji in the reflection as well, leaning over a stainless-steel counter consulting the prep list for tonight's dinner service. He takes a black Sharpie from the pocket of his apron and puts a quick slash through each item as he recites them out loud to himself.

I come up behind him and cast my arms around him slowly; my touch puts him at ease. He curls his left arm up to hold my arms in place and continues to mouth ingredients one by one to make sure he hasn't forgotten anything. It sounds like sweet nothings being whispered to me in a romance language I barely understand.

Benji crumples the list, a sign he's successfully on track with everything from the dehydrated goat's milk to emulsified caramel, and I snap out of my schoolgirl daydream. He turns to face me, shuffles a few steps back in his worn kitchen clogs and bends down to shake out his longish dark hair.

I know what he's about to do. And for as ordinary as it is, especially to girls like me who *routinely* wear their hair like this, watching Benji shimmy a hair tie—my hair tie—off his right wrist to tie his mane into a disheveled topknot is like the start of an exotic dance. For anyone who says the man-bun trend isn't their thing, they're lying.

The hair tie snaps when Benji tries to take it for a third lap around his voluminous bun.

"Goddamn it!"

"Relax, babe," I tell him as I zip open my makeup bag and pull out a spare. Crisis averted, I think to myself as I put another mental tally in the "Saves the Day" column.

He reties his white apron for the umpteenth time over a tight black T-shirt that shows off his tattooed-solid arms. I know for a fact he doesn't work out (unless you consider lifting fifty-pound boxes of pork and beef off the back of a pickup truck getting your reps in) but somehow he's been blessed with the body of a lumberjack. The only thing missing is the ax, which has been appropriately swapped out for an expensive Santoku knife custom-engraved with some filigree and his initials: BZ.

No doubt he's got the "hot and up-and-coming chef" thing down: tattooed, confident, exhausted and exhilarated. Hard to believe this isn't a casting event for *Top Chef.*

Harder to believe this is the man I get to take home every night.

"FUCK! Are you kidding me, Sebastian? Where the fuck is the lid to that thing?" Benji's words effectively snap me out of the trance I was in danger of being lulled into. It takes me a minute to realize what happened: his sous chef, Sebastian, has pressed Start on a Vitamix full of would-be avocado aioli, except the lid to the blender is nowhere to be found. Green schmutz has gone flying, marking up Benji's pristine apron like the start of a Jackson Pollock piece.

"Sorry, chef. I got it on now." Tail between his legs, Sebastian gets back to work as Benji furiously wipes at the streak with his bare hand. He's making it worse.

"Benji. Breathe." I grab his half-drunk can of LaCroix and pour a little onto a clean kitchen rag. While tending to the stain in the hot kitchen, I look directly into those deep brown eyes and give him a reassuring smile. He smells of cigarettes and sweat, garlic and onions. It's intoxicating.

"I know, Allie. This is just...huge for me. Huge for us. The press is going to be here tonight." He wipes some sweat off his brow.

"And my parents," I whisper.

"Oh god, them, too." He releases the tension by cracking the bones in his neck. A poor substitute, I imagine, for his true preference: a shot of whiskey.

But even a slug of 120 proof wouldn't take the edge off the fact that Benji's pop-up dinners are the new It Thing. People salivate at their screens just waiting for him to Tweet out the next time and place he'll be cooking. Why? Because he's the hottest chef in Chicago and you can't taste his food at any restaurant. So when he announces a dinner, it's a mad, server-crashing race to claim one of only twelve spots at the table. And when everyone wants to see how the reformed addict is faring, they'll cancel all their plans for the day on the off chance they'll be one of the first to submit a reservation request, followed by prompt prepayment—which all goes to me, the fan-favorite girlfriend of Benji Zane.

I can't blame his followers for the obsession. Our flash-in-the-pan love story was covered by the most-read food blog earlier this spring, and since then, there have been myriad articles chronicling his love-hate relationship with hard drugs and high-end cooking. Between his unlikely relationship with me, his checkered past and his unmatched kitchen skills, Benji's managed to divide people like we're talking about health-care reform or immigration.

Half see him as a prodigy in the kitchen who was given a second chance when some no-name poster child of millennial living suddenly inspired him to get clean. The other half of Chicago views him as an all-hype hack who uses the media attention to rob his patrons of their hard-earned money so he can get his next score.

Fuck those people. Because the Benji that I know, that I live with…well, he's a stand-up guy whose brunch—and bedroom—game happens to be on point.

"Listen, babe," I say. "What did I tell you? I'm not going to let you down tonight, okay? I'll pace the seating however you need me to. I'll greet the press and spot the critics, too. We got this, okay? I believe in you." And I do.

I don't always agree to help Benji at his pop-ups—usually I just accept the reservation requests and keep the books straight. But tonight is different. Benji told me yesterday that he's got an outstanding dealer debt to pay off and so he's oversold the dining room by about twenty-five chairs to try to make a little extra cash. Without me here to help host a guest list of this size, this highly publicized dinner would look and feel more like a dysfunctional family reunion. Something I'm sure the piranha-like press would love to write about.

I wanted to be pissed about this little "oops" moment. How careless could he be? Now, by over-inviting a horde of geeked-out foodies, and in the past, by racking up a $2,000 coke bill. But he assured me it's just one of those things that *needs* to be handled in order for him to move on with his sobriety. And that's what I signed up for by being his girlfriend: unconditional support and a back that would never turn on him.

He's even arranged for Sebastian to be the one to hand over the cash tonight after the last diner goes home. Consider it just another example of how hungry people are to work alongside Mr. Zane. The same set of hands is willing to debone fifty squab *and* pay off gangbanging drug dealers from the South Side, all in the same night.

I don't blame Sebastian, though. There's something about Benji that makes you want to strap in for the ride. It's like rushing a sorority: you'll do what you need to do to get in, because ultimately, you end up part of something bigger than yourself. I just don't think any of us know what that *something* is yet.

At least that's the way I see it from my vantage point, which is currently the groin area of a brand-new apron that was marked with an unsightly stain until I stepped in.

"See, babe?" I say. "All clean."

Benji pulls me in for a kiss, his hand cupped around the back of my neck. With my French twist fragile in his palm, I feel the stress in the kitchen disintegrate. I'm no superhero, but if I were, my power would surely be managing to make it all okay for him, every time. It doesn't even matter that there's garlic burning in a sauté pan, my lipstick is now smeared, or that my work email is probably blowing up with a hundred notifications an hour.

"You're my rock, babe," he tells me, tucking a few strands of loose hair behind my ears. I love hearing that I'm doing a good job, because it's not always easy.

"Okay, so here's the final guest list," he says, getting back to business. Benji hands me a piece of paper from the back pocket of his charcoal-gray skinny jeans. At the top, *Aug. 20 Pop-Up* is underlined in black marker. I give the list a quick once-over.

"So seating begins at seven, tables are set as rounds and the largest group is a party of six. Simple enough," I say.

"Well, it's more than just ushering people to their chairs." He tenses back up. "After everyone's seated, I'll need you to run food and bus tables if we get in the weeds."

"Weeds?"

"Busy as shit."

"Ah. Okay."

"And water. Constantly. You should be carrying the pitcher and filling any glass that's lower than two-thirds."

"Got it."

"Pay attention to what people are saying. Any issues, come find me immediately."

"Obviously."

"And as we're wrapping, make sure you call a cab for anyone who's too drunk to drive. The last thing I need is bad press about a deadly DUI from someone I fed."

"Anything else, your highness?" I jest to lighten the mood. I get that he's on edge, and rightfully so. So am I, to be frank. This mini romper won't be forgiving in the derriere area should anyone drop a fork while I'm rehydrating them. I also barely know the difference between kale and spinach, and am about to play hostess to a room full of people who are jonesing to fire off a photo or two of this year's culinary celeb couple to their judgmental social sphere. It's a lot.

"Very funny. And, yes, there is one more thing. Mark and Rita just texted me. They can't make it tonight. Couldn't find a sitter for Maverick or something."

While it would be great to finally meet Benji's sponsor, Mark—and his wife, Rita—I'm okay with the last-minute cancellation. Two less comp seats means more profit and less work for Benji. It also means two less people who I need to impress on the spot. Especially people whose job it is to spot bullshit. They'll be missed by Benji, I'm sure, since they're basically the parents he never had, from what I gather. But hopefully he'll just shake it off.

"I'm sorry, that sucks. It's tough with kids," I say, like I know.

"Yeah, it's whatever. I told them we'll see them next weekend. Anyway, can you just promise me something?"

"Of course."

He looks me dead in the eye and says: "Promise that you'll fuck me after this is all done."

Blood rushes to places it hasn't since I lost my virginity on Valentine's night my freshman year of college. I know, I know. That's totally cliché. But what was your first time like? Okay, then. Let's not judge.

Speaking of clichés, now would be a good time to mention that I fell for the bad boy. And being "that girl" doesn't end there: just imagine a more basic version of Selena Gomez with a day-old blowout, tucking her leggings into Uggs when the temperature falls below seventy degrees. Give or take a pumpkin-spiced latte and a *Real Housewives* viewing party, and you've just about got me—Allie Simon—pegged. I'm the last person someone like Benji Zane would want to date and the first person the food blogosphere has been able to confirm he actually is dating. I give him a wink and turn toward the dining room. I've got a little time before our first guests are set to arrive and I need to get my game face on. I need to feel less like someone whose superhot boyfriend wants to ravish her across the very counter the amuse-bouches are being prepped on and more like someone who knows on what side of the plate the fork goes.

Tonight's pop-up is in a small ballroom on the forty-fifth floor of a high-rise luxury apartment building way up on the North Side. For a Friday night, it'll be a bit of a clusterfuck for anyone who lives in the heart of Chicago, the Loop, or out in the suburbs like my parents, to get up here, but the views of the boats on Lake Michigan and the sunset reflecting off the buildings in the skyline will be so worth it. This summer evening is the kind of night Instagram was made for.

How Benji secured the venue this time is a doozy. He put an ad on Craigslist: "Party Room Needed." Said he couldn't pay money for the space, but would leave all his leftovers behind *and* the secret to "a roasted chicken guaranteed to get you laid." Thirty minutes later, some teenager whose parents live in the building dropped off the keys to the penthouse floor. It never ceases to amaze me the things people will do just to feel like they have a personal connection to the Steven Tyler of the food world. Alas, here we are.

I push on the balcony door handles fully expecting they'd be locked. But they pop down with ease and the warm summer wind hits me in the face. I grab the railing, close my eyes and suck in that city air.

I don't breathe enough. Not like this, deep and alone. I have to admit that being Benji's girlfriend sometimes feels like sitting in the passenger seat as he drives 110 miles per hour on the freeway in a jalopy with no seat belts. It's easy to get overwhelmed, but I remind myself that Benji came into my life for a reason. Every douchey, going-nowhere guy I dated before him was worth it because they led me to him: a beautiful genius who knows exactly who he is and what he wants. A guy with talent, charisma and nothing but pure adoration for me. So what if he had a flawed start? All that matters is that I stopped the top from spinning out of control and now we're good. We're really fucking good.

Just then my phone, which I have stashed in my bra (hey, no pockets, okay?), buzzes with a text. I dig around in my cleavage and read the message from Benji.

2-top off elevator. It's time, babe.

My feet are aching and I'm sweating, but as far as everyone can tell by the smile on my face, I'm having a grand old time filling water glasses. By now, we're more than halfway through the service, and so far, Benji's only used the bottle of bourbon in the back for a caramel-y glaze on the dessert course, not to ease the kitchen chaos. In fact, in the ten or so times I've popped my head in to check on him, he appeared to be keeping his cool entirely.

"And how are you two enjoying your evening?" I say, hovering over a couple at a round-top table I haven't checked on yet.

"There she is." My dad wipes his mouth as he stands up to give me a hug. My god, he's wearing a wool suit and a silk tie. Overdress much?

"What do you think of the food?" I ask.

"It's outstanding, Allie. Say, can we get another one of those sriracha Jell-O cubes?"

"Goodness, Bill, don't embarrass me like that. Just ignore him, Allie. Although, yes, the sriracha cube was…" My mom, Patty, closes her eyes, puckers her lips and explodes an air-kiss off the tips of her fingers. I think that's mom code for amaze-balls.

"I'm really glad you guys could make it," I say. And I mean that. It's not easy to accept the fact that your daughter is dating the most talked-about, tattooed chef in the Midwest, let alone show your support by attending a BYOB makeshift dinner party on the far North Side.

"Wouldn't miss it for the world. And, hey, I couldn't figure out how to get the flash on this dang iPhone to work, but I took a bunch of pictures," my dad says. "You'll have to explain later how I'm supposed to send them to you."

I'm positive they will all be blurry, but it's the thought that counts.

"Is Benji going to come out?" my mom asks, playing with the pearls on her necklace. Her question captures the attention of strangers sitting across the table and now everyone's eyes are on me.

"We'll see," I say, knowing that answer isn't good enough. Not for anyone in the room who paid to be here. "You'll have to excuse me. I've got to keep checking on other tables. Love you guys."

As I make my rounds, everyone seems to be gushing over the fifth and final course of the night: grilled fig panna cotta with a bourbon, honeycomb drizzle over vanilla bean gelato. I hear one person whisper it was better than Alinea's dessert. Another says she just had a foodgasm. At that, I set down the water pitcher and offer to clear a few dirty plates back to the kitchen. When no one is looking, I dip my pinky into some melted gelato and run it through a glob of the bourbon honey before quickly licking it off my manicured finger.

Heaven. Pure heaven.

Even though there's no negative feedback to report to the kitchen and everyone is stuffed, I can tell people are saving room for one more culinary delight.

They want to see Benji Zane.

Put it this way: sure, the tenderness on the squab was on point. And, yes, the scoop of gelato was spherical as fuck. But as rock-star as his dishes may be, these people are here for something else entirely. They've ponied up to get up close and personal with Benji Zane and not just because he's easy on the eyes. To them, this is the Reformed Addict Show. It's their chance to witness firsthand if he's turned over a real leaf this time, or if he's just moments away from the downfall more than a few food bloggers think is coming.

My money is on the former.

Does that make me a naive idiot? Maybe. But these people don't know Benji like I do. The one thing I'm sure of is that I am Benji's number one supporter. If I waver from that, I know the chances of a slip are greater, so it's not something I'm willing to do. Especially not since we live together. I mean, *you* try staying ahead of the curve when your roommate has a kinky past with cocaine.

"Benji?" I say, cracking the kitchen door open a few inches. "Can you come here a sec?"

He puts down his knife roll and heads to the doorway, tapping Sebastian on the way over and telling him to take five.

"What is it? Everything good?" I can see the anxiety in his eyes. Whether it's an audience of one or a roomful of skeptical diners, Benji cuts zero corners when it comes to his cooking. He wants tonight to go seamlessly, and if he's not pulling a huge profit in the end because of some dealer drama, well, then, his reputation among these unsuspecting people needs to be the thing that comes out on top.

"Everything's great," I whisper. "But are you going to step out? I think people want to applaud you. They loved everything. Honestly, it was the perfect night."

Benji's not shy. Not by a long shot. But I can tell he's delayed making his cameo until I offered up the reinforcement that people really are waiting in the wings like Bono's groupies.

"Really?" he asks.

"Really. Look at table eight. Bunch of food bloggers who wet their panties when they ate the deconstructed squash blossoms. I'm pretty sure they'll have a full-blown orgasm if you just come out and wave to them."

He peers over me to check out the guests. Table eight is all attractive blondes with hot-pink cell phone cases who must have taken a thousand photos so far. I'd worry, but when your reckless love story has been chronicled on every social media platform since its hot and heavy start, that makes it pretty official: Benji Zane is off the market, folks. Has been since the middle of May.

"Alright, fine. Give me a sec."

Benji ditches his apron and grabs my hand. Together, we walk into the dining room and all chairs turn toward us. I feel a bit like the First Lady, just with a trendier outfit and a more tattooed Mr. President by my side. I bite back the urge to wave to our adoring fans.

"I just want to thank everyone for coming out tonight. I hope you enjoyed the food. It was my pleasure feeding you. Feel free to stick around and enjoy the view or see Allie for a cab if you need one. Good night, everyone." Benji holds our interlocked hands up and bows his head.

The crowd goes wild—well, as wild as forty diners who have all just slipped into a serious food coma can go. It's a happy state, the place Benji's food sends you. Kind of like how you feel after a long, passionate sex session. When done, you've got a slight smile and glow on your face, but just want to lie down for the foreseeable future and possibly smoke a cigarette.

I spot my father standing in the back, filming on his phone as my mother claps so hard, her Tiffany charm bracelet looks like it's about to unhinge and fall into what's left of her dessert. Seeing them both smile proudly across the room at who their daughter has wound up with warms my heart. It's been an uphill battle, but I'm confident we've won them over.

Benji whisks me back to the kitchen, and before I can congratulate him on a successful evening, he pushes me up against the walk-in fridge. His tongue teases my mouth open and I am putty in his hands. With his right hand, he pulls down the collar of my romper, exposing my black lace bra. He frees my breast and kisses my nipple. My neck turns to rubber and my eyes roll back.

"Benji," I pathetically protest, very aware that all that separates us from a roomful of people who are currently picking a filter for a photo of the two of us holding hands is a swinging door that doesn't lock.

He continues kissing my neck, my breast still exposed. "I couldn't have done any of this without you, Allie."

"Oh, really?" I say, recognizing that the natural high he's on is most certainly fueling whatever is happening here. He slips a hand up my thigh.

"You made everyone out there have a good time tonight."

"I know," I playfully agree. He pulls my panties to the side. I know where this is going.

"And now it's my turn to get in on it."

Before I know it, he's inside of me and we're officially having sex against a cooler with forty people standing fifteen feet away, two of whom are my doting parents.

Sex between me and Benji has always been explosive. It's like he knows exactly what I need and where to touch me without me having to give a lick of instruction. Sex has never been like this in my entire life. Granted, I've only got about five solid years of experience, but nothing rivals what Benji has introduced me to in the last three months. There's virtually nothing I'll say no to with him. Pornos, toys and now public places. Who am I?

I'll figure it out *after* I get off. A few hushed moans later, and I'm there.

"You did so good tonight," he whispers in my ear as he helps adjust my outfit. "Now I need you to go back out there and get everyone to leave so I can fuck you again over that balcony with the view of the lake in the background. Okay?"

I come back down to earth and reply, "Yes, sir."

Back in the dining room, I brush shoulders with Benji's sous chef, who's on his way back to his station. I give Sebastian a nod and return to my post, trusty water pitcher in hand.

There are a few stragglers left in the dining room, including my parents, finishing the last sips of their BYO selections. From what I can tell as I clear empty dishes and put the tips in a billfold, people liked dinner. They *really* liked it. The average gratuity being left on the prepaid meal is about fifty dollars cash per person.

After subtracting the dealer's cut, it's looking like we'll walk with about $2,000 cash for ourselves and I can't help but feel like a bit of a cheat. I know nothing about this world—this high-end foodie club that I got inducted into overnight—yet people are emptying their wallets of their hard-earned cash to show their gratitude for what we've done. Do they realize just hours ago, the black squid ink from course two was being stored on ice in my bathtub? Regardless, we need the money. Benji may have kicked his expensive habit, but I'm the only one with a steady job right now, and being a social media manager for Daxa—yes, the organic cotton swab brand made famous by Katy Perry's makeup artist on Snapchat—isn't exactly like being the CEO of Morgan Stanley.

"Excuse me, where is the ladies' room?" a tipsy guest asks. Benji might not have taught me how to sous vide a filet mignon, but he did tell me you always walk a guest to the bathroom when they ask. I promptly put down the dirty glasses and the wad of tips and walk the boozy babe to the loo.

Upon my return, I nearly collide with another guest, this one quite a bit soberer.

"Allie." The prim-looking thirtysomething woman with a bleached-blond pixie cut says my name matter-of-factly. I stand up straight; this chick has *CRITIC* written all over her face.

"Yes, ma'am. Can I help you? Do you need a taxi?"

"No, thank you. I just wanted to give you a tip."

"Oh, that's so kind of you. You can actually just leave a gratuity on the table."

"No, I meant, like, some advice."

I tilt my head to the side and try not to lose my grip on my smiley service. She's five foot nothing, but her demeanor is as bold as her bright red lipstick.

"I'm not sure Benji would be cool with you leaving a billfold with what I'd guess is about $2,000 in it just sitting on a table in a room full of drunk people who don't know that it's time to go home. It would behoove you to keep an eye on your shit."

She jams the billfold into my chest and proceeds to walk right past me to the elevator bank.

And just like that, I've officially been felt up twice in one night.